MORE PRAISE FOR FREDERIC BEAN'S
PANCHO AND BLACK JACK

"With Pancho and Black Jack [Bean] has reached a new plateau. It will twist your mind and even crack your neck a little. Read this one without delay. You can't help but enjoy the action and enlightenment."
—Max Evans, author of *The Rounders* and *The Hi Lo Country*

"Here is magic. Frederic Bean has a genius for bringing historical characters to life. This is an utterly absorbing book, richly told by someone who has combed Chihuahua in search of one of the great stories of this century. And when you're done, you will never think of that fierce, bloody foray into Mexico in quite the same light. Bean combines massive research with a story-telling gift so profound you'll care deeply about each character, and they will linger in your mind long after you've turned the final page."
—Richard S. Wheeler

"Convincing, action-packed, masterful...Bean paints an accurate and exciting picture...A terrific story."
—*Roundup Magazine*

ABOUT THE AUTHOR

Author of thirty-four western and historical novels, Frederic Bean has spoken at numerous writing workshops throughout the country. As a member of the Western Writers of America, he served as the 1995 Spur Awards Chairman and as Spur Judge for numerous WWA awards. In addition to his writing, Mr. Bean has worked as a cutting horse trainer, livestock auctioneer, and magazine editor. He currently resides in Austin, Texas.

HELL'S HALF ACRE

FREDERIC BEAN

B
BERKLEY BOOKS, NEW YORK

HELL'S HALF ACRE

A Berkley Book / published by arrangement with
the author

PRINTING HISTORY
Berkley edition / December 1996

The Putnam Berkley World Wide Web site address is
http://www.berkley.com/berkley

ISBN: 0-425-15584-6

BERKLEY®
Berkley Books are published by The Berkley Publishing Group,
200 Madison Avenue, New York, New York 10016.
BERKLEY and the "B" design
are trademarks belonging to Berkley Publishing Corporation.

PRINTED IN THE UNITED STATES OF AMERICA

10 9 8 7 6 5 4 3 2 1

AUTHOR'S NOTE

In its heyday it was called "the Paris of the Plains." At the beginning of the cattle drive era it was a jumping-off place for immense herds of longhorns bound for eastern beef packers up the Chisholm Trail. During its violent twenty-five-year history it could boast more murders per square yard than any other piece of real estate west of the Mississippi, although it was a small area compared to most other frontier towns, a few city blocks in the heart of Fort Worth, Texas, not far from a railroad station. At one point in Fort Worth's history, by vote of the city council, no more permits were issued for whorehouses until more churches could be built, when a census showed that houses of prostitution outnumbered churches by two to one.

Not all of the Acre's commerce was given over to pandering. The Standard Theater and Bar at the corner of Rusk and Twelfth streets insisted upon a public policy, "there being no smoking allowed among women, no drinks sold to those already intoxicated nor bare anatomies exposed on stage, and no swearing, profane language allowed, or coarse vulgarities." A policy, however, is only as good as its enforcement. Court records tend to show the Standard Theater was, at various times, charged with numerous infractions of city liquor and obscenity ordinances. A few other establishments tried to maintain a mantle of public respectability; rarely, however, did a gaming house or saloon refuse to offer what its clientele wanted. Liquor, women, and gambling were the core of the Acre's industry. For a quarter of a century, few places on earth served up any more of all three.

Opium was available, although not as widely as it was in places farther west. Laudanum (distilled opium) was sold over the counter at many apothecary shops and addiction to it was not infrequent among the Acre's prostitutes. Epidemics of venereal disease sometimes occasioned a wholesale discharge of women who worked the "cribs," for word as well as disease spread quickly among trail hands between Fort Worth and Abilene. A few Kansas Territory physicians were known to brew batches of potash solution in giant cauldrons, the only known treatment for strains of gonorrhea coming up from Texas along with the herds. By the time an afflicted cowboy reached Abilene, his case was usually severe enough to warrant immediate and rather painful medical attention.

Crooked gambling was by far the most profitable vice in the Acre. Some city constables enforced honesty with a wink, due to generous bribes. A "hands off" policy prevailed among Fort Worth policemen until some of the city's blue-blooded citizens began to lodge weighty protests.

Murder was another matter. So long as the Acre's own seedy residents killed each other there was hardly an official stir at the Tarrant County Courthouse, prevailing sentiment being that a form of natural population control wasn't all that objectionable. But when a blueblood or a visiting well-heeled customer happened to step in front of a bullet or a knife, massive manhunts combed every establishment and back alley until someone was caught. At times there were whispered suspicions innocent men went to the gallows in order to satisfy the public hue and cry to end Fort Worth's violence. Public hangings often attracted huge crowds of cheering citizens who apparently felt justice was being served by hanging anyone from the Acre for the city's most recent crimes. Newspaper accounts often mentioned that the doomed man's place of residence was known to be Hell's Half Acre, a verdict of presumed guilt by association readers came to expect when an "execution by means of a rope" was ordered by area judges. Lemonade and sugar cakes were sold at these hangings by aggressive vendors who also purveyed paper fans for those who might feel faint at the moment death's door dropped out from under the accused.

If gambling were the most profitable enterprise in the Acre, by far the most popular attractions were the women. Beauty drew lonely, exhausted trail hands from their bedrolls on the prairie to smoke-filled dens where watered liquor helped stimulate what some cowmen described as limitless lust. A cowboy earned thirty dollars a month, which he could easily spend in two or three nights with the Acre's women. Being broke in the wilds of Indian Territory on the way to Kansas was seldom as bad as a yearning for female companionship where there was none.

The average age of Fort Worth prostitutes was just under eighteen. Womanhood not yet in its full flower was a sought-after commodity. Madames overseeing the Acre's whorehouses understood and provided as many youthful crib prostitutes as they could find, often tempting girls as young as thirteen into what was a gilt-edged profession for those blessed with good looks. Careers in prostitution were understandably short for most women. Disease, pregnancy, and alcohol abuse took an early toll. But in her prime, a pretty young girl might earn thousands of dollars before she found herself with a dwindling clientele. Older prostitutes usually drifted into supporting trades around sin parlors: laundress or cook or cleaning woman.

Hell's Half Acre became almost legendary for its variety of beautiful prostitutes, and perhaps for that reason alone it was to prosper like no other district of its kind in the West during the cattle drive era, outlasting places like Dodge City and, best known of all, Abilene. Almost every Acre resident could tell a story of strife, wicked excitement, and sudden danger. The Acre was home to the famous and the infamous. It was the last place Butch Cassidy and his Wild Bunch were together, before fate began to deal them a losing hand. Dozens of notorious gunmen and some of the West's most desperate killers frequented Fort Worth at one time or another. Thus it is no wonder area lawmen trod lightly along the Acre's streets when rumors began to spread that wanted men were in the vicinity.

Hell's Half Acre began as a district known for its vices in the 1870s. Before the turn of the century its streets ran red with blood. By the year 1901, only one murder was committed in a twelve-month period in the entire city of Fort Worth. An article in the Fort Worth *Daily Gazette* stated that the cost of doing all forms of illegal business in Hell's Half Acre had become prohibitive. Criminals were going elsewhere. ''The Paris of the Plains'' was finally closed down due to public pressure and less tolerant attitudes by city officials. Its time had come and gone with the passing of the trail drive era, and now only the stories remain of the Acre's lurid past . . .

HELL'S HALF ACRE

I

Fetch me another bar of lye, Annabelle!"

She heard her mother's request and yet she hesitated. Near the back of the wagon a young cowboy continued to watch her with interest.

"Comin', Ma. Be right there."

The boy chuckled. "Better hurry up, Annabelle," he said, slouching against a wagon wheel with a piece of straw in his mouth, "or your ma's liable to take a strap to your backside."

"Go away, Tommy Joe!"

"Can't make me."

She put her hands on her hips. Anger flashed in her dark brown eyes. "Leave me alone!" she cried. "Me an' Ma's got laundry to do. Ain't you got nothin' to do besides stare?"

He rolled the straw across his tongue. "I like starin' at you because you're right pretty, Annabelle. Ain't no law against starin', is there?"

A flush crept into her cheeks—she hoped he wouldn't notice because it was night. "Nobody likes bein' stared at. Go away."

"Can't make me."

She turned to the back of the wagon for a bar of soap. A sap knot popped in one of the fires, spraying the ground with red sparks. She sensed Tommy Joe was still looking at her.

"Hurry up with that soap, child!"

"I'm comin', Ma." She smoothed the front of her flour-sack dress before reaching for the lye, just in case Tommy Joe hadn't gone someplace else when she turned around.

"You're too pretty to do laundry, Annabelle," he said. "If

you wanted, you could do plenty other kinds of work.''

"I'm helpin' Ma. She ain't well.''

"You oughta be wearin' pretty dresses an' perfume, the kind comes from over in France.''

She took a bar of soap from a drying mold and covered what was left with canvas. "My ma's sick,'' she said again. "She ain't able to do all this laundry by herself.''

"She's dyin', ain't she?''

Annabelle didn't want to think about it now. "Go mind your own business, Tommy Joe Booker. We've got work to do.''

"It's called the consumption. Most folks don't live more'n a few months afore it eats 'em up.''

She wheeled around. "It's none of your affair, so please go away.'' A breath of wind swept a stray curl over her forehead and she brushed it away with the back of her hand, feeling a trace of sweat on her brow. This summer's heat had been terrible, making work with boiling kettles so much harder on her mother. "Please go away, Tommy Joe. Don't talk about my ma that way. She can't afford to go to no doctor right now an' you know it.''

"I seen it afore. Folks start coughin' up blood an' such.''

A tear formed in the corner of each of her eyes. "Don't talk like that. Ma's gonna be okay soon as we can afford for her to see a doctor out west. That's where folks go when they've got her kind of sickness, in case you didn't know.''

"There ain't no cure for the consumption. I heard Miss Rose say that to somebody.''

"An' what does she know? She runs a sin parlor. She ain't nothin' but a scarlet woman of the night.''

"Maybe. But she knows 'bout the consumption.''

"Fetch me that soap, Annabelle!'' her mother cried again, and now there was impatience in her voice.

"I gotta go,'' Annabelle whispered, starting around the back of the wagon.

"I tol' Miss Rose how pretty you was. She said to tell you if you wanted, you could work for her down at the Pink Lady.''

"I'd rather die!" she said, heading for rows of cooking fires where cast iron cauldrons bubbled softly in the night, smelling of lye and cooked sweat and mesquite smoke, a combination that sometimes made her nauseated.

Doris Green looked up from stirring one of her kettles with a mesquite limb. "What kept you, child?" she asked. Her gaunt face had a sweaty sheen to it. Dried blood crusted on her lips. She looks so frail now, Annabelle thought.

"I was hurryin'," she lied.

Doris looked past her into the dark. "Tommy Joe was huntin' you a while ago. That boy's no good, Annabelle. He ain't worth nothin' or he wouldn't work fer that fallen woman, cleanin' spittoons an' Lord knows what else in her den of iniquity. A man who takes up with sinful women can't expect no righteousness to come to him in this life or the next."

She gave her mother the soap. "He cleans out chamber pots, is all, Ma. That don't mean he's taken up with bad women. He told me he makes real good money workin' for Miss Denadale, much as two dollars a day on busy days."

"She's a fallen woman!" Doris snapped, tossing lye into one of the kettles. "God won't have no mercy on that boy's soul if'n he don't stay away from that place. Honest folk wouldn't consort with women of such low breeding."

Annabelle risked a glance behind their wagon where Tommy Joe had been standing. "He don't consort with 'em, Ma. Leastways I don't think he does. He ain't old enough for consortin', is he?"

Doris stirred her boiling kettle vigorously, as though she meant to stir away Tommy Joe's sin. "He's plenty old enough. I see the way he stares at you." She coughed up a mouthful of raw blood and spat it into the flames. Tears streamed down her face. "You stay clear of that boy or he'll lead you to the devil's own temptation."

"I can tell you're feelin' real poorly, Ma. Let me stir it for a spell."

Her mother handed her the stick. "A girl your age shouldn't be workin' over no lye kettles. Sixteen is too young for bein' around this much strong soap. Lye will age your skin some-

thin' terrible. Don't git none if it on your hands or near your
face. Soon as we git enough money together we'll leave this
dreadful town. Doc Collins said a dry climate will be good fer
what ails me.''

"Is what ails you called the consumption?"

Doris nodded, patting a bun she pinned in her graying hair.
She was not quite thirty-three, Annabelle remembered, yet she
had begun to age rapidly as soon as the coughing spells commenced.

"That's what Doc told me it was. He said if we was able
we oughta move out west to Arizona Territory.'' She looked
into her daughter's eyes. "It's right hard fer two women to
make enough money to travel that far, but we'll make it somehow. With them laundry kettles we can cook our way out
yonder.''

"Bein' a laundress don't make much money, Ma. We hardly get enough to feed ourselves an' that ol' mule. Ain't there
better ways to make money?''

"It's honest work. The Lord will provide.''

"The Lord hasn't done all that well by us lately. We nearly
starved last winter . . .''

Doris slapped her hard across the mouth with the back of
her hand. "You hush that kind of talk, girl!''

Annabelle dropped the stick to touch her lips, stepping back
from her mother's angry stare. "All I said was that we was
real hungry, Ma,'' she stammered, crying bitter tears. "Ain't
you ever gonna get tired of bein' poor?''

"Words like them come from the devil's own mouth, Annabelle. You've been listenin' to that Tommy Joe Booker.
Don't never let me hear you say the Lord don't provide. It's
blasphemy. Now, you git away from me so's I can do honest
work without havin' to hear no daughter of mine blaspheme
the Lord's good name.''

"I'm sorry, Ma. I know you've been sick.''

"Git! Go off in the darkness with Satan's disciple, if you
can't keep a civil tongue in your head. There's no shame
comes from bein' poor or knowin' hard work. Leave me be!''

Half-blinded by tears, Annabelle ran away into deep shadows far from the fires, still clasping a hand over her mouth where her mother had struck her. She ran down an alley behind the railroad station, getting as far from the public campground as she could before she stopped. Her shoes were covered with mud by the time she quit running, and she smelled a putrid scent. When she looked back down the alley, she saw she'd been running through a latrine ditch behind Union Station.

Sniffling, her sides heaving, she wiped mud and urine from her worn high-button shoes by rubbing them against depot bricks. Salty tears wet her cheeks. In the dark no one will see me cry, she thought.

Then she heard a distant melody, a piano and a banjo playing somewhere to the north. "It's comin' from that bad place," she whispered to herself. Her mother never allowed her to go there at night, when sinful behavior was practiced.

She trudged to the end of the alley, avoiding the ditch and its disgusting odor. Peering around a corner, she saw brightly lit windows on both sides of a wide street. Horses and carriages were tied in front of every building. People strolled along wood sidewalks enjoying night's cooler air. The music was louder than before. Another piano banged out a faster tune somewhere to the east.

"It's only a couple of blocks." She said it quietly as if to reassure herself.

She crossed two pairs of empty railroad tracks, lifting her skirt to cross each rail. All around her was quiet, save for the happy sounds coming from Hell's Half Acre.

"It's a fitting name," her mother had said one time as they set up their canvas lean-to and laundry kettles near the red brick depot, so travelers could avail themselves of clean clothing. It was a public campground for poor folks who couldn't buy a room. "You're forbidden to go there at night, Annabelle. In the dark the devil encourages more of his evil business because no one wants to be seen conducting themselves as a sinner."

She kept to one edge of the roadway until she crossed a side street. Darkness hid her approach toward the saloons.

Something akin to curiosity kept her walking closer, like a voice telling her it was okay to have a look at what was going on.

Near the first saloon she hesitated, staying back in shadows below a slanted roof to watch a cowboy walk beside a pretty young girl in front of the windows. The girl wore a red silk dress and stockings and high-heel, lace-up red leather shoes. Her golden hair was tied up in a red ribbon. A small red handbag dangled on a strap from her shoulder.

"She's so beautiful," Annabelle whispered. A desperate longing for fancy clothes kept her standing there a moment.

What would it be like to wear a silk dress? She'd touched the hem of one in a garment store window in Nacogdoches as they came west from San Augustine this spring, right after her mother was told she had lung sickness. It was silly, to dream of what a silk dress would feel like. Silk dresses cost a fortune. A poor farm girl from East Texas couldn't afford any silk. Her mother said she'd owned a silk dress once, before Chester died, but she had sold it to buy cotton seed the next fall.

The girl giggled happily, saying something Annabelle couldn't hear. "They're having a nice time," she told herself quietly. She could see how the girl's face was painted red with spots of rouge.

Farther up the street she saw a sign above the Pink Lady Bar and Gaming House for Discreet Gentlemen. She had been wanting to ask Tommy Joe what a discrete gentleman was, only she figured he probably wouldn't know and asking him anything meant he would be staring at her the whole time. She guessed it had something to do with men who consorted with scarlet women. Consorting was one thing she knew a little about. Timmie Witherspoon had consorted her with his finger down at the creek one time and it hadn't felt good, after he promised that it would. She also knew older men didn't use their fingers for that. Alice Barnes told her it was a pecker that did a man's consorting, the snake-like thing they urinated through. She claimed something else came from it when a man consorted, a white jelly that was sticky, only there wasn't all that much of it. Those were forbidden things to think about or talk about anyway, if someone wanted to be considered a decent person.

The girl in the red dress led her cowboy inside a place with a sign above it that said "The Stockmens' Retreat," passing through a pair of batwing doors. "They'll be consorting in no time," Annabelle said aloud, wondering about it, why the cowboy would pay money to do it. Cowboys were almost as poor as laundresses, Tommy Joe had said.

Annabelle looked down at her cotton dress, faded from too many washings and long use. "I can't go no closer or somebody will laugh at how I look." Her shoes were run over, needing boot black, and she hadn't brushed her hair.

She heard carriage wheels rattling behind her. When she turned, she saw a shiny black surrey coming around a corner—it would pass by the spot where she was standing and whoever was inside might see her. But there was no place to hide and thus she stood perfectly still, hoping she wouldn't be noticed by any of its passengers.

The carriage drew alongside her hiding place. A woman in a low-cut black evening dress, with flowing red hair, sat stiffly on the buggy's rear seat. She saw Annabelle and said something to her driver, a man dressed in long coattails and dark trousers.

The surrey came to a halt. The woman peered out from the shadow below a fringed canopy.

"What are you doing there?" she asked in a gentle voice.

"Just watchin' for a spell."

"Watching what?"

"What's goin' on here."

"Do you like what you see?"

"I like those pretty silk dresses an' stockings, ma'am. One of the girls was wearin' this red dress with matchin' shoes an' a handbag, an' her outfit was awful pretty." It seemed wrong to talk to a stranger so freely, but the woman sounded nice.

At that, the woman smiled. "Would you like to have a red silk gown of your own, my dear?"

She thought about her answer. "Kinda depends, I reckon.

If I had to do somethin' bad in order to get one, I might not want it so much.''

Her smile widened. ''What do you mean by something 'bad'?''

Annabelle felt the beginnings of embarrassment. ''Consortin' is what it's called, ain't it?''

''Consorting? Isn't that a word from the Bible?''

''Yes, ma'am. My ma uses it all the time.'' She looked at her shoes quickly. ''To tell the honest truth, I don't reckon I know all that much about it, really.''

''Nothing bad happens here. Pretty girls wear pretty dresses and they have fun with young men. Does that sound bad to you?''

''Not exactly. My ma say's it's sinful, what they do in some of these places.''

''Would you like to see what happens inside? Nothing bad can happen to you if you only want to look. I promise you won't have to do anything wrong.''

Annabelle's throat felt dry. ''I reckon maybe I would like to see it once, but all I'd do is look.''

''Climb in, my dear. My driver will take us there.''

With her heart pounding, Annabelle approached the carriage. ''My name's Annabelle Green,'' she said.

''I'm Rose.'' She extended her hand to help Annabelle into her surrey.

''Ma'll whip me somethin' terrible if she ever finds out.''

Rose smiled. ''Then it will be our secret, Annabelle. She won't ever have to know. You can see for yourself that nothing bad goes on inside the best places here . . . just some fun, and then I'll take you home whenever you're ready.''

The woman's smile was reassuring. ''Maybe just for a little while, ma'am.'' She accepted Rose's hand and climbed in the buggy before it resumed its slow journey up the street.

Even in the dark Annabelle could see how beautiful Rose was, although she was older, wrinkling a little around her neck. She wore the sweetest smelling perfume and dressed so nice. When the carriage hit a bump her generous bosom quivered above the bustline of her gown. "That's a mighty pretty dress, too, ma'am."

"Why, thank you, Annabelle. Why don't you call me Miss Rose? Ma'am sounds so formal."

Annabelle relaxed some, until the carriage passed a noisy saloon where loud music and gales of laughter echoed from inside. Lighted windows gave her a view of crowded rooms, so many people it appeared they had to be standing on one another's toes. "I never saw so many folks in all my life, Miss Rose. There ain't hardly room for another soul in there."

"Business is good where everyone is having fun. That's why so many gentlemen come to my place."

"You have your own place? Which one is yours?"

"It's called the Pink Lady."

Her heart began to beat rapidly. She noticed her palms were sweating. She knew what went on there because of Tommy Joe, and now she also knew whose carriage she was riding in as they drove deeper into the heart of Hell's Half Acre.

2

They entered a three-story building by a rear door, after driving down a muddy alleyway reeking of garbage. A bearded man in a black suit with a gun under his coat peered outside upon hearing buggy wheels, bowing politely to Miss Rose before he came out to help her down from the carriage. Piano music and off-key singing came from all over the district, too many different tunes to distinguish one from another.

"Evenin', Miss Denadale," the man said, giving Annabelle a quick look of appraisal in light from a red railroad conductor's lamp hanging from a hook above the door. "We're plenty busy tonight, but it's been quiet enough. Ain't busted any skulls yet, but it's still early."

"It's a Friday," Rose said, as if that should explain. She showed Annabelle inside, to a darkened storeroom where kegs of whiskey and beer gave off not altogether unpleasant scents. They took a set of creaking wood stairs to another locked door. Rose turned a key and entered a large, lamplit bedroom. The biggest four-poster bed Annabelle had ever seen sat against one wall, a canopy over it made from a white gossamer material, its mattress covered by a lavender bedspread. A deep burgundy rug lay on the floor. Red velvet drapes hung over a pair of windows.

"Is this your room?" Annabelle asked, wide-eyed, halting in the threshold to stare at finery everywhere—a polished wooden dressing table and mirror, a nightstand with a green oil lamp burning clove-scented oil, a freestanding clothes closet with all manner of intricate carvings on its doors.

"Do you like it?" Rose asked, beckoning her inside.

"I never saw nothin' like it before, Miss Rose. It's the most beautiful bedroom in the whole world. That bed is big as a wagon an' the canopy's got so many frills hangin' off I swear it took somebody a year to make it." She came into the room slowly and closed the door behind her.

"Would you like to have a room like this for your own?"

"I surely would. Only I'd have to be rich, which we ain't."

"Some of my girls have nice rooms with expensive furniture."

Annabelle was puzzled. "You mean your daughters?"

Rose smiled warmly. "Some of my girls are like daughters to me. I practically raised them." She took a seat on a bench at her dressing table and turned up the wick on her lamp, spreading more light around the room, then she casually ran a brush through her long red hair while Annabelle examined everything again.

"They ain't your blood kin, those girls?" Annabelle asked.

"No, my dear. They work for me."

She understood. "They consort with cowboys for money here, don't they?"

Rose nodded. "In a manner of speaking. They're having fun. Having fun pays very well for a woman who's pretty. Like you."

"I'm not pretty. Not that kind of pretty, anyways. Tommy Joe says men like women with big . . ." She couldn't finish it when the word got stuck in her throat.

"Bosoms. Some men like them big and some like them smaller. It depends on the man. You're very pretty, Annabelle. Beautiful in a natural way."

Annabelle was listening to music coming from downstairs, a piano tune she recognized, "Camptown Races." But when she thought about what Rose's girls had to do to make money, her face grew dark. "I could never consort with men for pay, Miss Rose. It's against the scriptures." She walked over and sat on the edge of the bed, feeling how soft it was.

"I never argue over scripture with anyone," Rose said. "I think that's a personal matter. But when a young girl wants to have some of life's finer things, new clothes and a nice room in a hotel, she should think about how to get them. Becoming one of my girls at the Pink Lady gives you a chance to make money, a lot of money. Some girls get tired of being dirt poor.''

''Me an' Ma are what you'd call dirt poor, I reckon. She's been real sick an' we can't afford for her to see a doctor yet. We take in public laundry down by the train station.''

''You could make enough money for her to see the best doctors in Fort Worth, if you worked for me. I can't think of a better reason to earn a lot money, if it was going to help take care of a girl's sick mother.''

Annabelle looked at the floor. ''She wouldn't understand if I made money that way. She's got the consumption. A doctor told her we needed to move out west where it's dry, on account of her lungs. Besides, I ain't nowhere near pretty enough to make that kind of money. My bosoms ain't big enough and I hear folks say I'm too skinny.''

Rose put her brush aside. ''Come over here to the mirror. I want to show you how pretty you can look in the right dress, with your hair fixed up in ribbons. We'll just pretend you wanted to look good for a handsome young cowboy. I'll let you put on one of my evening gowns and a pair of silk stockings, so you can see how different you look.''

''I hadn't oughta, Miss Rose. It wouldn't seem right, since I ain't gonna consort like you want me to. I couldn't do nothin' like that. It'd kill my ma, an' I'd be too bashful anyways. If it's all the same, I'd better be goin' home. Ma's got a lot of laundry to do tonight an' she's too sick to do it by herself.''

Rose got up slowly and went to her closet. She took out a bright red dress with a lace hem and lace around the neckline. ''Try this on just for fun. Then I'll take you home, if that's what you want.''

It was a beautiful dress, shimmering softly in lamplight. ''That's for sure the prettiest dress I ever saw in my life,'' Annabelle whispered, tingling all over when she thought about what it would feel like against her skin. ''I never saw one with so much pretty lace . . .''

"Try it on. It's about the right size, maybe a tuck here and there."

Annabelle got off the bed. "I'm not wearin' any underwear, Miss Rose. I never owned a corset. They cost a lot of money an' with me bein' so skinny, Ma said I didn't need one."

"With young breasts like yours you don't need a corset. I have a garterbelt and some stockings you can try on, and a pair of red leather shoes. First, let me brush your hair and put it up in ribbons. You've got naturally curly hair, don't you, my dear?"

"Yes, ma'am."

"That's always a help. Men like soft, curly hair."

"Now, Miss Rose, I told you I wasn't gonna consort with no men. But I sure would like to try on that dress . . . just to see what I'd look like wearin' it."

Rose said, "Try it on. I'll be the only one who sees you in it, if that's what you want. Let's have a look at your hair . . . I'd wear it up, I think, so it'll show off your pretty face."

Standing before the mirror, Annabelle was scarcely able to speak when she gazed upon her reflection. Her figure filled out almost every curve in the dress, and the tops of her breasts were brimming over its neckline. Her hair fell in ringlets down her slender neck. A red silk bow held a fan of curls atop her head. Spots of rouge made her cheeks glow pink in soft light from the lamp beside her. Red shoes over a pair of white silk stockings made her resemble the girl she'd seen on the boardwalk going into the Stockmen's Retreat.

"You're a very beautiful young woman," Rose said, admiring her work from a distance. "In fact, you may be the most beautiful woman in Fort Worth right now. Men would come from all over creation to pay you a call when the word got out."

Annabelle blushed. "I could never do nothin' like that at all, Miss Rose. My ma would die a thousand times if she knew I done such a thing."

Rose adopted a stern expression. "She may die anyway if

you can't afford to take her to a good doctor soon. No doubt she can use some medicines for her pain."

"She's always in a lot of pain. I can see it on her face."

"I'll give you some laudanum for her. Tell her to take two spoonfuls several times a day."

"You'd do that for us? For her? How come you're bein' so nice when you don't know me hardly at all?"

Rose took a brown bottle from her dresser drawer. "Because I like you, Annabelle. You seem like a sweet girl who needs some help." She gave Annabelle the laudanum. "Now, just for fun, let's go downstairs so you can see what goes on in the parlor. All we're going to do is have a look around. You can meet some of my girls and see how nice they are."

"Will they stare at me? Will there be menfolks down there?"

"When they see how pretty you look in that red dress, a few gentlemen may stare at you, but that's part of the fun. You can pretend not to notice them."

"I ain't so sure we oughta do that. I told you I'm kinda on the bashful side . . . I'm liable to blush."

"All the better. A girl who blushes when a gentleman looks at her is twice as pretty. Come now, we'll go downstairs for a minute or two, just long enough for you to see how much fun all of them are having."

Annabelle looked at herself in the mirror again. "It don't hardly look like me," she said, turning slightly, noticing how her breasts appeared to have grown larger and her hips were round in places she hadn't paid attention to before.

Rose opened a door into a carpeted hallway. "Come with me," she said, smiling again. "We'll only stay a moment and you won't have to do anything bad."

After a final glance at herself in the mirror, Annabelle followed Rose into the hall. She felt giddy, light-headed, as though she might faint. They came to a stairway, and now the music was much louder and she could hear the hum of conversation, scattered bits of laughter above the piano. Cigar smoke and vague sweet scents came from downstairs as they took the steps and descended into a lavishly furnished parlor crowded with dozens of men and women.

Before Annabelle and Rose reached the bottom step, heads were turning and a hush fell over the room. A bald piano player stopped his tune—he pointed to the stairs and shouted, "Gentlemen and ladies, meet Miss Rose Denadale, proprietor of the Pink Lady!"

Scattered applause began and ended abruptly when Rose put up her hands. "I'd like you to meet a friend of mine, boys," Rose said in a throaty voice, then she gave Annabelle a wink. "This is . . . Belle."

Whispers spread among groups of cowboys and better-dressed drummers and businessmen from all corners of the place. An older cowboy took a deep bow and said, "Howdy there, Miss Belle. You're near 'bout the prettiest female I ever saw in all my borned days, and I've seen more'n just a few in my time."

Another round of polite applause came from everyone, including half a dozen of Rose's girls. Annabelle knew she was blushing from all the attention. She did her best to smile, wondering why Rose had introduced her as Belle. And it appeared that every man in the place was staring at her then. For reasons she couldn't explain, their stares didn't make her feel the least bit uncomfortable, not after she got used to it.

Rose turned to her and asked quietly, "Do you see how much fun they're having? See how all the men are watching you? You are the prettiest girl in the room."

"Not prettier than you, Miss Rose."

Rose regarded her with a curious look. "No, I'm quite sure you're prettier than I ever was, my dear. And if you are as wise as you are pretty, you'll turn your good looks into a fortune. I can show you how it's done."

Annabelle gave the parlor another sweeping glance. Men were still staring at her, and most were smiling. Until tonight she'd never really thought of herself as pretty. Was it only a dress? Or could Miss Rose be right about the way she looked. Even a few of Rose's girls were watching her and she thought she could see a trace of envy in their eyes.

The piano player began playing again, when the hush gripping the Pink Lady's parlor had lasted too long.

"I'd best be goin' back now," Annabelle said, "before my ma gets worried."

"Of course, my dear. Just remember what you saw tonight. I wanted you to see it for yourself. If you ever get tired of being poor or if your mother needs money to visit a good doctor, you'll always be welcome here."

Annabelle had turned to go back upstairs, when she noticed a man in a bowler hat and suitcoat watching her. He winked and smiled, then he tipped his hat to her and raised his glass in a toast.

"To the most beautiful gal in town!" he cried. "Real nice to meet you, Belle, and I'm lookin' forward to seeing you again sometime."

She hurried up the steps before her blush deepened, but she had to admit all the attention made her feel very special indeed. For the first time in her life, she *did* feel pretty.

3

Cody Wade decided, on the eve of his twentieth birthday, to change his luck. A cowboy's luck was seldom ever good, considering the nature of his work. Coaxing a cow into doing anything it wasn't inclined to do was always a chore, and if the cows were of the Mexican longhorn variety, his job went from tough to downright impossible. Life for most cowboys was a series of disasters from which they were often lucky to survive. Tangled ropes tended to wrap more frequently around a careless cowboy's hand or his boot. Horns were much more than decoration on Mexican cows, having been put there by the Almighty Himself for the sole purpose of goring a cowboy's thin hide or a horse's flanks. Stampedes and flooded rivers, cattle rustlers and marauding Indians, added to what was already a weighty contest favoring cows over cowboys. Thus Cody made up his mind to change professions and leave riding herd for city life, selecting Fort Worth as the best place to begin a new career.

Trouble was, he hadn't decided what profession to enter yet, waiting until he got a good look at whatever Fort Worth might be able to offer. Riding up from Waco with his partner, Newt Sims, they talked about their options as the skyline of Fort Worth came in sight.

"There's the dry goods business," Newt offered, rolling his plug of chewing tobacco to the other cheek. "A man can prosper in dry goods, so I hear." Newt was missing a finger on his left hand due to an accident with his rope when a dally failed around his saddle horn, and he, too, sought a change in occupation before he found himself entirely fingerless.

"Takes money," Cody said. "Where the hell are we gonna get any goods, dry or otherwise, with just twelve dollars between us? We need to investigate lines of work that don't require much in the way of start-up capital."

"We could sell these horses, Cody, an' our saddles, too, in order to get a grubstake. It don't appear we'll need either one if we ain't gonna hire on with another cow outfit."

Cody made a face. "We'd be afoot an' there's nothin' more undignified than a horseless cowboy."

"But we agreed we wasn't gonna be cowboys no more."

"Whatever we're gonna be I don't think we oughta attempt it without a horse an' saddle. It's a comfort to know I can up an' ride off if I take the notion. Walkin' just ain't my style. We can find work if we look. There's plenty of professions besides cowboyin'. Maybe I'll decide to be a dentist."

Newt frowned. "You'd have to go to dentist's school, Cody, an' you never was much when it came to book learnin'. Miss Jones told you, back when we were kids in school, that your ears wasn't connected to your brain, remember? She said you never did listen to a word she spoke."

"That was different. What she was sayin' didn't interest me all that much."

Newt spat off one side of his horse. "Bein' a dentist don't sound all that good to me . . . pullin' teeth while some poor bastard is screamin' his head off on account of it hurts so bad. Ol' man Tucker got up out of a dentist's chair back in Waco one time an' gave his dentist a terrible ass whippin'. There used to be this big sign over the dentist's office sayin' extractions were almost painless. Tucker claimed nothin' ever hurt him so bad in all his life. My pa told me about it. There ain't no such sign hangin' on Elm Street no more. Somebody painted over the painless part."

"Maybe I'll take up the blacksmith's trade," Cody suggested. "I can shoe a horse, only it's a hell of a lot of work. I'd be more inclined to use my brain instead of my back. A strong back is what it takes to be a blacksmith an' it don't hurt none to be stupid."

"Some broncs kick real hard. Blacksmithin' can be dangerous as hell. Kyle Weatherby ain't got no kneecap in his right leg on account of a bay mare mule. His right leg's straight as a fence post ... won't hardly bend at all. He was laid up for months after it happened.''

"I'll think of somethin'," Cody promised. "The one thing I ain't gonna do anymore is cowboyin'. No more cattle drives up a long trail like the Chisholm for me, Newt. I nearly drowned up on the Red last year when that river was flooded. I figure Lady Luck was tryin' to tell me somethin'. I'll find work someplace or another an' it damn sure won't be swingin' a lariat rope. I'd just as soon shovel shit for a livery stable.''

Newt's expression said he wasn't so sure. "I'm gonna try to find somethin' that don't require usin' a shovel if I'm able. No more post holes, either. I've strung about all the fence I care to.''

"Fort Worth will have plenty of opportunities," Cody said as they came to a shallow creek south of town. He stopped to water his horse and gazed down at his reflection, rubbing blond beard stubble sprouting from his chin. "First off we'll hunt up a bathhouse an' make ourselves presentable. Then we'll look for some respectable form of employment.''

"Sounds good to me," Newt remarked, wiping sweat from his face with a soiled bandanna. "We could use gettin' some laundry done while we're at it. My best shirt an' denims need a boilin' somethin' fierce. Wouldn't care to be downwind from 'em myself.''

Cody grunted. "We might even avail ourselves of a couple of sportin' women tonight. My sap's been on the rise ever since I got word Millie Anderson up an' married Willard Cobb. I hadn't poked Millie in quite a spell but it was a comfort to know she'd be agreeable to it whenever I wanted.''

Newt seemed troubled by Cody's suggestion. "We ain't got no extra money to spend on sportin' gals. We'll have to stable our horses an' feed ourselves. We'll need to hire a room, an' I'm damn sure gonna buy a jug of decent whiskey. That don't leave us much for necessities.''

Cody argued, "A woman can be a necessity sometimes. Depends on how long a man's been without.''

"There ain't many cheap women down in Hell's Half Acre. I ain't so sure I'll have the price. Besides that, it can be a bit on the risky side to walk them back alleys where cheap women sell their favors. A man can get robbed or maybe killed, if he ain't real careful. The Acre is plumb full of hardcases who'll kill a man for what he's got in his poke."

Cody touched the butt of his revolver absently. He carried a Mason Colt .44-.40 on his right hip and considered himself more than ordinary when it came to shooting, although he'd never been in a position where he'd killed anyone with a gun. He could hit a bottle at forty paces with a fast draw and once shot an Osage cow thief in the leg while crossing with a herd up on the Canadian River. He'd been carrying a gun since he was fourteen. "We can handle ourselves," he told Newt, touching a spur to his horse when it lifted its muzzle from the stream.

They rode toward Fort Worth as dusk purpled the prairie. A westerly wind curled dust away from their horses' heels. In the back of his mind Cody knew opportunity awaited him there. All he had to do was look for it.

Her old wagon looked untrustworthy, its wheels tilted at a dangerous angle due to excessive wear on axle hubs. The woman who ran the laundry appeared sickly, pale, off her feed. She took their bags of clothing and piled them beside a cooking pot. A sign painted on the side of her wagon advertising that laundry was done cheap had drawn Newt and Cody to this public campground on their way into town.

"They'll be ready tomorrow," she said. "Dry an' folded, but I don't do no mendin' without extra charge, or no ironin'."

"How much?" Cody asked, noticing a girl standing at the back of the wagon, although it was too dark to see her as clearly as he wanted.

"Four bits a bundle. You won't find it no cheaper at one of them Chinese places."

Cody saw the girl a little better when she came closer with a bar of soap. "I never did trust no Chinaman to do laundry the way it oughta be, ma'am." He reached in his pocket for money as the girl walked to a boiling kettle with lye. "The price sounds all right to me." In light from the flames he could see the girl was very pretty. He thought of a way to make their conversation last. "Your wagon looks like it could use some repairs. I'm a right good hand when it comes to fixin' wagons. Maybe I can have a look at it for you in the mornin'."

"We can't afford no high-priced repairs, mister. Our wagon ain't much to look at but it gits us where we're goin', me an' my daughter." There was a suggestion of a warning in her voice when she made mention of the fact that the girl was her daughter.

He handed her fifty cents, finding he was unable to take his eyes off the pretty girl adding soap to one of the pots. "I can take a look. Won't be no charge for that. When we come back to pick up our clothes tomorrow, I'll see what it needs. Sometimes a wagon only needs a little adjustment here an' there."

She was suspicious. "Maybe it wouldn't be our ol' wagon you was interested in takin' a better look at. You been eyein' Annabelle since you got here."

Cody grinned and quickly turned his head. "Sorry, ma'am. I reckon I was lookin' some," he said in a quiet voice, hoping the girl wouldn't hear.

"Your laundry will be ready tomorrow by noon. If you still hanker to take a look at our wagon, we'd be obliged, but we ain't got any money so don't figure to make a payday off us—" All at once the woman coughed, gripping her sides. She turned away and wiped her mouth with a handkerchief.

The girl hurried over to her mother, ignoring Cody and Newt. "You okay, Ma?" she asked softly, concern furrowing her brow. In light from the fires Cody saw she was even prettier than he had first thought, although she was younger than he'd imagined, hardly a full-grown lady yet.

When the woman nodded, Cody said, "We'll be headed to town so's we can find a place to stable our horses, ma'am." He spoke to Annabelle. "Hope your ma feels better real soon."

"Thank you," she said, dark eyes meeting his for a moment. "Your clothes will be ready." She smiled a little, and when she did, Cody's heart corkscrewed like a pitching bronc.

"I'll have a look at that wagon, too," he added, wishing he'd shaved at the creek before they rode into town. He was thankful for the dark just then, since it would hide the color he felt in his cheeks, and a week's growth of beard. "Like I told your ma, there won't be no charge if I can tighten them hubs some. Won't take but a minute or two."

"That would be very nice of you."

"My name's Cody, Cody Wade, an' this here's Newt Sims." He pulled off his battered Stetson in gentlemanly fashion, hoping his untrimmed hair wouldn't offend her. He'd been meaning to get a haircut before they left Waco and hadn't gotten around to it in time.

She acknowledged Newt with a slight nod, but her eyes were on Cody. "Pleased to meet you both."

The woman turned around, patting her lips with her handkerchief, giving Annabelle a hard stare. "Git back to them kettles, girl. Clothes won't git clean by themselves."

"I'm goin', Ma. I was only bein' polite to our customers." Her gaze flickered briefly to Cody again, then she went to one of the cauldrons and began stirring its contents with a stick.

"We could fetch you some firewood, too, ma'am," Cody offered as he turned for his horse. "Appears that stack you got is a bit on the low side. I'd guess it takes a lot of wood to do so much laundry."

"We'll fetch it ourselves, young man," she said. "We ain't got money to pay for no firewood."

Cody swung a leg over his badly worn Steiner roping saddle and gathered his reins in one hand, wondering how a sick woman and a slightly built girl could chop and haul enough firewood to keep their kettles going. He touched the brim of his hat. "Be seein' you around noon," he said, trying to sound friendly about it.

When the woman merely nodded, he reined his horse. From the corner of his eye he caught Annabelle glancing at him, although she did it in such a way that her eyelashes mostly covered what she was looking at.

He tapped spur rowels against his dun's ribs and struck an

easy trot away from the campground. Newt rode up beside him in the dark. A few blocks away music and lights in Hell's Half Acre were like a beacon coming from the center of town.

"That ol' woman went plumb mean when she seen the way you was starin' at her daughter," Newt said, when they were well out of earshot.

His remark irritated Cody some. "What do you mean, the way I was starin', Newt? Why, I hardly noticed that girl at all. Come to think of it, I can't even remember her name."

"Her name was Annabelle an' you know it as well as me. You like to have stared holes through her just now, besides offerin' to fix her wagon an' cut down half the trees this side of Fort Worth so they'd have firewood."

"You're imaginin' things. I was just bein' neighborly."

"Horseshit, Cody. You got yourself downright moon-eyed over that gal. It wouldn't have surprised me none to see you step on the end of your tongue."

They swung their horses down Rusk Street. Cody decided it was pointless to deny his fascination with Annabelle. "She was mighty pretty, all right. Biggest brown eyes I ever saw an' the curliest, softest-lookin' hair. Her teats didn't look all that big, come to think of it, but she don't appear full grown. If I was to venture a guess, I'd say she's about fifteen or so. Maybe a little older . . . a year or two."

Newt chuckled. "She damn sure got your number. You nearly got flustered when you told her our names."

Farther up the street they could see couples walking along the Acre's boardwalks and hear half a dozen pianos, each playing a different tune. For the moment Cody forgot about Annabelle, when he remembered nights he'd spent here in the middle of Fort Worth before starting up to Kansas with a herd of cows.

"We're gonna have us some fun tonight," he said. "Let's get these horses put away an' find us a few shots of whiskey. Maybe a woman later on."

Newt made no objection to Cody's ideas as they rode abreast of the Stockmen's Retreat.

4

The Oasis Bar sat at one edge of the district known for its support for the undertaker's trade. Dead men were carried out so often, some said, they scarcely drew notice from regular patrons. A sign above the door claimed it was "Fort Worth's Safest Place Because Our Walls Are Lined With Lead." Dark stains on its wood floors were a mixture of blood and tobacco juice—when a spitter's aim was wide of a spittoon. Bullet holes in the ceiling leaked when it rained. The price of a drink was fifteen cents for a variety of whiskey known as Bull's-Eye, the name of which also served notice to more cautious customers that on occasion, more than watered down liquor might be included in an evening's entertainment. Gunshots were as commonplace inside the Oasis as complaints about the bad smell. The Oasis was at the bottom of a low hill where sewer ditches collected from better places farther up Tenth Street. It was here, due to the price of whiskey, where Cody and Newt lingered over their first drink of the night.

"It's good to be out of a saddle for a spell," Newt said as he knocked back a shot of Bull's-Eye. For the moment he couldn't quite catch his breath. "Damn, that stuff burns!"

Cody eyed his drink. The Oasis was known to color its home-brew corn whiskey with tobacco juice or whatever was at hand. A shot of Bull's-Eye was also rumored to kill stomach worms, while opinion was divided as to whether it cured or worsened some other forms of intestinal distress. "We've spent our last days in a saddle, Newt. From now on we'll be in another type of business."

"I sure hope you're right." Newt signaled the bartender for

another drink, of better whiskey, when his throat cooled.

Cody took a tentative sip from his glass. His tongue burned, and somewhere there was a suggestion of turpentine. "I know I'm right. You an' me are done with the cattle business forever. If they were payin' a hundred a month, I wouldn't sign on with a cowherd headed to Kansas, not even with Charlie Goodnight. I hope I never see the southern end of a cow again, or hear another bovine bawl in the middle of the night. I'm even tired of the taste of beef. If I had my choice, I'd eat chicken or pork the rest of my natural life."

Newt considered it. "We could raise pigs, I reckon, only I ain't sure I could stand the stink. If everybody else is as sick of beef as we are, pork is gonna get real popular. A chicken is mighty hard to raise, so they tell me. They get diseases. I'm a bit more inclined to vote we raise some hogs if we're stayin' in the livestock business. Then there's sheep to think about, only I ain't all that excited about callin' myself a sheepman. Sheep can be real sickly an' everybody knows how much a cowman hates a man who raises sheep."

"They're born lookin' for a place to die," Cody said. "Sick sheep are always a problem. I'd rather raise almost anything but lambs. It robs a man of his pride."

"Leastways we agree on that."

"No sheep. I reckon I'd feel nearly the same way 'bout us raisin' pigs."

A commotion outside made them glance to the door. A voice cried, "I'll kill you, you son of a bitch!"

Cody noted that the bartender immediately reached for his shotgun and then cradled it in the crook of his arm while keeping an eye on the batwing doors, although he seemed unruffled by the disturbance and continued to pour Newt's drink.

"Those dice are loaded!" the same voice declared.

A quiet spread through the Oasis, until someone spat loudly into a spittoon. Heads turned to hear what was going on.

"Go for your gun, you yellow bastard!" another man shouted, as Newt's glass was set in front of him.

"That'll be two bits," the barman said, sounding almost

too unconcerned about death threats beyond his doors.

Newt dropped a quarter on the bar. "Is there gonna be any shootin' out there?" he asked. Everyone in the Oasis heard his remark because of the quiet. Someone chuckled.

The bartender swept Newt's money into his palm. "I wouldn't care to bet against it," he said, watching the doors again. "If a man wanted to go broke, he'd bet against there bein' a shootin' on Tenth Street tonight. Most any night, for that matter."

Cody saw a man outside in a square of light cast on Tenth Street by an Oasis window. He was hunkered down like he meant to reach for a pistol strapped to his waist. Boots clumped heavily down a boardwalk in front of the saloon when passersby made haste getting away from the scene of a potential conflict. Soon there was another silence.

"You know goddamn well those dice are crooked, Jake! I seen you switch 'em when it was my pass. Ain't no pair of honest dice rolls sevens four times in a row."

"You're callin' me a cheat, Ike. Them's fightin' words. Go for that iron you're carryin' or give me an' apology."

A bearded cowboy standing next to Cody said softly, "That's Jake Ketchum, the one standin' in the light. He's faster'n most gents with a six-shooter an' he sure as hell knows how to throw crooked dice. If this was a horse race, my money'd be on Jake."

"You ain't gettin' no apology outa me," Ike swore, before Cody could ask who the other man was. "You the same as stole my money."

"Now you're callin' me a thief. I'm gonna have to kill you, boy, unless you apologize."

It seemed both men were more inclined to talk than shoot, when suddenly, through the pane of glass Cody saw Jake claw for his pistol.

A gunshot thundered up and down Tenth Street. Someone let out a groan. For a few seconds Jake appeared frozen to the spot, until something made him relax. Piano and banjo music stopped higher up the hill when the Acre's musicians recognized gunfire.

A pair of spurs rattled outside, sounding like their owner was having trouble keeping his feet. Cody watched Jake lower his gun, then boots staggered across the boardwalk toward the Oasis.

A cowboy near one of the windows said, "Ol' Jake just shot a hole through Ike Joiner."

A man stumbled through the batwings holding his belly, with a stream of blood pouring between his fingers. He looked young and frightened, his face a sickly shade of white. He made a turn for the bar, reeling, leaving a trail of blood across the floor.

"I'm shot," Ike gasped. His eyes were rounded with fear and pain. Slowly, his knees buckled. He sank to the floor, landing on his knees as though he meant to pray. No one made a move to help him.

"Jesus," Newt whispered, glancing over to Cody. "Somebody oughta fetch him a doctor."

"There ain't a sawbones in Fort Worth who'll come down here after dark." The bartender spoke with assurance. "We got us a veterinarian who sees to bullet wounds until mornin', only this feller don't look like he'll last that long."

A pair of cowboys came over to Ike. Ike looked up helplessly, without removing his hands from his belly. Blood pattered on the Oasis floor like gentle rain and in spite of a thick cloud of cigar smoke a coppery smell reached Cody's nostrils. Each cowboy held one of Ike's shoulders to keep him from falling on his face.

"Send for ol' man Grimes," the barman said, "if he ain't too drunk to walk already. Tell him to bring his medicine bag."

Someone hurried through the batwings, stepping wide of a man in a rumpled suit coat and baggy trousers stuffed into stovepipe boots, who came swaggering in. Cody recognized Jake Ketchum the moment he saw him even though he'd only seen him briefly through a window.

Jake scowled at Ike Joiner kneeling on the floor. "The son of a bitch called me a cheat. Claimed I switched the dice on him an' he went for his gun.'' Jake still carried his pistol loosely at his side.

"He ain't carryin' no gun, Jake," a whiskered cowboy said from the back of the room.

Jake's expression turned angry. "The hell he ain't! Open up his shirt—he's got a bellygun. He went for it plain as day."

Cody watched one of the cowboys holding Ike upright on his knees examine the front of Ike's shirt. "No gun," he said in a somber voice, like he'd known all along there wasn't.

"That means you shot an unarmed man." Cody said it before he had time to think. Everyone in the Oasis heard him.

Jake's dark eyes come to rest on Cody. "I say he had a gun. Maybe he dropped it out there in the dark someplace. Who the hell are you?" he snarled.

Cody shrugged, feeling suddenly naked and foolish for having said anything. It wasn't his affair. "Nobody in particular," he replied soft and low. "Just sayin' what was on my mind."

Jake's fingers tightened around the butt of his pistol, yet he kept it beside his leg for now. "Keep your goddamn nose outa business that ain't yours, sonny, or I'll give you a dose of the same lead poisonin' I gave this no-account son of a bitch."

In spite of the danger, Cody felt his temper rise. "Might not be quite so easy," he said casually, wishing he'd kept his mouth shut from the start. His mother claimed he'd inherited a bad temper from his father, always getting him into trouble. "I have a gun," he added needlessly, since it was in plain sight.

Jake's eyes narrowed. "You must fancy yourself a shootist, boy, sayin' those words to me." The challenge was unmistakable in Jake's tone.

It was so quiet in the Oasis every patron could hear Ike's blood dripping on the floor, until someone coughed.

"I don't claim to be no shootist," Cody replied as he edged away from the bar, "just an average cowboy who hates to see a man get shot when he ain't carryin' a gun." He let his right hand dangle near his .44-.40, all the while knowing he was acting like a crazy man, butting into trouble that wasn't his.

Jake's expression slowly changed to amusement. He gave Cody a one-sided grin. "You're hardly more'n a snot-nosed kid, but I swear you won't live long enough to see another birthday if you keep talkin' like that to me, sonny. I'll kill you 'fore you can sneeze."

Ike groaned, doubling over until his head hit the floor. He began pissing in his pants, but hardly anyone appeared to notice. All eyes were on Cody and Jake Ketchum.

"Like I said, that might not be so easy." Cody wondered if he could draw and shoot before Jake brought his gun up. He had to be loco to even consider it. He'd ridden all the way to Fort Worth looking for a new line of work, not a gunfight. What was he thinking?

Jake's grin disappeared. Cody watched his right hand, the hand holding the gun.

"Let's see how fast you are, boy," Jake hissed, clenching his teeth in anger. "Go for that gun whenever you're ready..." A noise coming from the boardwalk forced Jake to hesitate, when heavy boots clumped to the swinging doors.

A towering figure in a black suit coat and pants came into the Oasis. A flat-brim hat of the same color hid most of his face in shadow, although not all of a graying handlebar mustache with waxed ends decorating his upper lip. He carried a sawed-off twin-barrel shotgun in his left fist. His coattail was swept behind the butt of a revolver holstered low on his right leg.

"Evenin', Marshal Hull," the barman said offhandedly, as if they knew each other too well.

Jake turned around to face the much larger man, and when he did, his fingers relaxed on his gun. "I can explain, Cordel," Jake began, pointing to Ike. "This feller accused me of tryin' to cheat him with the dice, an' then he reached into his shirt for a gun."

Hull's gray eyes circled the room. The badge on his lapel read "City Marshal." He looked down at Ike, then back to Jake, and when he spoke his voice was like a rasp across iron. "Who saw it?" he asked.

No one said a word.

"It happened outside," the bartender explained. "Besides that, all my customers have got real bad eyesight. It's mighty dark out there tonight, so I don't reckon nobody saw a thing."

Cody's anger had a considerable distance to go before it cooled down—the muscles in his right arm were still tensed. He spoke to Marshal Hull. "I'm pretty sure the gent with the hole in him didn't have a gun. Could be there's one lyin' out there in the street, but I don't figure it's likely."

Hull watched Cody a moment, then he gave Jake a withering stare. "Is that so, Ketchum? Was this man you shot unarmed?"

Jake gave Cody a backward glance. "The kid's lyin'. I'd swear on my mammy's grave I saw the feller reach for a bellygun inside his shirt."

The marshal noticed Jake's pistol. "Drop that gun on the floor. We'll take a look outside. Somebody bring us a lantern so we can see who's tellin' the truth. There've been times when you had trouble with your memory, Ketchum. Last month you forgot you borrowed a drummer's pocket watch and his ring."

Jake still clung to his revolver. "That was all a mistake, Cordel. I found that watch an' ring in the alley."

Very slowly, Marshal Hull raised the barrels of his shotgun and placed them underneath Jake's chin. "I told you to drop the gun an' I never tell a man the same thing twice." His thumb drew one hammer back, making an ominous clicking noise when it cocked. "I'd hate to scatter pieces of your skull all over this ceiling, Jake, but I damn sure will if that gun don't hit the floor now."

Jake's Colt thudded to the floorboards.

Hull spoke to the barkeep. "Bring a lamp out here. If I don't find a gun out front, this owlhoot's goin' to jail. Judge Warren will charge him with attempted murder." He took another look at Ike before he prodded Jake with his shotgun. "Somebody needs to send for Doc Grimes if it ain't already too late."

"He's comin'," a customer said, as the crowd came forward to follow Marshal Hull and Jake outside.

It required less than five minutes to determine there was no gun in the street. Cody stood on the boardwalk to watch the proceedings, finally able to control his temper by now. No one came to attend to Ike while everyone looked for a weapon.

When the marshal was satisfied, he turned to Jake. "Walk in front of me to the city jail, Ketchum. Remember I'll be sorely tempted to blow you in half if you try anything dumb. Keep your hands where I can see 'em all the time."

"I was framed," Jake protested, giving Cody an icy stare before he felt shotgun barrels touch the small of his back. He stiffened.

Hull noticed Cody standing nearby. "I'm grateful for what you told me. Jake's got everybody in this end of town scared of him. Glad to see you ain't one of 'em." He pushed his prisoner forward up Tenth Street.

As Cody and Newt were ready to go back inside, the bearded cowboy who spoke to them earlier motioned Cody aside. "If I was you, I wouldn't turn my back on none of Jake's friends, stranger. He'll be after revenge for what you told Cordel Hull."

"I'm obliged, mister, but I'll be okay. Thanks anyway."

Newt caught Cody's arm. "Have you lost your damn mind, ol' friend?" he whispered, peering into Cody's eyes like he'd seen a ghost. "Why didn't you keep your mouth shut?"

He thought about it. "Hardheaded, I suppose. It sticks in my craw when some gent runs a bluff or uses a gun on another man who can't defend himself."

"What in tarnation made you think Ketchum was bluffin'?"

Cody knew what it was, something his pa taught him about a fight of any kind. "You can see it in a man's eyes when he ain't all that sure of himself. He don't look at you exactly straight. If you've seen it before, you get to where you recognize it."

Newt wagged his head. "You've taken leave of your senses, partner. I'd say you damn near got yourself killed . . ."

"Let's have another drink, Newt. The night's still young."

They returned to the Oasis just in time to hear a silver-haired veterinarian reeking of stale whiskey pronounce Ike Joiner dead.

5

Annabelle carried another basket of wet clothes to one end of a drying line as the morning sky paled with first light. Warm breezes from the south caused a stirring among garments hanging along sagging lines fastened to their wagon and nearby mesquite trees. All night, as she carried damp laundry to clotheslines, she thought about that moment in the Pink Lady when she'd been the center of attention, the polite applause they gave her, the way she looked in a borrowed silk dress and stockings. What a wonderful moment it had been. But at the same time, there was something wicked about it, something sinister and somehow filled with foreboding, as though an inner voice warned her of dire things to come, should she go there again.

Her back was aching as she afixed wooden clothespins to each piece of sodden laundry. Wet clothes were heavy, requiring more effort to hang up than her ma could manage lately. More and more as time passed, there were fewer things Doris could get done on her own. Her sickness had weakened her much faster than she'd expected, and when she coughed, more blood than ever came from her lungs. Annabelle still had the bottle of laudanum in a pocket of her dress, waiting for just the right moment to tell her mother how she got it. Or would it be better not to tell her the truth? How could she explain having it? Admitting she'd gone down to Hell's Half Acre after dark would anger her mother so much that she wondered if any benefit from the medicine would be worth it.

Doris was seated by a wagon wheel, on her old milking stool, when Annabelle returned with her empty basket.

"That's the last one, Ma. Why don't you lie down in bed for a spell?"

"It's too hot in that wagon, child. The breeze feels nice." She gave Annabelle a sideways look. "I'm sorry I hit you like I done," she said quietly, then she closed her eyes and rested her head against the wheel rim.

"It's okay, Ma. I know you didn't mean it. Since you been sick, you ain't nearly so patient like you used to be. Back when I was real small, you always told me the Lord would provide, only it don't seem He cares much about folks with the consumption, or He wouldn't let you feel so bad."

"It ain't the Lord's doin'. It's the devil's work goin' on inside me on account of my sins."

"You ain't no sinner, Ma. If there ever was an angel on this earth it's you."

"I was a sinner once," she said, in a voice so small Annabelle almost failed to hear her. "That was before I married your pa."

"I can't hardly believe that, not about you. You was always the gentlest person in the world. An' if you did happen to allow a sin or two a long time ago, surely the Lord has forgiven you for it by now." She sat on the ground and took her mother's hand.

Doris opened her eyes, staring off at the sunrise like she was some other place in her mind. "It was a long time ago, child. I was 'bout your age, a year younger."

"What happened?"

"I can't git up the gumption to make myself talk 'bout it now. It ain't the sorta thing a child oughta hear anyhow."

"I surely do wish you'd stop callin' me a child, Ma. I'm a full sixteen years old, not some sugar-teat baby. I do my share of the laundry an' seein' after our mule. I cut a right smart of firewood, too. I'm old enough to be called a woman an' treated that way, don't you think?"

Tears formed in her mother's eyes yet she continued to stare at the horizon. "I reckon you are," she sighed after a bit. "I jus' can't help thinkin' of you as my baby girl. It's hard for a mother to let go of her children sometimes. Hardest part is to think of 'em as full growed enough so's we can talk 'bout things like we should. There's a hundred things I oughta tell you, only I can't git up enough gumption to do it, seems like. Lately I've been reminded I may be runnin' out of time to git things said.''

"Don't think about dyin', Ma. It ain't nearly time for that yet." She squeezed her hand gently, reassuringly.

Doris blinked away eyelids full of tears and she still could not look at her daughter. "I been thinkin' about it real hard. I know I ain't got long. I'm gettin' mighty weak these days an' when I cough, there's more'n more blood. My time's comin' soon an' all I can think about it what'll happen to you when I'm gone to be with the Lord. You'll be all alone, without no family."

"I can make it just fine. Stop frettin' over me."

"I do fret, Annabelle. We got no money. Only this ol' bit of a wagon an' boilin' kettles. A smooth-mouth mule. A few old clothes. I wanted you to have a better life . . ."

"Life ain't so bad. More money would be nice."

"Money's hard to come by. Folks ain't inclined to part with it 'less you got somethin' they really want. Most everybody says they want clean clothes, only there's too many folks who'll do a laundry cheap." She sniffled, wiping her cheeks with a bloodstained handkerchief. "When I die . . . you won't have any money or no place to call your own, nobody to keep you safe from sin till you're old enough to know better."

"I'm old enough to make it on my own. You fret too much about what'll happen to me. I'll make it just fine." She made up her mind it was time to tell her about the laudanum. "I met this real nice lady. She was in a fancy carriage. When I told her about your sickness, she gave me a bottle of laudanum. She said take two spoonfuls when you're hurtin' real bad."

Doris gave her a questioning look. "Who was this here real nice lady, Annabelle?" She eyed the bottle with suspicion and did not take it when Annabelle removed it from her dress pocket.

"I didn't ask her name," she lied. "I was walkin' down by

the train station after you slapped my face, an' when she seen
I was cryin' she told her driver to stop. She asked me what
was so bad that I was cryin' like that. I told her my ma was
sick, so she gave this to me. She said it'll help.''

"Did you promise to pay her money for it?"

"She didn't want any money."

"Medicine's real expensive. Don't make any sense, hard as
times are, that she'd give it to you for no reason."

"She said she wanted you to have it, is all. She was a nice
lady. Rich as a queen, too. That carriage probably cost more'n
a house."

Again, Doris eyed the bottle without taking it. "It don't
seem right, that she didn't ask for no money. Rich folks ain't
got much sympathy for them that's poor, usually. Seems like
she would have wanted money, or somethin'."

Annabelle couldn't tell her what Miss Rose really wanted,
a girl to consort with cowboys at the Pink Lady. But hadn't
Miss Rose said she couldn't think of a better reason for making money if it was to take care of a girl's sick mother? "She
didn't ask for no money, Ma. But wouldn't havin' some
money so you could go to a doctor be better'n hurtin' so
bad?"

"Where would we git that kind of money?" She finally
took the bottle and held it in her lap.

She knew she couldn't tell her what Miss Rose had said.
"I was only wishin', Ma. But it sure would be nice to have
some, so you could stop hurtin' all the time."

Doris fingered the bottle absently. It was clear her mind was
on something else. She watched the rising sun. "There's no
time left for wishin'," she said. "When somebody's dyin',
they know these things. There's hardly no time left for me to
tell you what a young woman needs to know. I kept tellin'
myself we'd have a chance to talk when you got older, only
I ain't gonna be around then. I gotta learn you about menfolk
an' havin' babies, besides all them evil things the devil's
gonna tempt you with. This life is full of terrible temptations.
Wrongful actions are sure to give the devil his due. You can't
let temptation take you off the path to righteousness. Fill your

spirit with the word of the Lord an' don't ever give in to temptation or you'll be punished by the wrath of God almighty. I'm gonna die young because I was a sinner, Annabelle. Don't let Satan take you down the wrong road, not even once!''

''What did you do that was so awful?''

She held the bottle of laudanum up to the light. ''When the time is right, I'll tell you,'' she whispered, as more tears came streaming down her face. She took out the cork and drank a long swallow. ''Time we got back to them clothes. I've got foldin' to do before them two young cowboys come at noon.''

''That tall one was real nice an' polite, only he acted like he was embarrassed when I spoke to him. He was handsome, too. He said his name was Cody.''

Doris corked the laudanum and put it down, drying her tears with a finger. ''Cowboys are mostly shiftless drifters who never settle down. They've hardly ever got any money or an inclination to do hard work if it can't be done from a horse. Don't take no fancy to a cowboy like him. Bein' handsome don't make him a good man or a hard worker.''

''He offered to fix our wagon an' cut some firewood.''

''We'll see. Until this wagon is fixed, it wasn't nothin' but an empty promise. Same goes for the wood. Lots of men can make big promises, but only the best keep 'em.''

''I'll help with the foldin' an' see to the mule. We're near out of corn.'' She stood up and then patted her mother's shoulder. ''Don't you worry none, Ma. We'll find a way to get enough money so you can visit a doctor. I'm old enough so I can help to make us some extra.''

Doris came stiffly from her stool, looking ghostly pale when morning sunlight shone on her face. ''It's better to be poor an' live a God-fearin' life. We won't take any charity in no regular way, but if you see that nice lady again, you can tell her I'm mighty grateful for the medicine.''

''I'll tell her. If I see her again. Soon as we get done with foldin', I'll fix us some frybread an' bacon.''

They began taking clothes from some of the lines, folding them neatly in small piles. Annabelle was remembering the young cowboy and she made a special effort to fold his shirts and pants free of wrinkles.

He was nice, she thought. Broad shoulders and narrow hips, a quick smile. She wondered how he would look in daylight. And was it true, what her mother said, that all cowboys were drifters who never had money?

She remembered the crowd downstairs at the Pink Lady. A man in a nice suit and bowler hat had spoken to her, and he looked as though he had enough money to afford better things.

Why did everything center around money? she wondered. What was it that made money so hard to earn? Miss Rose promised she could make a lot of money by working for her. What would it be like to do that? How could she ever take off her clothes with a stranger and consort with him? It would be the most awful thing she could think of.

Later that morning, as she was tending to their mule, giving it the last ears of corn they had, Tommy Joe Booker came walking through the trees with his hands in his pockets. He saw her and grinned.

"Miss Rose said you came to see her last night."

"Hush that kind of talk, Tommy Joe, or Ma will hear you."

He stopped a few yards away, toying the ground with his boot toe. "Are you thinkin' about goin' to work for her?"

"Never! I'd rather die!"

"She tol' me you came downstairs in one of her red dresses, an' that the whole place clapped real loud and whistled."

"Didn't nobody whistle. It wasn't like that at all."

"She said you was the prettiest gal in Fort Worth, when you got dressed up. She never said nothin' like that before about no other girl."

"She was only bein' nice."

He wagged his head. "Nope. She tol' me you was so pretty that if you wanted, you could make half the men in the county pay to see you. She said you could be rich."

"That was a terrible thing to say, that so many men would do somethin' like that. There's good men, too, like my pa was. He'd never have paid no scarlet woman to consort with him."

"Maybe. But there's plenty of them that will." Tommy Joe

said it like he knew what he was talking about. "Some gals down at Miss Rose's place see five or six men every night. That's a whole bunch of money, almost more'n there is in the whole world."

"Five or six in one night?" She couldn't believe any woman could consort with so many.

Tommy Joe's blush was hiding his freckles. "For a fact," he said. "I carry out the pots, so I'd know."

Annabelle shucked the last ear of dry corn. "How much does a girl make when they do somethin' like that?" she asked without really thinking about the nature of her question.

"Maybe four or five dollars. Depends if she's pretty."

Now she was blushing. What was she doing talking to a boy she scarcely knew about something so private?

But she counted it up to herself. If Tommy Joe was telling the truth, some girls at Miss Rose's were making nearly twenty-five dollars a night. "Wouldn't be long till they'd be rich," she said.

"You could be rich," he promised. "Miss Rose said so."

She caught herself thinking about what it would be like to have as much money as she could spend. She'd have as many new dresses as Miss Rose, and a room like hers with a canopied bed and fine furniture, even rugs.

"I'd never do it, regardless. Now, go away, Tommy Joe, so I can finish helpin' Ma with the laundry. Quit botherin' me with all your fanciful tales about bein' rich. God-fearin' women do not sell themselves for money."

6

The August heat became oppressive before noon most days. Doris lay on a pallet below a canvas roof of their lean-to that gave shade from the sun's fierce glare. A dose of laudanum had been enough to put her to sleep despite the heat, allowing Annabelle to make herself as presentable as she could before Cody Wade's arrival. She hadn't wanted her ma to notice when she changed to her best dress, a pale blue with a button missing in front which gave a view of the tops of her breasts, not too much. She examined her face in a mirror they kept in an old jewelry box. Long ago, they'd sold what few trinkets they had in the box to get enough money to eat—a silver brooch, a ring, and Chester's old pocket watch that wouldn't keep time. But the little mirror was useful and now, as she looked at herself in it, she fashioned her hair the way Miss Rose had, ringlets dangling down her neck, a fan of curls on top tied in a piece of dark blue ribbon. She'd taken a quick standing bath in their covered wagon, using a cloth and a bucket of water, scrubbing her face and neck the most so no dirt would show where sweat plastered airborne dust to exposed skin. She wished for something scented, like that wonderful perfume filling the room at Miss Rose's place last night, so she'd smell as sweet as those other girls. But perfume was very expensive, even common lilac water, thus she made ready for Cody without it.

She glanced down at the cleft of her bosom self-consciously and felt her face coloring. Would he stare? Her blue dress was made of cotton and it showed long use. Would he laugh at the way it looked?

She smiled at her reflection. She'd brushed her teeth with the last of a box of baking soda, hoping her ma wouldn't notice it was gone. Now, as she looked at herself one final time before putting the mirror away, she wondered what Cody would think. Was it silly to hope he'd notice her and maybe feel a bit of attraction? He was handsome, and even if he was a cowboy who drifted from place to place, that made him no different than they were as they headed west toward Arizona Territory, wherever that was.

She glanced at the sun and saw it was almost noon. Cody's bundle of laundry was folded and as ready as she could make it. Now there was nothing to do but wait.

She ambled slowly to the shade of a mesquite and rested a shoulder against the trunk, thinking, remembering last night and the strange feelings she had had while all those men were staring at her, the applause. The old cowboy had bowed and said she was "near 'bout the prettiest female I ever saw in all my borned days and I've seen more 'n just a few in my time." But that handsome gentleman in the bowler hat had toasted her with his glass and called her "the most beautiful gal in town," calling her "Belle" the way Miss Rose had. He'd also said he was looking forward to seeing her again sometime.

She recalled things Tommy Joe said, how some of Miss Rose's girls were visited by five or six men in a single night. It did not seem possible, but then what did she know about that sort of thing, having only consorted once in her life and that with Timmie's finger?

"I could never do it for money," she whispered to herself as a warm breeze rustled her skirt, tousling her hair, rattling dry mesquite beans above her head. "I just know I couldn't." But as she said it, she thought about making twenty-five dollars in only one evening, more than she and her ma made in a whole month doing laundry, and then there was the cost of firewood and soap.

Was Tommy Joe telling the truth?

Down the street from the campground a few passengers began to gather in front of the railroad station. "Train must be late today," she said idly. A passenger train came every day at noon when it was on time. She watched the road for any sign of Cody and his friend and saw no one. Dust blew across the road in big swirls now and then. Between gusts dirt settled back to earth in layers, like powder.

"I wish he'd come along soon." She worried that sweat might stain her underarms, and that the wind would muss her hair. Was he coming at all? Or had he forgotten about his laundry?

She tapped one foot impatiently and then noticed her shoes, a coating of dust. She licked her fingers and wiped them off as best she could, frowning at how badly worn they were. "It would sure be nice to have enough money to buy a new pair of shoes. I would get red ones, like Miss Rose's, the ones she let me wear." The silk stockings felt so smooth when she put them on. She had to be shown how to use the garter belt, never having put one on before. Back in San Augustine, she'd examined one at Bingham's General Merchandise, although not too closely since her ma warned they were expensive.

"Everything's expensive. Everything worth having . . ."

A gust of wind lifted her dress briefly, showing her legs, only no one was there to see them. The campground was empty this time of year. When trail herds began forming later on, the place would be crowded, Tommy Joe said. Tommy Joe lived across the creek in a two-room shack with his pa. His pa was very poor, a carpenter by trade, and they were as poor as the Green family from San Augustine, she judged. Tommy Joe worked at the Pink Lady because they needed the money. One time he told her that his pa got drunk most of the week and that was the reason they were so poor, not because he was a carpenter. His ma had run off with a traveling drummer because his pa beat her when he got drunk.

She examined the road again, looking for Cody. "Wonder if he'll come at all," she said quietly, folding her arms across her chest, which made her breasts swell where the top of her dress was open. She hadn't really noticed until last night how much bigger she'd gotten there, or how much rounder her buttocks were. Her old dresses didn't show much of her figure, and they couldn't buy from a bolt of new cloth so she could sew a new one. It was so terrible being poor, she thought.

Her ma still slept soundly underneath the canvas in spite of the heat, and for that she was grateful. It would be better if she were asleep when Cody and his friend came, so they could talk a bit and get to know each other. If they ever came at all.

She watched the road, pensive, recalling what it was like to be the center of attention in a room full of people for once in her life. She felt a trace of sorrow because it was over so soon and now she was back to being plain and going unnoticed. Today, no one would notice her because she wore an old dress and worn-out shoes. Unless Cody liked the fact her button was missing.

The locomotive chugged loudly into Union Station, pulling its load of passenger cars and boxcars, hissing steam from couplings and fittings like a giant dragon from a book Annabelle read when she was in school. Someone, she couldn't remember who, had slain the dragon with a sword.

She watched the train grind to a halt, wishing she could be one of its passengers just once. She'd never ridden a train, nor was it likely she would since train tickets cost money. Only the richest folks rode trains, Ma said. Everybody else rode wagons.

Passengers dressed in all manner of finery climbed down from the cars. Women opened parasols to keep sun from their faces. A man wearing a flat-brim hat and gunbelt got down from a car and looked both ways several times, like he was expecting to be met by somebody. He gave Annabelle a passing glance when he saw her standing by the tree, then he strode off in the direction of the Acre, carrying a black valise.

Annabelle sighed, feeling lonely. Doris still slept and that was a blessing. There was no sign of Cody or his companion. If he didn't come soon, Ma would be waking up and that would keep Annabelle from talking to him freely, maybe even flirting a little if she found the courage.

More passengers boarded the train and all at once the steam whistle blew. Seconds later a conductor cried, "All aboard!" as the locomotive hissed loudly again. The string of cars began to move slowly away from the station. Annabelle wished with all her heart she was riding on it to wherever it went. Almost any place would be better than where she was now, she thought.

Soon the last railroad car was out of sight behind rows of buildings. She could still hear the locomotive chugging after it was gone more than a minute. The sound faded and there was only the sigh of wind passing through mesquite branches again.

Two men walked past the station heading in her direction, and when she saw them, she recognized Cody and Newt. They seemed in no particular hurry, wearing different shirts today—she was quick to notice those things, being in the laundry business. Her heart beat a little faster now.

She looked down at her bosom, and in a moment of daring she unfastened another button at the top so that a good deal more of her breasts showed. If her ma woke up while she had so much skin exposed, there would be a sermon on the subject. But for now she slept and that alone was enough to give Annabelle more courage to see if she could interest Cody the way a pretty woman interests a man.

She did her best to walk slowly and calmly toward the wagon where their clothing lay on a blanket. Before they came too much closer, she took a look at the tops of her breasts. It was almost indecent, how much of her bosom was showing, but remembering the way Miss Rose's dress showed her cleavage, she left the button as it was.

"Howdy, Miss Annabelle," Cody said, when he was close enough for her to hear him. He grinned and tipped his hat. But when he came a few steps nearer his eyes strayed down, and that's when a look of surprise crossed his face.

"How are you, Cody?" she asked, halting by the wagon with a bit of a turn to her waist. She only smiled at Newt, not wanting to encourage him falsely.

Cody sauntered up, glancing at her bosom again before he let his gaze return to her face. "I'm just fine, I reckon. I hope it ain't bein' too forward if I say you're lookin' mighty pretty today."

"Why, thank you," she replied, hoping her blush didn't show too much. She wanted to tell him he looked handsome, only that didn't seem very ladylike. She couldn't help noticing how Newt stared at the front of her dress. "Your laundry is ready. I did all I could to get most of the wrinkles out." Hadn't he said she was looking mighty pretty?

"I'm obliged." He looked past her. "Is your ma feelin' a bit better today?"

"It's nice of you to ask, but she's not well. She has the consumption. She's sleepin' right now."

He grinned again, resting one hand on the butt of his gun. He seemed very sure of himself and she liked that. He was tall, taller than she remembered, over six feet. He had bright blue eyes the color of a sky and blond hair that needed a trim. His shoulders, what she could see of them underneath his bib-front shirt, were muscled like a man who was no stranger to work. He had a strong chin, which Ma always said was important since men with weak chins were prone to be weak-willed. She decided Cody was one of the most handsome men she'd ever seen, even if he was only a cowboy.

"Would it be all right with your ma if sometime," he asked, "I came to pay you a social call? We could walk downtown to a place I know an' maybe get some lemon pie or even some ice cream, if you'd want."

"I'd like that very much, only I don't think Ma'd let me go. She has this notion that I'm too young for . . . that sort of thing."

His eyes fell to her cleavage again. "She's sure wrong as she can be about that, Annabelle. You're plenty old enough, it looks like to me."

She knew her blush was deepening, and in a curious way she found she liked the feeling. "That's nice of you to say, but I don't think it'd change Ma's mind about it." She took a quick look in the direction of their lean-to. "I suppose I'd be willin' to meet you at this place some evenin', if you wanted. I couldn't be away too long."

"I'd like that, Annabelle," he said quietly, sincerely. "If you want, we could meet there this evenin' early, maybe eight or so. It's called the Emporium, on the corner of Sixth Street. We can get whatever you like there. Sweet stuff, mostly. Candy and cakes an' pies. And they serve the best lemonade. I sure hope you'll decide to come.''

''I'll try,'' she told him, ''if I can get away without upsetting my ma.''

''See you around eight, then,'' he said, taking his laundry as, once again, his gaze wandered down the front of her dress. ''You won't be sorry. It's the best pie you ever ate.''

He departed with Newt, glancing over his shoulder a time or two before they rounded a street corner. Annabelle watched them leave from the corner of her eye, pretending not to notice. As soon as they were out of sight, she buttoned her dress, then she smiled to herself.

''Maybe I am pretty,'' she said softly, returning to the back of the wagon to open the jewelry box. ''Maybe I am old enough to have myself a young man.'' She wondered if Cody really liked her, or was it that he liked what he saw where her dress was open? He seemed to be sincere when he said he hoped she'd come to the Emporium. Just thinking about it made her heart beat faster.

When she looked in the mirror, she saw something different, something she couldn't identify. Her face looked just about the same, but there was something in her eyes that was very different—yet she couldn't explain what it was. Somehow, she had changed. Or was it only her imagination . . .

7

Damn," Cody whispered, with his clothes under his arm, leading Newt along Main Street to their boardinghouse in Maddox Flats, where they shared a four-bit room. "She's nearly the prettiest girl I ever saw in my whole life, Newt. An' did you notice how her dress was open?"

"Couldn't hardly keep from noticin'. She ain't as flat in the chest as I figured the first time I saw her."

"She sure as hell ain't, and she's got a face so smooth it's like it was painted on. Biggest brown eyes I ever did see. She got me to wonderin' how old she is, after what she said about her ma not lettin' her go no place yet."

"Maybe eighteen or so. She's young, and poor as a church mouse. You plumb forgot about fixin' her wagon."

Cody stopped in mid stride and shook his head. "You shoulda reminded me. I promised I'd look."

"Your mind was on other things, partner. When you seen what was hangin' outa the front of that dress, you went dumb as a post. I wish you coulda seen your face."

He looked back toward the campground thoughtfully. "If I go later on, when her ma's awake, it might seem like I meant to come back all along. I said I'd chop 'em some firewood, too . . ."

"You've lost your senses over a woman, choppin' down trees and fixin' wagons for free. Maybe you've come down with a case of the heatstroke."

He gave Newt a weak grin. "I may have lost my senses but I sure as hell ain't blind. I'll go back later this afternoon, so they'll know I'm a man of my word." He continued walking up Main until they came to Fifteeth Street, turning east with Newt keeping silent. A few working man's bars were opening early, since this was Saturday. A boy was sweeping out a place called Maude's as they came abreast of the doors. Cody took a look inside and saw the city marshal talking to a man behind the bar. He stopped to hear what was being said, and that was when Marshal Hull noticed them standing out front.

Hull pushed away from the bar. He came through a pair of swinging doors, squinting when sun hurt his eyes, until he tugged down the brim of his hat.

"I remember you," he said, not in an unfriendly way. "You were at the Oasis when I collared Jake Ketchum for murderin' that boy from Big Spring."

Cody nodded and offered his hand. "Name's Cody Wade. I was there last night. I told you the other feller wasn't carryin' a gun. Too bad he had to die that way."

Hull appraised Cody carefully before he spoke again. "Jake and me are well acquainted over the years. He's one of them back alley characters we breed from time to time, like leavings at the bottom of a whorehouse piss pot. I aim to see to it he stretches a rope for shootin' that unarmed boy. I just wanted you to know I'm grateful for what you said in front of him and everybody else down there. Maybe I oughta warn you Jake's got friends who'll be unhappy. You handled yourself right well, but I wouldn't make a habit of turnin' my back on too many folks for a spell. Jake is a yellow bastard. He's liable to have somebody take a crack at you from behind."

"I'll be careful. Jake's kind don't worry me much."

Hull's eyes narrowed a little. "That's mighty strong talk." He examined Cody's gunbelt. "Are you any good with that thing?"

"I get by reasonable well in a tight spot. My pa taught me how to shoot."

The marshal was still searching for something. "Was your pa anybody special with a six-gun?"

"Some said he was a long time ago. They said he was quick

on the draw an' could hit what he was aimin' at might' near all the time.''

"What was your pa's name? I don't recall nobody by the name of Wade right offhand . . .''

"John. He went by Johnny. He's been dead six years or so. Got killed by a runaway horse down in Waco. He'd be about your age, I reckon.''

Hull said the name softly. "Johnny Wade. Seems I heard it someplace before. I can't remember just now.''

Cody was a bit embarrassed. "He had a price on his head. We hardly ever saw him when I was small. He did his time for a bank robbery down in San Antone. Five years he was away over at Huntsville. When he came back, he was changed. Started breakin' horses, until one of 'em broke him up real bad. He was a good hand with a bronc.''

For the moment Hull seemed satisfied. "Just watch your back side, son. Jake's got some mean-natured friends. Are you goin' up the Chisholm this fall like most trail hands?''

"No, sir, I ain't. I'm givin' up the cowboyin' profession to find another line of work. I'm lookin' for a job.''

Again, the marshal appraised him closely. "You appear to be big and strong. I may be lookin' for a jailer in a few weeks. I gotta warn you it ain't easy work and sometimes the drunks get a little rowdy. It pays fifty a month and a bed. Come by my office sometime and we'll talk.''

Cody frowned. "I hadn't figured on bein' no lawman. It can get kinda risky, from what I hear.''

"It's no job for a tenderfoot. If you're scared easy, you'll only last a day or two. This is a tough town. It takes hard men to enforce the law here.''

"I never said I scared easy, Marshal, only that I heard it got kinda dangerous wearin' a badge around Fort Worth lately. A deputy sheriff told me about it last year, how he had to be real careful in Hell's Half Acre at night.''

"Think it over,'' Hull said, idly watching the kid sweeping a boardwalk in front of Maude's Place. "Where're you stayin' while you're in town?''

"Adams Boardinghouse over in Maddox Flats. We're

sharin' a room right now, till we can do better."

The marshal grunted. "That ain't exactly the best neighborhood. Watch your ass down there after dark." He made a
turn to go west and paused. "Seems this town in gettin'
tougher all the time. I just got word George Curry got off the
noon train. I tangled with Flatnose Curry once. It wasn't a
church picnic that time and I don't expect it'll get no better.
You think about the jailer's job, son. Might be you're just the
man I'm needin', if you've got backbone." He sauntered off
in the direction of Main Street before Cody could say anything
more.

Newt nudged his ribs. "That'd be a laugh, Cody, the son
of Big Johnny Wade becomin' a lawman. Your pa'd flip over
in his grave if he knowed it. He hated lawmen worse'n a
preacher hates sin."

"He mellowed some after he got out of prison," Cody explained, turning for Maddox Flats. "I remember he told me
not to take up robbery or break no laws if I could help it, on
account of prison was such a bad place. It broke his spirit, he
said one time, like breakin' the spirit in a wild horse. He
changed after he did that five-year stretch. Maybe he wouldn't
be all that set against me bein' a lawman."

Newt remained unconvinced. "I still say he'd sunfish right
outa his grave if you pinned on a badge. Folks down home
wouldn't believe it either. You never was known for bein' a
real law-abidin' type a few years back. You stole a good-sized
share of old man Fuston's watermelons an' peaches, and there
was the time you took that candy jar right out of the front
window at Curtis Johnson's store."

"That was while Pa was in prison. I wanted to be like him
so I did a few robberies. That was kid stuff."

They both laughed, walking through a quiet section of the
Acre devoted to smaller whorehouses, to reach a poor district
by the name of Maddox Flats, where down-and-outers lived
in shacks and shabby little hotels. Cody recalled his boyhood,
after what Newt said. It had seemed like a lonely time while
his pa was in prison. His mother worked at odd jobs and ran
a small farm where they lived on what a garden would pro-

vide. It was hard back then being the son of a gunman and bank robber. Almost everyone knew about his family and John Wade's crimes. Newt had been his best friend, being from a poor family himself, and they'd just naturally been thrown together by circumstances when they were kids.

Newt said, "They were harmless things, stealin' peaches an' candy, Cody. But decidin' to be a lawman might not be so harmless. You could get killed."

"A jailer is different. You lock 'em up and feed prisoners for regular lawmen. Nothin' dangerous about a plateful of pinto beans twice a day."

Newt appeared to be troubled. "I reckon that means you an' me wouldn't be goin' into business together, like we planned."

"If I took that job, it'd only be temporary," Cody promised. "It wouldn't be the sort of thing I'd do permanent."

They came to their boardinghouse and trudged up a set of sagging steps. Somewhere inside they heard someone laughing as they let themselves in.

Upstairs, rooms were hot during the heat of midday and Cody decided to head back to the laundry wagon to keep his promise, as well as to get another look at beautiful Annabelle. She was too pretty to push from his mind and maybe, with luck, she'd meet him at the Emporium tonight so he might really get to know her over a piece of sweet lemon pie.

"Pleased to make your acquaintance, Miz Green," he said, as he removed his hat, remembering his manners. "I came back to see about your wagon."

The woman didn't trust him and it showed. "You already got your laundry."

"Yes, ma'am, but you were asleep an' I feared it might wake you up if I made too much noise."

Annabelle was stirring a kettle, hardly paying any attention to what was being said. He'd noticed that her dress was buttoned up the front now.

"We can't pay," Mrs. Green reminded him.

Cody put on his hat. "I understand, ma'am. I'll see what I

can do without it costin' money.'' He walked to a rear wheel and bent down. "Just like I figured. This hub nut is loose. Your axle's worn some, but a good tightenin' and some grease will fix most of the wobble.'' He took a rusted hub wrench from the wagon box and rolled up his sleeves. Annabelle glanced his way when he began tightening the nut. Two full turns required every ounce of strength he could muster since the threads were badly rusted, but when he was done the wheel stood straight the way it should.

"There. It'll roll true now,'' he said.

Mrs. Green watched him attend to the other wheels while her daughter busied herself with boiling clothes. Every now and then Annabelle would look his way and give him a half smile, only when her ma wasn't looking.

After tightening all four nuts, he took their grease bucket from where it hung under the wagon bed and applied a heavy coat of grease to each axle hub. He was sweating in late day heat by the time he finished.

"It's done,'' he told the woman, returning the bucket to its proper place. "Mind if I wash off my hands?''

Her expression softened some. "Over yonder's the washtub. There's a bar of soap an' a cloth.''

He walked to a wooden bucket and soaped his palms, all the while sneaking looks in Annabelle's direction when he could. She appeared to enjoy their secret exchanges and smiled whenever her mother's back was turned. Mrs. Green added wood to fires under the kettles until Cody's hands were clean and dry.

He approached the wagon, being careful not to pay any notice to Annabelle just then. He spoke to her ma. "I told you I'd cut some wood, Miz Green. If you'll show me the axe . . .''

"We can't pay,'' she said darkly, worried again that he would ask for money.

"There won't be no charge, ma'am.''

His offer only concerned her more. "Why would you cut some wood an' not want no money?'' she asked, peering under the brim of his hat so she could see his eyes.

He hooked his thumbs in his gunbelt. "I reckon because

it's real clear you folks could use some help. I know what it's like to be poor.''

"Don't make any sense. Nobody does somethin' for nothin'.''

Cody shrugged. "I fixed your wagon best I could. It needs new axles before too long, but it'll run true now. I never said I wanted any money.''

"We don't take charity neither. Not regular. We're obliged for what you already done, but we'll fetch our own firewood—''

"He's only bein' neighborly, Ma,'' Annabelle interrupted, as she stopped stirring a kettle. "It won't hurt nothin' if we let him chop us some wood.''

The woman gave her daughter a cold stare. "You tend to them pots, child.''

"Yes, Ma.'' Annabelle's face turned red—she tried to hide it by turning her back on him.

"I'll be goin' then, Miz Green,'' he said, "if you're sure I can't help with that wood.''

The woman watched him for a time. Something he saw in her face told him she guessed what he was really up to, although he couldn't quite be sure.

"I don't want to appear ungrateful, Mr. Wade, but we don't need no more of your help. Me an' my daughter have still got our pride, even if we ain't got no money. We know how to chop wood. You done us a service fixin' them wheels. Now it's time me an' her got back to work. We're obliged for what you done.''

He backed away and turned toward town. "You folks have a pleasant evenin', ma'am,'' he told her, walking off like he never intended to come back.

8

He wore his best navy bib-front shirt and the only pair of denims he owned that weren't faded nearly white. He'd brushed his Stetson as clean as he could get it and done what he could for his boots with blacking. He even cleaned and oiled his gun, not that she'd notice something like that. After a bath in an iron tub behind Adams Boardinghouse, he'd shaved again and done his best to run a comb through his thick hair, borrowing a splash of rose-scented hair tonic from Newt as a final touch.

He sat at a table looking out on Sixth Street with his back to the wall, drinking a fizzy sarsaparilla concoction that was too sweet for his liking. No distilled spirits were served at the Emporium—he would have much preferred a whiskey to settle his nerves, thinking about Annabelle and how beautiful she was. But as eight o'clock came and went, his spirits began to sink. She isn't coming, he thought sadly. Maybe she couldn't. Maybe she decided against the idea.

A few patrons gave his gun and holster wary looks, as though a sweetshop wasn't the proper place for a man carrying a pistol. He drank his sarsaparilla dejectedly until twenty past the hour. Dark was settling over Fort Worth and now he was sure she wasn't coming after all.

A young woman hurried past a front window, where she stopped abruptly when she came to the door. His heart skipped a beat as he recognized Annabelle, and then he noticed that she unfastened a button at the top of her dress before she opened a glass-paned door to come inside.

He swallowed, hoping his nervousness wouldn't show, and

got up to offer her a chair. She came over to his table, smiling.

"Sorry I'm late," she said, sounding out of breath. "Ma was dead set against me leavin' just now. She figures I was up to a meanness of some kind."

She took the chair he held out for her, showing off more of her bosom than he had seen before, because now he was looking down into her dress.

"I'm sure glad you came," he said, wishing he'd thought of something better to say to start off with. He sat down opposite her and pointed to a row of glass cabinets where all manner of sweet things were displayed. "Try a slice of lemon pie first an' then we'll top it off with ice cream."

"That'll be so expensive, won't it?"

"Don't worry about it, Annabelle. I just got paid off from my latest cattle job in Waco. I've got plenty of money to spend on a pretty lady."

She blushed so deeply he thought she might burst.

"You say the nicest things, Cody."

A waitress came over, eyeing the bulges where Annabelle's dress showed off milky skin. "What'll she have?" the woman asked in a slightly disapproving way.

"Bring us two slices of lemon pie, an' a sarsaparilla for the lady. We'll be havin' ice cream later on."

Their waitress departed for the cabinets, leaving them alone again. Cody made himself a promise right then he wouldn't stare at Annabelle's chest, knowing he'd better make a first impression that showed he could be a gentleman.

"I just love the smells in here," Annabelle said, examining rows of candy jars, cookie jars, and slices of pie and cake along a glass-topped counter. "I've never been here before."

"It's no fun bein' poor," he admitted. "We were awful poor when I was a kid. We couldn't afford to go to places like this."

"Seems we've been poor all my life," she said. "Times, we hardly have enough to eat. Ma keeps tellin' me the Lord will see to it that we don't starve, but lately He ain't been seein' to it like somebody should."

"Havin' money can be downright wonderful," Cody

agreed. "I still remember what it was like not to have none. My pa was gone for quite a spell when I was little an' that made it extra hard on Ma to make ends meet. We never had enough money."

"I take it you've got plenty now." She examined his face in a curious way, paying particular attention to his chin. But the look in her eyes was not critical of what she saw.

"I've got enough to get by, I reckon. And just today, the city marshal talked to me about a job down at his jail. It pays real good. Fifty dollars a month."

Her brow furrowed a little. "You'd be around bad men most all the time, wouldn't you? You'd have to be very careful."

"That part don't worry me none. I've been around my share of bad men on cattle crews headed up the Chisholm Trail to Kansas, an' there ain't hardly any place on earth worse'n Abilene."

"You look like you're strong," she said, blushing again, and now she averted her eyes.

"I can handle myself," he said, as their slices of pie came on a tray. He grinned. "Taste that, an' tell me if it ain't the sweetest you ever ate."

She took her fork and ate a bite of lemon custard pie with a thick layer of meringue on top. "It's so delicious," she said, licking her lips—he noticed how full her lips were. Then she drank a mouthful of sarsaparilla through a straw and smiled until her face fairly beamed. "This is what heaven's like, everything tastin' sweet, don't you suppose?"

"Got no idea what heaven's like," he told her, being careful to talk without his cheeks being full.

"My pa's up in heaven," she said, eating more pie.

"So's mine, I reckon, only maybe he went to the other place first on account of some bad things he done."

"What did he do that was bad?"

Cody wondered if he ought to tell her. "He robbed this bank down in San Antone a long time ago. He was mean with a gun, so I heard folks say. He went to prison when I was a kid. Soon as he got back, he broke wild horses for a livin'.

He didn't rob nobody else or carry a gun after that.''

"Did he kill people?"

"Ma told me he did, but that was back when he was younger."

"How did he die?"

"A wild horse ran away with him. Bucked him off an' broke his neck. He laid there in bed for three whole weeks, then he up an' passed away in his sleep. The doctor told Ma he was bleedin' inside. Wasn't nothin' anybody could do.''

Annabelle said, "I'm sorry, Cody. I know what it's like to have your pa die. My pa died of fever. He got these red spots all over him an' wouldn't eat. It like to have killed my ma to see him die so slow. She cried all the time an' prayed somethin' fierce, only it didn't appear to do no good."

"It's just you and your ma?"

She nodded. "And now she's dyin' of the consumption. She can't hardly breathe sometimes an' coughs up all this blood. I guess I'll be on my own pretty soon, but that's okay. I'm tired of that wagon and doin' laundry day and night. Movin' from one place to another all the time, never havin' any friends. We're on our way to Arizona Territory, where it's supposed to be good for the consumption on account of it's so dry."

"I hear there's lots of wild Indians. Apaches."

Annabelle finished her pie and put down her fork. "It won't make no difference 'bout Indians," she said quietly. "Ma ain't gonna live long enough for us to get there. She gets a little weaker every day."

Cody leaned across the table. "A girl pretty as you hadn't oughta be havin' so many troubles."

"You're only sayin' that. I know I'm not as pretty as those girls at the Pink Lady or the Stockmen's Retreat. But it's nice of you to say it anyway."

He wondered how she knew about places in the Acre. "Have you been to the Pink Lady?"

"Just once. I met Miss Rose Denadale and she took me there to see what it was like. She let me borrow one of her dresses. I only wanted to take a look inside."

"How old are you, Annabelle?"

"Sixteen. I'll be seventeen before Christmas."

"You look older." As he said it, his eyes traveled down to her breasts for a moment. "Too bad about your ma an' her case of the consumption. What'll you do when ... she's gone?"

"Haven't made up my mind yet." She glanced at a clock behind the counter. "I'd better be goin' or Ma will pitch a fit. Thanks for the pie and soda water."

"What about ice cream?"

"Some other time, maybe."

"I'd like to see you again, if you're agreeable."

She chewed her bottom lip like she had to think. "I reckon I'd be agreeable. Some nights when it's real late Ma gets tired an' she goes to sleep. Maybe then we'd have more time ... just to talk, if you know what I mean."

"Any particular night?"

She thought again. "Mondays are the ones. We get a lot of laundry on Mondays an' she gets real tired. If you happened to come by real late Monday night, I might be able to slip away for a little while." She drank the rest of her drink quickly.

"I'd like that," he said softly.

She got out of her chair and made as though she meant to run out the door, until she stopped and came over to his chair. "I'd like to thank you for a nice time an' these wonderful sweets. If you'd care to see me again, come this Monday."

He stood up and reached for her shoulder. "I'd like that a whole lot, Miss Annabelle Green. You can count on seein' me this comin' Monday night late. I'll give a whistle from them trees on the south side, so you'll know I'm there."

She stared into his eyes like the two of them were alone in the place. "I'll only come if Ma's asleep," she whispered, then she stood on her tiptoes and gave him a quick kiss on the lips before she wheeled and hurried out the door.

He was so surprised by her kiss that he couldn't think of a thing to say until she was gone. He stood there a moment while their waitress came over and said, "You owe half a dollar, cowboy."

He paid the bill with his mind elsewhere, on Annabelle's soft lips and the swell of her breasts where her dress was open. He remembered the way she looked at him, the sound of her voice when she talked about her pa and her ma, and being alone. She was only sixteen and yet she seemed to be more of a woman than any he had ever known, but in a special way. An innocent way.

He walked out front and looked down the street. Two blocks away, he saw her running as hard as she could toward the campground, with her skirt flying behind her.

"She's scared to death her ma will find out," he whispered to himself.

He'd never known a girl he felt he could love before. Most girls his age shunned him because of his family's bad reputation and poverty while he was growing up. A son of John Wade was not welcome at the homes of better families—the offspring of a man who'd been to prison for bank robbery wasn't invited to parties or many social gatherings. The few women he'd known were mostly crib girls or those who came from the same humble beginnings as he. None of them had ever touched his heart before.

But as he watched Annabelle Green disappear around a street corner, he experienced feelings he couldn't explain, a longing to hold her in his arms for a while, the desire to be near her and hear her gentle voice. She was unlike any girl he'd ever met or wanted to meet. He couldn't recall ever feeling this way.

"She's so damn pretty," he said, tingling all over from her kiss and being so near her. His stomach did a flip-flop and he noticed his palms were sweating.

Streets through the Acre darkened with the coming of night as he strode back toward Adams Boardinghouse. He thought about the job at the marshal's office. If he had steady work and some money, perhaps Annabelle's ma might be less resentful toward him when he came calling. Or was he getting too far ahead of himself wishing for something like that?

He passed a man in a flat-brim Stetson watching Rusk Street from the porch of the Standard Theater. He wore a low-slung gunbelt. His face was hidden by deep shadows, but there was something about him that made Cody uneasy. He could almost feel a pair of eyes following him as he swung down Twelfth Street on his way back to Maddox Flats.

9

She lay sweltering in late summer heat through most of the night, unable to rid her mind of Cody. She couldn't sleep. A breath of wind swept through their lean-to, helping to lessen the perspiration beading on her skin. Her nightdress was so damp it clung to her body, but it was heat of another kind that kept her awake, a warm sensation lingering in her groin while she remembered Cody's lips, the way she felt when he stared at her breasts or looked so deeply into her eyes. The warmth was a feeling she experienced more and more lately, sometimes awakening her from a sound slumber. There were times when it was so intense her arms and legs trembled.

She got up quietly when sleep wouldn't come, being careful not to wake her mother. Walking barefoot, she crept away from their wagon, entering a mesquite thicket that would take her down to a shallow creek running past Tommy Joe's house. There was a pool where she could wade and cool off if nobody was around, and at this late hour no one would be.

She came to the bank of the creek and stopped to listen for a while, making sure she was truly alone. On the other side she could see that the windows at Tommy Joe's place were dark, as they should have been at three or four in the morning. She wriggled out of her nightdress and hung it on a mesquite limb, then she stepped into dark water reflecting light from stars overhead and let out a sigh.

"That feels better," she whispered, enjoying the coolness surrounding her feet and ankles, bending down to cup water in her hands.

She covered her body with water, her chest and belly and

her groin where the troubling warmth lingered. Gooseflesh pimpled on her arms and thighs, down her back when she splashed water over a shoulder. She thought about how nice it would be to have a cast iron bathtub like the one sitting in a corner of Miss Rose's big bedroom. Someone would carry pails of cool water to her tub and she could lie in it for hours, with scented crystals sprinkled in her bath making handfuls of soft bubbles. Someone had told her about those bubbling crystals . . . she couldn't remember who.

"I'd have to be rich," she told herself, gazing up at bright stars winking at her from a black velvet sky. Why did everything pleasurable have to cost so much money? Like lemon pies and bathtubs and silk dresses and red leather shoes and silk stockings. As she waded deeper, the water soon reached her knees. Mud from the bottom clung to her feet, oozing between her toes. She went a bit deeper until the surface almost touched her pubic hair and there she stopped, listening to the faint sound of a piano coming from Hell's Half Acre.

"Their fun lasts all night," she said quietly, turning her face toward the music. She remembered coming down the stairs at the Pink Lady wearing that beautiful red gown. Every man in the room was staring at her. It felt sinful, and at the same time wonderful, to feel those stares. No God-fearing woman should have been enjoying it and yet she had. Why? She'd always been so bashful and shy around men. Until now. Until last night.

"What's happenin' to me?" she wondered aloud. Very slowly, she traced a fingertip through the soft hair between her thighs, still listening to the piano while fever in her groin began to increase.

A few moments later she shuddered and let out a soft groan. She looked down at herself, feeling naughty, dirty, all the things her ma said went with wickedness and evil.

She started to cry. What was going on inside her? Why was she doing wicked things, thinking wicked thoughts? It seemed as though someone else controlled her now. Was this the work of the devil Ma always warned her about?

"I'm not a God-fearin' woman anymore," she whimpered,

with her palms pressed to her face. Tears fell down her cheeks
to the surface of the pool, making tiny ripples.

Off in the distance she heard a loud crack. It startled her
and she cocked an ear toward the sound. Was it a gunshot?
When she heard it again, she was sure it was shooting, coming
from the Acre. She rubbed her eyes dry. Two gunshots, and
then silence. Not even the piano played now.

She lowered herself into the water until it reached her chin
and remained perfectly still for several seconds listening to the
quiet around her. Hearing those shots reminded her of the
danger always lurking in the Acre. Hardly a week had passed
since they came to Fort Worth when someone wasn't killed
there.

"It ain't all pretty dresses an' pretty bedrooms," she said.
Her voice traveled too easily across the water and echoed back
from the trees, reminding her to speak very softly.

The water felt good and she stayed submerged in it awhile
longer, thinking about how she'd changed. Beginning with a
night at the Pink Lady in a borrowed dress, she'd felt different
suddenly, no longer herself. Kissing Cody Wade so brazenly
at the Emporium in front of dozens of people was something
she'd never have done before. And just now what she'd done
to herself with her finger was something she'd only recently
discovered, and she knew it was wrong, somehow, probably
against the scriptures. Opening the front of her dress when
Cody came to pick up his laundry had to be the work of Satan
inside her, and she'd done it again at the Emporium in front
of everybody.

"And I'm always thinkin' about money," she whispered.
"Ma would say that was wrong, too. I even asked Tommy
Joe how much money a scarlet woman makes . . ."

So many thoughts crowded her mind at once she couldn't
sort them out. Later, she stood up and walked slowly to the
edge of the creek, letting her skin dry in a cool night breeze
while she sat beside the water on a flat rock with her knees
bent under her chin. Staring at the reflections of stars on the
water, she gave in to another dark mood and began to cry
quietly, wondering why she was changing.

"I'm becomin' a scarlet woman," she sobbed, "always thinkin' about money, kissin' Cody the way I done, comin' down them stairs dressed like a whore! Ma's preachin' don't do me no good. I let the devil get inside me." She broke down then and cried hard, until her sides were heaving and she was gasping for breath. All alone on the creek bank, she emptied her heart and her soul to an indifferent night sky.

Gradually her crying grew less. She stared across the water through tear-rimmed eyelids, feeling spent, overwhelmed by what was happening to her, powerless to control it. She knew it must be the work of Satan himself. No other explanation made a bit of sense.

At some point she dropped off to sleep with her head resting on her knees—that was before someone touched her arm gently and asked, "Was you asleep, Annabelle?"

She jumped, although even in the dark she knew his voice. She opened one eye and then the other. "What are you doin' here, Tommy Joe?"

"Wonderin' about you. Wonderin' why you're sittin' here on this rock plumb naked sound asleep."

Suddenly, she remembered her nightdress and covered herself as best she could with her arms, tucking her knees tightly under her chin. Her mind was racing for some sort of answer and a way to get him to leave. "I went for a swim. Now, go away! Can't a girl get a minute's privacy?"

"I seen you sittin' there an' figured maybe somethin' was bad wrong, Annabelle. I was on my way home from work when I seen you an' I got worried you might be sick."

It was too dark for him to see her nakedness clearly so she calmed some. "I'm okay. Just feelin' bad, is all."

"How come you're feelin' bad?" He stood behind her on the bank of the creek so all he could see was her back and bare legs unless she moved.

"Thinkin' about bein' so poor. Wishin' I had some money so I could buy things, and send Ma to see a doctor."

"I'd lend you some if I had any. Pa takes most of mine so's we can eat an' so he can buy whiskey."

"That's okay. You need money as bad as us anyway."

He cleared his throat. "There's a way you can make all the money in the world. If you went to work for Miss Rose you'd be rich in no time. She said so."

She glanced across the stream at nothing in particular. "I can't, Tommy Joe, even though the devil's inside me now. I don't think I could do that for money."

"What do you mean, the devil's inside you?" he asked softly, squatting down on his haunches behind her.

She wondered if a boy of fifteen would understand. "I been havin' terrible thoughts. Wishin' I had money, thinkin' about a grown-up thing."

"What sorta grown-up thing?"

"You wouldn't understand. You're too young."

"Maybe not. I know about how a man sticks his pecker into a woman. I peeked through keyholes plenty of times at Miss Rose's, so I know plenty 'bout that."

For a time she was silent, wondering if she should ask him a very private question. "Does it hurt a woman the first time, you reckon?"

Tommy Joe didn't answer right away. "I wouldn't know 'bout the first time. Some of the girls carry on like it feels so good they can't hardly stand it. I never saw one act like it hurt."

"Timmie Witherspoon's finger hurt," she confided in a tiny voice, deeply embarrassed to be talking about that sort of thing with a boy she'd only known a few weeks, yet still wanting to be informed by someone who knew. "He swore it would feel good, only it didn't."

Tommy Joe said, "You ain't never had no pecker stuck in you. I could tell by the way you acted."

She sighed. "No, I ain't. I was only wonderin' if you knew whether it hurt the first time like Timmie's finger did." She looked over her shoulder. "Tell the truth, Tommy Joe. Have you ever been with a woman?"

"Two times," he said, sounding prouder than she thought any decent boy should. "I was with Miss Nellie the first time. She done it for free. Second time I paid five whole dollars to Miss Allene. I saved some money my pa didn't know 'bout.

I got three more dollars hid behind our hog shed. I'm gonna do it again soon as I've saved up enough.''

"Who'll you do it with this time?" she asked without caring all that much who it might be.

"I ain't rightly sure jus' yet. But if you was to work for Miss Rose, I promise it'd be you."

She looked at him again, angry that he would say something like that. "You hush that kind of talk! I never said I'd do it for money. I was just curious if it hurt, that's all."

He looked askance. "If a man's pecker ain't too big, I can't see how it'd hurt."

Annabelle noticed a warmth in her groin again. Why was it there when she was only talking to a kid like Tommy Joe Booker? "Is yours big?" She didn't really care, she thought.

"Not big as some. I'd take an oath I wouldn't never let it hurt you."

Sitting in the dark, she smiled where he couldn't see her. "Then yours is little, ain't it?"

"Not all that little. If you want, I'll show you."

"You wouldn't dare!"

"If you wanted to see it, to see how big it was, I would."

Something made her turn around, curiosity perhaps, or was it the heat spreading slowly through her abdomen. "If you ain't too scared to show it to me, I ain't afraid to look at it. Only I'll bet you won't do it."

"You gotta promise you won't laugh."

"And what if I do laugh?"

"I won't never show it to you again, that's what."

"You won't do it, Tommy Joe. You'll think of some excuse."

He straightened up, standing over her, and began unbuttoning the front of his pants.

10

"You hadn't oughta do that," she warned, keeping herself as well covered as she could with her arms and legs. No decent girl would allow a man to show off his pecker like this, and yet a part of her, a part the devil was controlling now, was curious to see what it looked like.

"You dared me to. You said I wouldn't." He opened his fly and reached inside his pants.

A wave of excitement made her shiver. "If the devil hadn't gotten inside me, I wouldn't even take a peek at it. I want you to know it ain't really me wantin' to see it."

He pulled out his pecker and held it in his palm. "See, it ain't so awful big that it'd hurt. Miss Nellie showed me how to put it inside her real slow at first. That's how a man's supposed to do it, she said. Miss Allene said she didn't care how I done it, that it didn't make no difference to her."

Annabelle couldn't help staring at it, although she knew she shouldn't be looking at all. The warmth between her thighs began to intensify. Even at night she could tell Tommy Joe was bigger than Timmie Witherspoon's finger. She looked a while longer and she supposed it was because the devil inside her wanted a better look at it. "Why would you pay so much money to a girl to stick it inside her?"

He grinned a little, like he was embarrassed. "On account of it feels real good, better'n nearly anything in the world."

Her breathing became noticeably faster and that strange new feeling of excitement grew stronger. "It's dumb, to waste money like that."

"Some girls do it for free. Miss Nellie said she wouldn't

ask for no money from me because I was nice to her. I told her I never had poked a girl an' she told me I oughta know how, so she showed me one night when she didn't have no gentlemen who'd pay. She said I was old enough to learn how to poke a woman.''

"She called it bein' poked?"

"That's what nearly everybody calls it.''

"You ain't but fifteen, Tommy Joe."

"That's plenty old enough, Miss Nellie said."

"I would never do it for free, or for money. It's wrong to do it either way."

"No it ain't. Miss Nellie told me it's the oldest profession there is. Women have been doin' it for money for a thousand years. Some folks claim it's a bad thing, but if it's so awful bad then how come so many discrete gentlemen come to Miss Rose's place to pay a girl to do it?"

"What's a discrete gentleman?"

"I ain't exactly sure. Somebody with money, I reckon."

She examined his pecker more closely, seeing how thick and long it was. "I just know it would hurt. It's bigger'n Timmie's finger. A lot longer, too."

"It wouldn't hurt, Annabelle, if I put it in real slow."

"I'd never let you put that thing inside me. Wouldn't make any difference how slow or fast it was."

"One of these days you'll put one inside you if'n you aim to have a baby. There ain't no other way."

"That'll be different. It'll be with my husband. Havin' a baby hurts, too, so my ma says. Folks have to tolerate some hurt now an' then, like when you cut your finger."

"It ain't the same. Bein' poked don't hurt none at all if it's done right. I never hurt Miss Nellie or Miss Allene. Fit jus' like it was supposed to."

"You talk like you know everythin' there is to know about it when you only done it twice."

He let go of it and his pecker stuck straight out by itself. "I don't reckon I'd call myself no expert on pokin', but I know a lot more'n you. Leastways I done it twice."

"A decent woman's supposed to save her virtue for her

husband. My ma told me that. Only a scarlet woman of the
night is sinful enough to take money from just anybody for
it.''

''Maybe so, only those girls down at the Pink Lady sure
make a lot of money doin' it. Miss Nellie told me it was a
whole lot better'n bein' poor, workin' for Miss Rose. I bet
she's got a dozen fancy dresses, an' no tellin' how many pairs
of shoes.''

Annabelle frowned. ''How come it does that, stickin' out
the way it is?''

''It gets hard when I wanna be with a woman, like I wanna
be with you now. It gets softer after it's over.''

''After white jelly comes out. A girlfriend told me.''

''It ain't exactly like jelly.'' He cleared his throat. ''I'll
show you, if you'll let me poke you right now. I'll give you
the three dollars I got hid behind the hog shed, an' I'll owe
you two more. I get paid next Friday an' I swear I'll pay the
rest.''

''You're insultin' me, to say I'd do it for money. It's the
same as callin' me a whore.''

''No I ain't, I swear, Annabelle. I only offered to give you
that money because I wanna poke you more'n any girl I ever
saw in the whole world. Three dollars is all I got an' I know
you ain't gonna do it for free. I'd pay the other two this comin'
Friday.''

She thought about having five dollars. She could buy cloth
for a new dress, some lilac water, so many things. Only, her
ma would ask where she got it and she couldn't tell her the
truth. ''That would make me a whore,'' she said softly. ''Besides, you an' your pa are nearly as poor as we are. It wouldn't
seem right to take your money. And I just know it would hurt
somethin' awful if I let you . . . poke me.''

''No it won't. You got my word.'' He edged a bit closer,
so his erection was close to her face. ''See, it ain't all that big.
I swear I'd put it in real slow so it wouldn't hurt you none.''

The burning desire between her legs ached for her finger so
it would stop bothering her, making her think wicked thoughts
she wished would go away. And what of Cody? If she were

to have the chance to marry him someday, she would be soiled by having done a thing like consorting with Tommy Joe for money. But that was a foolish notion, that a handsome cowboy like Cody would ever care to make her his wife, only wishful thinking. He wouldn't want to marry a woman who had the devil inside her anyway.

She stared at Tommy Joe's pecker, then at his face. In dim light from stars overhead he appeared to be pleading with her, by his expression. The warmth in her groin pulsed with the beat of her heart. "I'd have to think about it," she said, and when she said it, she couldn't quite believe the words had come from her own mouth, as if the devil had spoken for her.

"There ain't hardly time, Annabelle. It's nearly daylight."

"I'd only be doin' it to see if it hurt. So I'd know."

"I promise I won't let it hurt. I'd rather let my pa whup me with his razor strap than do anythin' to hurt you."

She gave in to her urges reluctantly, feeling that somehow she would never be the same. It wasn't just the part about whether or not it hurt her—it was giving in to what the devil wanted her to do. "You swear you'll do it real slow, an' that if it hurts you won't go no farther?"

"I swear," he said breathlessly, offering his hand to help her climb up the creekbank to a grassy place behind him.

She accepted his hand and stood up slowly, revealing all her nakedness. She fully expected to be embarrassed, letting him see her like this, and yet she wasn't.

"You're the most beautiful girl in the whole wide world," he told her, his voice quivering in an unusual way so it wasn't like his regular way of talking.

He led to her a spot of grass. His hand was trembling. She lay down beneath a mesquite limb where shadows were deepest as he took off his shirt.

He knelt down beside her. "You want me to kiss you first?"

"No reason for that," she replied, wondering why he asked a foolish question at a time like this. "All we're gonna do is see if it hurts me. Kissin' is for people who're in love, silly."

His trousers slipped down to his knees. He parted her legs gently—she could feel the tremor in his fingers when he touched her inner thigh. She lifted her head off the grass so she could see his erection when it entered her. He worked his way between her legs.

"You've got beautiful teats," he said hoarsely, bringing the tip of his erection lightly against her pubic hair.

"We ain't supposed to talk, are we?" she asked. Anticipation was making her groin ache in a most pleasant way and now she knew she'd been possessed by something so evil that it made her want to do wickedness. The devil had a way of making sin feel good.

She felt him penetrate her, but only slightly. A sensation so intense it made her gasp accompanied his entry and, suddenly, a spasm of pleasure turned her muscles to iron. He pushed a little deeper and stopped again as though he expected her to tell him it was enough.

"Does it hurt?"

"It don't hurt at all, Tommy Joe," she whispered. While it was her voice, she was sure it was Satan who said it.

II

A body lay in a spreading pool of blood near an overturned
brass spittoon. A kerosene lamp on a roof support shone down
on the dead man's beard-stubbled face. His mouth was open
strangely and only a closer look showed that part of his upper
lip was missing where a bullet had shattered his front teeth.
A fist-sized plug of scalp and brains dangled from the back of
his head where a lead slug fired at close range had exited.
Bystanders stayed back against the walls at Maude's Place as
a filmy layer of blue gunsmoke settled slowly to the floor.
Cody and Newt stood at the bar along with a few other patrons
who were unwilling to move until a stocky man with a smoking gun in his fist holstered his revolver. Cody had been telling
Newt about Annabelle, their meeting, how she up and kissed
him for no reason, and her promise to meet him late Monday
night if her ma was asleep. All at once a stranger had come
into Maude's, the man holding the gun, and just as suddenly
a cowboy nobody noticed before, who lay dead on the floor
now, wheeled away from the bar and reached for his pistol
without uttering a word.

"That's Flatnose Curry," someone whispered.

Cody's ears were still ringing from two gun blasts fired in
a small room and he wasn't quite sure he heard the name right.
A look at the stranger's nose convinced him the nickname fit.
His nose had been broken, or so it appeared, pushed flat
against his face so it was a wonder he could breathe.

Cody recalled what Marshal Hull told him, that he'd tangled
with Flatnose George Curry before. Cody had seen him draw
and he was quick, sure of his moves, as calm as still water

when he'd gone for his gun just now. Had it been fate that
took Cody and Newt to Maude's tonight to witness another
killing? Cody had remembered the place from his discussion
in front of it that afternoon, with Cordel Hull about a jailer's
job. A sign in a window said drinks were only ten cents on
Saturday night and that, more than anything, had been what
lured him and Newt inside. That same window was broken
now, by a bullet fired at Curry, a shot fired too late and wide
of its mark.

Curry lowered his gun. He glared at the men standing
around the saloon. "You all saw him go for his sidearm first.
It was self-defense. When the law comes, everybody better
have a good memory." He inclined his head toward the body.
"That gent there is Buford Davis, wanted for train robbery
and murder up in Laramie. He knew I'd recognize him, so he
went for his gun." Curry gazed across the room at Davis. "He
was too goddamn slow."

"I seen it all," a young cowboy said from a back corner.
"It happened just like you said. That Davis feller went for his
gun the minute he seen you come through them doors."

Curry seemed satisfied. He holstered his pistol and strode
over to the bar, keeping one eye out front like he expected the
marshal to come at any moment. He tossed a coin on the
counter. "Gimme a whiskey. The good stuff, none of that
goddamn rotgut."

A barman poured Curry a shot glass full of labeled bourbon
from a bottle underneath the bar. "Who's gonna pay for my
busted window?" he asked.

Curry shrugged and looked back at Davis. "See the gent
who shot it out. I didn't break your window."

"But he's dead."

The gunman's eyes narrowed. "It's none of my affair. I'd
ask somebody else if I was you."

Newt leaned closer to Cody. "Did you see how fast he drew
a gun?" Hushed conversation resumed around them. Drinkers
slowly returned to their tables and chairs. A few curious patrons went over to examine the bullet hole in Buford Davis's
mouth.

"I saw it," Cody replied. "He's quick enough an' his aim is mighty good. That's about all it takes."

"I'll go fetch the undertaker," someone said. A cowboy with spurs clanked across hollow floorboards to go outside, stepping carefully around the pool of blood mingling with spilled tobacco juice from the spittoon.

"That Curry's one mean hombre," Newt whispered, tossing back a third shot of ten-cent liquor, making no further mention of how it reminded him of the acid used to cure cow hides.

Cody wondered what Marshal Hull would do when he arrived to investigate the shooting. He had the marshal figured for a man who wouldn't back down from anybody. He thought about what Newt said. "Bein' fast with a gun don't make him tough. Toughness comes from inside, not bein' afraid of anything even when a man with good sense oughta be, like my pa was. He wasn't scared of nothin' on earth, if you didn't count prison."

"Remember what that big marshal said, that him'n Curry had crossed trails before? How it wasn't no church picnic?"

"I remember. It's liable to be a mite touchy when Marshal Hull shows up to find out about the shootin'. Hull don't strike me as havin' no soft spots. If Curry don't behave himself, he's in for a fight, if you ask me."

"Curry's expectin' the law. You heard what he said, 'bout how he wanted everybody to have a good memory when the law showed up."

"The dead man pulled iron first," Cody said, remembering the split second in time when Curry drew and killed his rival before Davis could get off a shot.

Newt signaled for another drink. "Like Curry said, he was too goddamn slow, Davis was."

Minutes passed while they idled over whiskey. Talk around the saloon was quieter than before. Everyone made it a point to avoid Curry. He stood alone at one end of the bar sipping his drink, watching the doors like he knew Cordel Hull was coming. Curious passersby came to Maude's shattered front window to peer inside. When most saw the body, they hurried off into the dark as quickly as they could.

An elderly man came from the back with a broom and a dustpan to sweep up the broken glass. Cody watched the sweeping disinterestedly, wondering what Hull would do when he saw George Curry and learned he was involved in a killing.

"Nobody's offered to move that corpse," Newt observed in a hushed voice. "I reckon everybody's waitin' for the marshal to get here. Looks like somebody'd cover him up, outa respect for the departed."

Cody toyed with his glass. "In this part of town it don't appear nobody's got much respect for the dead. I suppose that's why they called it Hell's Half Acre, 'cause only the devil gets his due down here."

A movement out front caught Cody's eye. A man dressed in a dark hat and suitcoat passed the broken window and pushed through Maude's swinging doors.

Marshal Hull stopped when he saw Curry. Curry turned slowly from the bar to face him. The two stared at each other, and all at once the room fell quiet again. Cody noted that Hull was not carrying his shotgun now, although his coattail was swept behind the butt of his revolver so he could get at it in a hurry.

"I heard you were in town, George." Hull's deep voice boomed in the heavy silence.

"I came in on the noon train," Curry replied quietly, acting about as unconcerned as a man could. "It's been a while, Cordel. Two or three years . . ."

"I see you've already killed a man," Hull said. He made it sound like he'd expected it all along.

"He drew on me first. Everybody here saw it. That's Buford Davis. He's a wanted man up in Laramie. We had a scrape up near Denver last year . . . a disagreement. He went for his gun as soon as he saw me. There was nothing else I could do but shoot him."

The marshal's pale gray eyes beheld Curry like they were on a snake. "I'll talk to some of the witnesses. In the meantime, hand over your gun. I'm holdin' you for questioning until a judge hears the evidence."

Curry stiffened. "I won't let you do that, Cordel. It was

self-defense. You've got no right to hold me.''

"The law says I can. You've killed a man in my jurisdiction and I can hold you till Judge Warren hears what happened. If it happened like you say, I'll return your gun and you'll be free to go.''

"You're bluffing," Curry snapped. "You can't hold me and you know it."

"Hand over the gun, George. Let's do this the easy way."

Lightning-fast, Curry pulled his revolver and aimed it for Marshal Hull's face. Hull hadn't made a move toward his pistol.

"Back out of my way, Cordel, or so help me I'll shoot you in order to get clear of this shit-hole town. I won't let you take me to jail."

Cody was surprised when Curry beat the marshal so easily at the draw. He couldn't figure why Hull made no attempt to draw.

Hull's flat expression showed no emotion whatsoever, like he was made out of ice. "Put that gun down," he said. It sounded like he was the one holding a gun on Curry, the way he ordered it so hard.

"You're not leaving me any choice," Curry warned, and as he said it, he cocked the hammer on his Colt. A clicking noise from a single-action ream dropping into place was the only sound when Curry got ready to fire.

Something stirred inside Cody's head, an urge he could never have explained to anyone else. Curry's back was to the bar and the rest of Maude's drinkers, thus he couldn't see Cody pull out his .44-.40 and bring it up, aiming for Curry's skull. His thumb drew the hammer back. "If you pull that trigger there'll be one hell of a big hole behind your right ear," Cody said, steadying his sights just below the brim of Curry's hat. When he said it, his voice sounded calm.

Very slowly, Curry turned his head to one side, just enough to see the muzzle of Cody's gun. His flattened nose gave him a menacing appearance. His eyes flickered from Hull to Cody again in a matter of seconds.

"Don't force me to use this," Cody said, when it seemed

a gun aimed at his head had no effect on Curry. Cody's gun hand was steady and his gaze never wavered when he met Curry's cold stare.

Curry's jaw muscles tightened. Cords stood out in his neck like ropes. He looked at Hull and snarled, "I might have known you'd have me covered from the back." Very slowly, deliberately, he lowered his pistol and let the hammer down. "Everybody here saw what happened, Cordel. Davis pulled a gun on me. I have a right to defend myself."

Marshal Hull glanced in Cody's direction, then he stepped over and took Curry's revolver. "You can tell it to Judge Warren in the mornin', George, after I get statements from some of the witnesses."

As soon as Curry was disarmed, Cody holstered his pistol and let out a quiet breath. Suddenly, after it was over, his nerves made him so jumpy he wasn't sure he could bring his drink to his mouth without spilling it down the front of his shirt. He picked up his glass and tossed the whiskey down as quickly as he could.

"Look behind you," Newt whispered.

Cody's head almost twisted off his neck as he turned rapidly to see what Newt was talking about.

Standing in the doorway leading into a back room was a man holding a shotgun to his shoulder. He wore a leather vest with a badge pinned to it. He was tall and skinny, with close-set eyes and a prominent Adam's apple that bobbed up and down when he said to Cody, "Nice work, cowboy."

Marshal Hull took a pair of manacles from his coat pocket. "Turn around, George, so I can put these bracelets on. You've worn this kind of jewelry before."

"It was self-defense," Curry said. When he turned his back on Hull, he fixed Cody with a steely look.

The clatter of iron handcuffs locking into place only made Curry madder. He glanced over his shoulder and spoke with his lips drawn into a thin line. "You're gonna be real sorry you did this to me, Cordel."

"Maybe," Hull remarked. He made a motion toward the back of the room with his free hand after he stuck Curry's pistol in his belt. "Cole, take our prisoner down to the jail. I'll be along directly."

The man wearing the star walked slowly along the bar carrying his shotgun leveled in front of him. When he passed Cody, he grinned with one side of his mouth, nodded, and continued to the front, where he put his gun muzzles against Curry's ribs. "March in front of me, mister," he said, prodding his prisoner out the doors.

It seemed everyone in the place was trying to talk at once as soon as Curry was taken outside. Some drinkers were telling Marshal Hull about the shooting while others described among themselves what they had seen. A few were looking at Cody now and then, yet no one spoke to him until a bartender brought over a bottle of his good labeled whiskey and said, "Have a drink on the house, mister."

Cody accepted, saying, "Thanks," as quietly as he could. He looked down at his glass and tasted it, calming himself.

He wasn't paying attention to what was going on elsewhere in the place until he heard someone walk up behind him. He did not care to talk about what he'd done and didn't turn around until he heard a hoarse voice he recognized.

"I owe you," Marshal Hull said. "That took plenty of guts, to call his hand the way you done. My deputy was too far away to use that scattergun without hittin' a bunch of innocent men."

Cody was a bit embarrassed when he faced the marshal. "To tell the honest truth I never saw your deputy standin' back there or I'd have thought twice, maybe. Seemed like somebody oughta do somethin' about the fix you was in, so I did what came natural at the time."

Hull's eyes wandered up and down Cody's frame, like he meant to figure something out. "We talked about a job down at the jail and I'm wonderin' if you're interested."

"I been thinkin' about it some."

"If you can handle the work, I might make you a deputy later on. Pays eighty dollars a month to begin with. It ain't an easy job down here in this district, but if you've got as much backbone as you showed here tonight, you won't have a problem.''

Everyone in the place was listening to what Marshal Hull was saying, making it that much harder to appear undecided about it. "I'll come by your office sometime, Marshal. I'd like to hear a bit more about it.''

Hull nodded. "I've got one more question. It's hard for me to tell how old you are and there's regulations.''

"I turned twenty last week.''

His answer apparently satisfied Hull. "Stop by my office on Monday, seein' as tomorrow's Sunday. We'll talk. You appear to have the makings of a man who can be trusted, even though you're a bit on the young side.''

Hull gave the room a sweeping look. "Anybody see anything different from what Flatnose Curry claims?'' he asked. "Did the dead man draw first?''

"That's the way it happened, all right,'' a cowboy at a table agreed, while several more shook their heads.

Hull glanced at the body. "Someone send for the undertaker. I'll have to let Curry go in the mornin'.'' He walked along the bar and went out, turning past the broken windowpane.

Newt was looking at Cody strangely when conversation resumed inside Maude's. "You've lost your damn mind, Cody Wade, pullin' a gun on Flatnose Curry like that. You'll be joinin' your pa six feet under before you know it. Have you forgot that Jake Ketchum is in jail on account of you, an' he's got friends?''

Cody didn't answer or offer an excuse for what he'd done. A choice had come along, a choice between riding herd on a bunch of unruly longhorns or helping to keep the peace in one of the most dangerous places he'd ever been. From what he knew about either job, neither one offered much in the way of a secure future.

12

Cody lay in the dark, staring blankly at a flyspecked ceiling while he thought about events at Maude's earlier in the evening. Someone in a room across the hall was snoring loudly—the bedroom walls at Adams Boardinghouse were paper thin. He remembered the look on Flatnose Curry's face when he saw a gun in Cody's hand, a look that should have frightened him. For some reason he hadn't been afraid of Curry then, and tonight, long after their confrontation was over, he wondered why a gunman with Curry's reputation didn't scare him like he should. Was it something to do with being the son of John Wade? Offspring inherited things such as looks from their parents, didn't they? He'd been told a hundred times that he looked like his pa, almost a spitting image, some said. But had he also inherited John Wade's inclination toward violence? Ma said he had his father's bad temper. Did he also have his pa's urges to use a gun the way he did before he went to prison? Was he destined by bloodline to be a bank robber, even a killer, like his pa?

A breeze fluttered curtains beside a single window overlooking an alley running behind the boardinghouse. Somewhere off in Maddox Flats a dog barked angrily over some intrusion. Cody lay on his back, unable to sleep, wondering what to do with his future now. Marshal Hull had as much as offered him the jailer's job and even promised that a deputy's position was available, if he could be trusted with so much authority. Of all the professions he'd considered since making up his mind to leave cattle herding, none was farther from his deliberations than becoming a peace officer. Perhaps it was because his pa had broken the law and gone off to prison that he hadn't thought about it. John Wade's reputation as a bad man had been a part of Cody's upbringing and he supposed he'd never viewed becoming a lawman as an option available to the son of a criminal.

Thinking about it, he wondered if he was cut from the right cloth to wear a badge. There was a saying among country folks, that a skunk couldn't change its stripes. He'd never been in any real trouble with the law, if you discounted kid stuff like those watermelon thefts and a stolen candy jar. He hadn't ever thought about robbing a bank like his pa did. But had he inherited some dark side he didn't know about? Was he potentially a bad man who hadn't found out yet who, or what, he really was? Thus far, his sole qualification for a lawman's job was that he'd been fearless when it came to facing men with mean reputations. And that was something his pa taught him early, not to back down from a fight no matter what, and to be ready to defend himself and his honor at any cost.

Turning over on his rawhide-webbed cot, he gazed out at the stars.

"You been flippin' over like griddle cakes," Newt mumbled sleepily. "How come you can't drop off?"

He sighed. "I reckon I'm thinkin' about that job offer at the jail, wonderin' if I oughta give it a try. I've been thinkin' maybe I wasn't cut out to be a lawman on account of what my pa done. I've heard it said meanness runs in families."

"You ain't never done nothin' mean, Cody. Fact is, you've got a real gentle nature, mostly. You was always bad to fight if somebody pushed you, but that ain't meanness. You're real gentle with horses."

"I suppose I was thinkin' more about a gun. My pa was said to be a killer when he was young, an' he went to prison for that bank robbery. Tonight, when I pulled iron on Flatnose Curry, it happened without me even thinkin' about it, really. I just know I'd have killed him, Newt, if he'd shot Marshal Hull."

"That wasn't meanness either, partner, that was plumb crazy. You done it before your brain was workin'. I'd call that reaction a mighty dumb reaction. Owlhoots like Curry are honest to goodness bad men. If you ever take a shot at him, you'd better be damn sure you kill him.''

"I wasn't scared of him. Wasn't scared of that Jake Ketchum either. My pa taught me not to be scared of nobody when it comes to a fight. You're either gonna win or you're gonna lose. Bein' afraid can make a man do the wrong thing, sometimes.''

Newt sat up in bed, peering across their starlit room at his friend. "If you lose in a gunfight, you're dead, Cody. How come you ain't scared of dyin'?''

He thought about it. "Pa told me there wasn't nothin' to be scared of, that dyin' is gonna happen to everybody someday. He said the worst kind of feller there is, is a coward.''

Newt lay back down in resignation. "Maybe your pa shoulda been scared of that runaway horse. Maybe he'd still be alive.''

"Knowin' Pa, he'd rather be dead than admit he was scared of a bronc. That's how he was.''

Newt watched the ceiling himself, thinking out loud. "Looks like you aim to take that jailer's job, by the way you're talkin' about it. Sounds to me like you already decided.''

"I reckon I am, Newt. And if my chance comes to be a deputy, I aim to take that job, too. I've nearly made up my mind on it.''

"We was plannin' to throw in together. All this time we've been talkin' about what we were gonna do.''

"I know, an' I'm sorry about it. We've been partners a long time. I sorta hoped you'd understand that this is an opportunity for me to make somethin' of myself.''

Newt was quiet a moment. "I reckon I do understand, only I sure as hell hope what you're makin' for yourself ain't a grave.''

Cody wanted to change the subject. So much had happened in the past couple of days to talk about. "That Annabelle is sweet as sugar, Newt. She's got eyes big as marbles an' the prettiest skin you every saw. When she looks at me with those big brown eyes, I get this funny feelin' inside an' I can't hardly think straight. She's got a smile that'll melt the ice off a frozen lake. When she kissed me, I got so flustered I couldn't think of a single thing to say, like I was tongue-tied or somethin'. I can't get her out of my head no matter how hard I try. She said she'd meet me Monday night an' I can't hardly wait for Monday to come.''

''Sounds like you're love-bit. I'll admit she's pretty, but you never was one to let a woman make a fool outa you. What's so special about her?''

''Can't rightly say for sure, only that she's beautiful and I think she likes me in a real special way. If I could buy her new dresses an' all sorts of fancy stuff, she'd knock a man's eyes out of his head, lookin' so good.''

''You ain't got that kind of money. Judgin' by the looks of their wagon, they're poorer than dirt. What with her ma bein' so sick it ain't likely they'll ever have enough money to buy her a new dress. You said her ma was dyin' from the consumption.''

''It's a fact they've come on hard times. If I got that job at the jail, I could buy her nice things.''

Newt rolled over on his side, facing the wall. ''I never did dream you'd get so moon-eyed over a woman, Cody.''

A moment later Newt began to snore.

Monday morning, Cody paused in front of a window of the city marshal's office to see his reflection, making sure his shirt was tucked in and his hair was combed before he put on his hat. All day Sunday he'd given as much thought as he could to the jailer's job and couldn't find a good reason not to take it. He had less than three dollars to his name, and being broke, without a better prospect for earning any money, the decision was easy enough to make.

He let himself in, finding a boxlike room with a desk and a chair against one wall. In a room behind a middle door he saw a row of iron-barred cells. To the left of the roll-top desk a gun rack held Winchester rifles and shotguns.

The deputy named Cole saw him come in, lifting a greasy

hat off his face while resting on a bench across the room. At the desk, Cordel Hull also noted his arrival and put down a sheaf of wanted circulars.

"Mornin', Mr. Wade," Hull said tonelessly. He got up slowly and offered his hand. Motioning to his deputy, he said, "This is Coleman Webb, one of my deputies. He's handlin' the jailer's job until I find somebody I can trust." He indicated a chair next to his desk. "Sit down for a spell. Let's talk a minute or two. I have a few questions . . ."

Cody pulled off his hat and took the chair, after nodding to Coleman Webb. He felt uneasy about the way the marshal referred to having a few questions.

"I looked through some old files," Hull began. "Now I know where I heard your pa's name before. Big John Wade rode with the Youngers for a while, before he got caught robbin' the bank down in San Antone. He was suspected of several murders, but a county attorney couldn't prove it. Wade did five years at state prison for armed robbery, but then I reckon you know all about it, since he was your pa."

"I never knew anything for certain about the killin' part," Cody told him truthfully. "My ma told me once that he'd killed some men a long time before I was born."

"I'm not holding his past against you, son. I needed to see why John Wade's name was familiar." Hull's eyes roamed over Cody the way a horseman looks at a horse. "Have you ever been in any trouble with the law?"

"No, sir. I stole a jar of candy from a store window when I was six, but the Waco sheriff let me off after my ma promised to whip me real good. I took some watermelons an' peaches from ol' man Fuston's garden one summer."

Deputy Webb chuckled.

Hull's face was blank. "What have you done for a livin'?"

"I've been up the Chisholm four times. Worked on Johnson's cattle ranch durin' the winters. I'm a decent hand with a rope and I can shoe most horses front an' rear. The kickin' kind I've had to throw to get the back hooves right. Mostly I've cowboyed for one outfit or another. I'm plumb sick of ridin' herd on a bunch of longhorns."

"You carry a gun," Hull observed. "And from what I've seen, you're not afraid of pullin' it. Have you ever shot a man?"

"Yessir. I shot this Osage Injun up in the Nations when he tried to run off some of Johnson's beeves. Got him in the leg. He wasn't hurt all that bad. He was bleedin' some, and claimed he was real sorry he took those steers when I caught up to him."

The marshal examined Cody's holster. "That's a shootist's rig. A cutaway holster ain't the usual gun outfit for a cowboy."

"It was my pa's gun and holster. He gave it to me when he got out of prison, sayin' he wasn't gonna carry it no more. He taught me how to draw an' shoot. Said every man oughta know how to use one, just in case."

Again, Hull looked him over so closely that Cody felt naked as the day he was born.

"You're stout enough to handle a troublesome drunk, but it's the gunplay I'm worried about. There's enough shootin' down here in the Acre most every night to keep a gunsmith in the ammunition business. A man who works for me can't be afraid of flyin' lead or the muzzle of a gun, but on the other side of things you'll be representing the law and you can't just shoot the first gent who waves a gun in your face. We try to end things peacable when we can."

"I understand, Marshal. I wouldn't say I'm trigger happy or nothin' of the kind."

"It's our job to try to talk a gun out of some drunk's hand before he shoots somebody. Most cowboys are peaceful when they sober up. It's when they're drunk that they can be a handful at times, so we do our best to disarm them. A jailer's responsibility is to feed the ones we lock up and to make damn sure nobody comes along to spring a prisoner out of jail. You'll clean up a cell now and then and sweep out the office. Carry food from the little café across the street twice a day to the ones we've got locked up."

"Don't sound like anything I can't do," Cody said.

"There's one more thing," Marshal Hull said, and he said

it like he wanted Cody to pay close attention. "Whatever you might happen to see or overhear inside this office is never repeated to anyone else. Nobody. Your mouth stays shut."

Cody didn't quite understand. What could go on inside the marshal's office Hull didn't want others to know about? "Do you mean official business?"

Hull's pupils became pinpoints. "I mean anything at all. If you see anybody come in to talk to me, you find something to keep you busy in the back until we're finished."

Still wondering what he meant, Cody said, "That's okay by me if that's the way you want it."

The marshal nodded. "Good. That's real important to bein' able to keep this job." He glanced over to his deputy. "Cole is gonna show you a few things if you're ready to start. Should you need to know anything, ask Cole. You get paid fifty a month and there's a little room off the back, just a cot and a washstand. Whenever you're ready, you can move your gear in. Remember what I said . . . you don't talk to nobody about what goes on around here."

With some misgivings Cody stuck out his hand, puzzling over what could be going on that no one else should know about. "I'm ready," Cody said, waiting for Marshal Hull to accept his handshake before he got out of the chair.

Hull took his palm, shook it once, and inclined his head in the direction of the door. "Go fetch your gear, Cody. I've got the feeling you'll make a fine jailer. If you take to the work like you oughta, it won't be too long before you'll be wearing a deputy marshal's badge."

13

"You seem restless, child. Maybe that preachin' yesterday done you some good. Hearin' the word of the Lord causes honest folks to think about the hereafter. Is that what's causin' you to keep lookin' in the mirror all mornin'? The preacher said we oughta take a hard look at ourselves an' the way we been livin' our lives. He didn't say you should be lookin' in a mirror."

"It ain't that, Ma. I've just got a case of the nerves, is all." As they did every Sunday, they'd gone to church, sitting in a back pew so nobody would notice they didn't have clothes as nice as most of the others' for attending a preaching. Ma insisted on going to church on Sunday no matter where their travels took them, and she always found twenty-five cents to put in the collection plate. Of late, they'd been attending services at the Fifth Street Baptist Church on Sunday mornings. Yesterday's sermon had been delivered on the subject of facing up to one's own sins, a topic Annabelle hadn't wanted to think about, after what she'd done with Tommy Joe. Sitting in that pew, she'd squirmed over every mention of personal sin and felt a sweat pop out in spite of the breeze blowing through the church windows. She even imagined that if God were in a vengeful mood he might decide to strike her dead with a lightning bolt before the final hymn was sung that morning. When the services were over, she felt like running all the way to their wagon to get away from any further discussion about sin and sinners.

"The word of the Lord will give you inner peace. You've got a case of the nerves for another reason. Is it on account of the young cowboy who fixed our wagon that you been primpin' today?''

"Why'd you ask that, Ma?" She stirred the kettle even more vigorously, wondering how her ma had known her mind was on Cody.

"Because you've been fussin' over yourself in that mirror so regular, like you was expectin' company."

"I wasn't fussin', Ma, only lookin' at myself and the way my hair gets all matted up. It's this steam from these laundry pots that's causin' it, an' that lye causes my eyes to burn somethin' terrible sometimes."

Doris was content to let it drop for now. She carried a few sticks of wood to build up the flames under another kettle. Last night she'd coughed up so much blood that Annabelle nearly cried. She felt sure that if her ma didn't see a doctor soon the coughing spells themselves would kill her before the consumption did. She got weaker every day it seemed, eating less and less, taking more laudanum, until the bottle Miss Rose gave her was just about empty.

Her ma came over to inspect the pot Annabelle was stirring, pushing a strand of damp hair from her forehead. Once she'd been pretty, before her sickness robbed her of beauty. Annabelle had seen tintypes of her when she was young, and it was easy to see a resemblance between mother and daughter, back then. Doris never said much about her youth, and a while back those tintypes had disappeared. And now there was her most recent mention of being a sinner sometime in her past, something she wouldn't talk about until she felt the time was right, making Annabelle all the more curious to find out what it was that was troubling her so.

"I've been thinkin' it's time to move on," she said. "We've got a little money saved ... enough to take us to the next town if we spend it careful."

"I hadn't wanted to leave so soon, Ma. You've been feelin' mighty poorly. Last night I worried you was gonna die from all the blood. Maybe you oughta rest up awhile longer."

Doris gave her a questioning stare. "It's that cowboy who's

makin' you feel like stayin', ain't it? You took a fancy to him an' he's taken a fancy to you.''

"That ain't so. He hardly noticed me when he worked on our wagon that time."

"I saw him starin' at you when he thought I wasn't lookin' and you done the same to him more'n once. You been actin' real strange lately an' I figure he's the cause of it."

"It ain't so, Ma. I was only lookin' at him because he's a real handsome man. Nothin' wrong with that, is there?"

"Depends. Depends on if he's honorable. Most cowboys are a shiftless type. He'll be goin' off with a herd one of these days an' you'll never see him again."

"You're wrong about him. He told me he's thinkin' real hard about takin' a job at the city marshal's office."

"When did he mention that? I never heard him say no such of a thing."

Annabelle's mind raced for an answer. "When he came to pick up his laundry, while you was alseep. He hardly said anything to speak of, but he did make mention of workin' for the marshal down at the jail."

She didn't believe her. "Don't lie to me, child. You've got that same look in your eyes you get when you ain't tellin' me the truth."

"It's true, Ma. How come you think I'm lyin'?"

"Because I was young once," she said, turning for the wagon. She walked away, bending over, clutching her ribs like they were hurting bad. She got to their canvas shelter and sat down on her stool with her eyes closed, rocking gently back and forth with a grimace twisting her face.

"What's wrong, Ma?" Annabelle put down her stirring stick and came over as quickly as she could.

"Jus' some pains," she whispered, bowing her head to hide a pained expression. Then she coughed, spitting blood all over the ground around her shoes. Another violent coughing spasm shook her and more blood came from her mouth.

"You gotta have a doctor right away," Annabelle said as she gripped her mother's shoulders. "Tell me how much money we got an' where you hid it in the wagon. I'll run to town an' get the closest doctor I can find."

Doris wagged her head. "Hand me that laudanum, child. We ain't gonna spend what little money we got. Doc Collins said I had to git to Arizona real soon . . . ."

"You ain't strong enough, Ma. You can't hardly ride a wagon seat, the shape you're in. Tell me where the money is so I can fetch you a doctor right away."

"No. Give me the rest of that medicine. I'll be all right in a little spell."

Annabelle let go of her shoulders. "You ain't gonna be all right and you know it, Ma," she said quietly. "You're dyin', and you won't let me help you by bringin' you a doctor." She looked at the blood spots, shining like new copper pennies in light from the sun. "You gotta have a doctor real soon or we won't ever get to Arizona."

She raised her head so she could see Annabelle. Blood was on her lips and chin and down the front of her dress. Tears ran off her cheeks and her eyes were slightly glazed over. "Fetch me the medicine," she said weakly. "Don't give me no more argument or I'll take a strap to your hide."

Annabelle stamped her foot angrily. "You always see to it that we've got money to put in some preacher's collection plate, but you won't spend none on seein' a doctor when you're sick. I say that don't make no sense. If givin' money to the church did any good, you wouldn't be hurtin' so bad right now."

A look crossed her ma's face, a widening of her eyes the way they did when she was really mad. "You speak blasphemy!" she said as loudly as she could. She pointed a trembling finger in the direction of town. "Git away from my sight, you thankless child! Go to the devil's den when you can't keep words like that inside your mouth. Leave me be or the wrath of God will strike us both down. No child of mine will blaspheme the name of the Lord, or tell me my hard-earned money hadn't oughta go for God's work!"

She wheeled and ran away in the face of her mother's fury, as tears flooded her eyes. She ran as hard as she could toward the railroad depot, dashing behind it, running through a muddy alley reeking of urine and excrement without thinking of her shoes or the smell. She ran blind, seeing her surroundings through a veil of tears, stumbling over obstacles, the latrine ditch, lumps of dirt, discarded whiskey bottles. By the time she reached the end of the alley, she was gasping for air. She came to a halt at the corner of Rusk Street. Looking north, she saw the sign above the Pink Lady.

"I could ask Miss Rose for some money," she sobbed quietly, as she tried to catch her breath. "She'd want me to work for her to pay it back . . ."

She understood now what it would mean to work for Miss Rose. She'd be doing the same thing she'd done with Tommy Joe on Saturday night, only she'd be doing it for money with strangers. When she'd allowed Tommy Joe to poke her, as he called it, it hadn't seemed so terrible bad and it didn't hurt like she expected it would.

She looked up at the sun, judging it was close to noon. The train would be coming soon, and unless she went elsewhere, all the passengers would see her crying with mud on her shoes.

"I'll talk to Miss Rose about it. Won't be no harm done if all I do is ask her."

She started up Rusk Street, keeping her face to the ground so no one would recognize her heading into the Acre's collection of saloons. When she came to the alley running behind the Pink Lady, she glanced both ways to see if anyone was looking and then hurried around a corner to clean her shoes.

Rose Denadale cooled herself with a paper fan. Her bedroom windows were open and still the August heat was oppressive, like someone had opened an oven door. She listened to Annabelle's story without saying a word until she was finished. In harsh light she didn't appear quite so pretty, sitting by a window. Deep wrinkles webbed around her eyes and across her neck. Little folds of skin encircled her mouth as though she'd been smiling too many years. Her red hair appeared slightly orange in daylight, with streaks of gray growing from her temples, which she tried to hide with a pair of tortoiseshell combs in front of each ear.

"So you see, Miss Rose, my ma needs to see a doctor real

bad an' we don't have enough money to pay for it."

"How sad it must be for you to watch your mother dying."

"It's plenty sad. She's got this notion about the Bible an' the word of God. She gives money to the collection plate every Sunday, but she won't spend none on medicine or goin' to see a doctor. That laudanum you gave her sure did help, only it's all gone, nearly."

"You want to help her, don't you?"

"I surely do. Only I ain't sure I can do it . . . I ain't sure I can let some stranger poke me for money. I'm real bashful when it comes to men."

"Perhaps if you had some experience you'd be less bashful."

"I had some . . . experience Saturday night," she said, turning bright red, "only it was with this boy I know an' I don't suppose that would be exactly the same thing as a stranger."

"You need experience with an older man, I think. I know a gentleman who'd be perfect for your first customer. He's a very quiet man and he wouldn't be rough with you or treat you in a way that would be unpleasant. There'd be nothing to worry about. In fact, he's a Fort Worth peace officer, so you wouldn't be in any danger or have a problem with a drunken cowboy your first time."

She sat on the edge of Rose's big bed clasping her hands in front of her. "I'd be real nervous, Miss Rose. That ain't the sort of thing I'd be inclined to do if I had a choice about it."

"Sometimes a glass of wine helps take the edge off a girl's nerves."

"I could never drink even one glass of the devil's brew, not for no reason. Ma says it's evil and the devil's own concoction, and that only the worst kinds of folks drink bottled spirits or use tobacco. Drunkenness is one of the worst sins."

Rose smiled. "Your mother puts a lot of faith in what the Bible says. Everyone has to make up their own mind about what's right or wrong. Plenty of people use spirits in moderation, but that's your choice. It was only a suggestion to help overcome a bit of nervousness."

Annabelle looked at her fine furniture, the canopy above her bed, and the soft rug around it. "This sure is a beautiful room, Miss Rose. I'd wish to have one just like it someday. All your pretty dresses an' shoes . . ."

"Wishes can come true on occasion. Because of your remarkable beauty you could have all this and more."

The compliment caused her to blush. "I've never felt I was pretty, not until the other night when you let me wear your red dress. I appreciate what you done for me, lettin' me see what it felt like to wear it."

"You were beautiful then and you still are, Belle. A dress can't make anyone truly beautiful."

"How come you keep callin' me Belle? My name's Annabelle."

Rose smiled again. "It seems to fit you, I suppose. I can call you Annabelle if you prefer it."

She shrugged. "Belle's okay. I was just wonderin'."

"Then Belle it is. Would you like for me to arrange a time for you to meet this older gentleman?"

"I hadn't exactly made up my mind yet." She swallowed hard, thinking about it. "I'd have to fix it so Ma wouldn't find out. I couldn't be gone all that long."

"Your mother needs a doctor soon. You said she was getting much worse."

"I know. Truth is, that wouldn't be the only reason I'd do it. I'd be doin' it so I could buy dresses an' stockings, shoes an' maybe some perfume. I'm tired of bein' poor and if that's a sinful notion, then I reckon the devil's inside me now. Ma ain't gonna be able to do laundry much longer, sick as she is, an' I'm thinkin' about what I'll do for money when she's . . . gone."

"You're a smart young lady to think about your future. I'll be able to help with that, if you work for me. I can promise you steady work and a nice room with plenty of good food to eat, and I'll even help out by giving you some advance money for a doctor and a new dress or two. Think it over, Belle. Let me know what you decide."

"I'll come back tomorrow, if that's okay."

"Of course. In the meantime, here's a little something for extras." Rose opened her handbag and took out a few banknotes. "Take this. Do whatever you want with it."

Annabelle looked at the money, counting five paper dollars in Miss Rose's palm. She was sorely tempted by it, although she knew that if she took it she would feel an obligation to agree to meet with the older gentleman. "I'd better not take it until I made up my mind. It wouldn't be right to take your money if I'm not gonna let nobody poke me."

"Take it anyway. You won't owe me a thing. I'll understand if you decide against arranging a meeting with the marshal."

She got off the bed and hesitated a moment. So many confusing thoughts clouded her mind at once. Five dollars seemed like so very much money.

In the end she took it and thanked Miss Rose before she went down the back stairs and then through the storage room. With the money clenched tightly in her fist, she ran toward the campground, wondering if she'd taken a first step down a pathway from which there was no turning back.

14

Rose walked to a bedroom window, looking beyond thick velvet drapes that helped keep out sunlight during early morning. She gazed across the odd assortment of rooftops in Fort Worth without really seeing them, thinking about the girl.

"Belle Green," she said softly, to herself. "I'll make her the talk of this town. Mayor Tompkins will pay thirty dollars to spend an hour with her if I tell him she's new to the business, and how young she is."

She thought about Cordel. Cordel liked his women young and beautiful and he'd be gentle and understanding with her the first time. Of far greater importance, she needed Cordel's cooperation to keep her gambling tables out of trouble. Having the marshal in her back pocket, so to speak, made staying in business so much easier when dealers and roulette wheels were making sure the odds were always heavily in the house's favor.

Remembering Belle, she smiled. The girl had no idea how truly beautiful she was—how beautiful she could be wearing the right clothing, using her charms the way she should. Rich men would pay generous sums to sleep with her. They would come from all over to see her, men who spent big money on cards and roulette and drinks and girls. Belle would become the Pink Lady's prime attraction, a drawing card.

"I have to find a way to convince her," Rose said, fanning herself. It would probably be simple enough. Buy her expensive things: dresses and jewelry, stockings and dressing gowns, lacy corsets, high heeled shoes to match. The girl's dying mother was pushing her closer to a decision, but it wasn't only that. Belle said it herself—she was tired of being poor, and if there was one thing Rose understood, it was poverty. Rose had been as poor as anyone could be, in the beginning, and only her good looks, an ample bosom, and a mane of flaming red hair gave her a way out of back streets along the wharfs of New Orleans. Now, almost thirty years later, she owned one of Fort Worth's finest and best-known gambling parlors as well as a two-story home in one of the better sections of town. She had enough money saved to travel across Europe if she saw fit, visiting places like Paris and London and Venice, staying as long as she cared to. Running a casino and whorehouse had been good to her and the time was coming when she could quit the business forever.

She left her window and went down to the storeroom to find Luther. Cordel needed to be told about the girl. Lately he'd begun to show less interest in Rose, saying he preferred younger women. She couldn't remember the last time Cordel was in her bed, and because of that, there was a risk he'd find a younger woman in one of the other gentlemen's clubs to show favor. Rose understood with a businesswoman's clear head that something had to be done to keep Marshal Hull's sympathies with the Pink Lady.

Luther Pierce was hunched over his desk in a room behind the bar, counting last night's receipts. He looked up when Rose came in, furrowing his bushy black eyebrows. He was a giant of a man with hamlike fists and a temper that could equal an angry lion's when someone pushed him as he oversaw operations at the Pink Lady and served as the Lady's business manager and general keeper of order. Rose trusted him, and slept with him on occasion, but only when he asked, although theirs was almost entirely a business relationship, spanning twenty years. He enforced strict house rules from everyone who worked for her and from customers who got too rowdy. Because of his size and tremendous strength he'd crushed a few skulls when he was mad, and when occasion warranted he knew how to use the gun he carried inside his coat. He could count money honestly and handle the meanest drunk, two very valuable assets for anyone put in charge of running a gambling casino and whorehouse.

"Afternoon, Rose," he said, shifting a stack of currency to one side of his desk. A safe stood open in a corner of the room. "We had a slow night, but it was Sunday. I've got the marshal's money counted out for the week. I was gonna take it by soon as I sealed the envelope."

Luther's tiny office was too hot for her liking; however it wasn't Luther's nature to complain. "I want you to give Cordel a message from me. In private, of course, after you give him his cut from the tables. Tell him I've got a new girl coming to work for me in a day or so. She's young, just sixteen, and she hasn't been with a man before. She's by far the prettiest girl I've had since we opened, and he can have her first. I'm making arrangements now. You can tell him I said she is, without a doubt, the most beautiful girl ever to work a house in Fort Worth. She may be one of the most beautiful girls I've ever seen."

Luther's puzzled expression became a leer. He shifted his bulk in the chair so he could see Rose's face in light from the oil lamp atop his desk. "Is she really that pretty? Sounds to me like she's mighty young to be . . . fully developed."

Rose began fanning herself. "She's a natural beauty. I've never met a girl with so much innocent charm. She'll need a bit of polishing with her manners and speech so she won't seem quite so backward. Right now she's as country as a butter churn, but I can fix that. You tell Cordel that as a special favor to him I'm saving her so he can be with her first. Tell him her name is Belle."

Luther picked up the stack of money and put it in an envelope, licked the envelope, and stuck it into his inside coat pocket. "We was needing a new attraction, Rose. They've got this girl down at Stockmen's Retreat named Marylou who's got everybody talking about her, and the Standard still has Miss Pearl. Lots of men go down to the Standard just to see what her chest looks like."

Rose made a face. "Pearl Hawkins smokes enough opium to put a team of oxen down. I fired her because of it. She can't make us or herself any money when she's unconscious half the time. I promise you that Belle will bring the crowds back. Just you wait until you see her. Now, give that message to Cordel, and be sure to tell him business will get better here real soon. Tell him to come see me, so I can tell him about Belle.''

Luther got up with no small amount of effort. In the last year his weight had risen to over three hundred pounds. ''Cordel wasn't too happy about last week's envelope. He said it wasn't nearly enough, like he thinks we're cheating him out of his fair share.''

At that, Rose chuckled. ''What's fair about having to pay a lawman under the table so we can run rigged games? He'd better not get too greedy, or come election time, he might find himself without a job. He'll be satisfied when you tell him about Belle and being first with her. That'll keep him quiet long enough for the girl to start bringing in more customers.''

Luther nodded and put out his lamp. ''This girl must be the prettiest thing west of the Mississippi. I never heard you carry on about a woman like that before.'' He put two large canvas bags of money away, then closed the safe and spun its tumbler dial.

''She is, Luther. All she needs is a bit of polish and some time to learn things she has to know.''

She walked with him out of his office and waited while he locked the door. In the front parlor, two Negro women were busy sweeping rugs and polishing furniture. A balding man in a white apron applied wax to a gaming table, and wiped the wood around the edges of a roulette wheel very carefully. Rose noticed a layer of dust on wood frames surrounding two large oil paintings of nude women hanging above parlor love seats.

''Don't forget to dust those picture frames, Fannie Mae,'' she said, examining every detail throughout the room with a practiced eye, making sure nothing escaped her.

One black woman replied, ''Yes, ma'am, Miss Rose. I was gonna get to them frames shortly.'' She hurried over to the wall with a feather duster as Rose walked to the front door with Luther.

Luther let himself out, pausing while he gazed up an empty

street. Until the sun went down, Hell's Half Acre was usually a quiet place. "There've been two killings this week," he said in a flat voice, like someone discussing weather. "Cole Webb told me George Curry is back in town, and that he already shot a man over at Maude's. They say it was self-defense, so the judge'll let him go. We can look for trouble if he shows up here."

Rose's expression hardened. "Men like Flatnose Curry are trouble wherever they are. I don't want him in my place. He'll scare off our best customers. We can't afford to have him come around. We'll have to do something."

"He's a hard man to discourage, Rose. If I get too rough with him, he'll use a gun on me and claim I drew on him first."

"Ask Cordel if he can do something about Curry. For the money I'm paying we're entitled to some protection from men like him."

"It's not that I'm scared of him," Luther explained as he touched the bulge of the pistol hidden inside his coat. "He's the type who'll do most anything to have some advantage. If I bust his head he'll only come back and we both know that won't be good for business. Half the men in this town are afraid of him because of his reputation as a shooter. You know I'm no fast draw artist, but don't think for a minute he scares me. I won't back down from him, gun or no gun."

She touched Luther's sleeve. "I never saw a man you were afraid of, Luther. But it wouldn't make good sense for you to let him push you into a shooting contest. Let Marshal Hull take care of it. That's what he gets paid to do."

He acknowledged her kind remark with a nod. "The marshal's tough, but he's getting like me, a little long in the tooth to be taking on gunfighters. Somebody said Curry drew on him the other night and Hull didn't even clear leather. Some young cowboy got the drop on Curry from behind or we'd be attending the marshal's funeral today."

Rose seemed puzzled. "Whoever that cowboy is, he may regret aiming a gun at George Curry's back. Curry isn't the kind who's likely to forget."

"This town is full of boys who think they're men because of a gun. The cemetery has got plenty who found out they were dead wrong. I'll talk to Cordel about Curry. Maybe there's something he can do officially that'll keep him away from the Lady."

Luther strolled off in the direction of Marshal Hull's office. Rose watched him until he reached the corner at Twelfth Street, then she went inside. Behind the bar she took down a bottle of imported sherry and a long-stemmed glass. What she needed now was a drink.

As she climbed to the top of the stairs, she recognized an odor coming from one of her girl's rooms—she knew which room it would be. At a door numbered "5" she stopped and knocked.

"Who is it?" a fuzzy voice mumbled.

"Rose," she snapped impatiently. "Open this door."

A stirring inside, then silence.

"I said open this goddamn door, Allene!"

"I'm comin', Miss Rose."

A tall, dark-haired woman appeared when the door opened a crack. She still had traces of beauty in her face, yet it had begun to fade with age, although when Rose counted up the years realized Allene couldn't have been more than twenty-five. The girl's eyes were glassy, hooded. "What is it, Miss Rose?"

"You know goddamn well what it is, Allene. I won't allow an opium pipe here. Get rid of it, and don't ever let me catch you smoking one in my place again."

"But I was only doin' a little bit . . ."

Unconsciously, Rose's fingers tightened around the bottle neck and glass. She pushed the door back with her foot, and when she spoke, her voice was a harsh whisper. "Look in a mirror, you stupid bitch! You've aged ten years since you started smoking that shit. I'll have Luther throw you out if I ever hear you've smoked it again. You'll be sucking off old men in back alleys for the price of a shoeshine!"

Allene stepped back, closing the front of her dressing robe with trembling hands as tears rushed to her eyes. "But, Miss

Rose, I need just a little bit once in a while or I get the shakes real bad.''

Rose made a face. "You're disgusting, Allene, worse than a drunk. Remember what I said—one more time and I'll have Luther throw you out. No girl of mine is going to smoke a waterpipe while she works at the Lady. You used to be pretty. Take a good look at yourself now.''

She wheeled away and walked stiffly down the hallway to her room, slamming her door behind her. Pouring herself a drink at the dressing table, she noticed how her hand was shaking when she brought the glass to her lips. She wondered if it was anger that made her hands shake, or was it her own dependence on liquor? As the years passed, she drank more and more when she noticed her own beauty fading. Sherry softened the sting of growing old, of what she saw when she looked in a mirror too closely. Of late she'd been unable to fall asleep without several glasses of sherry or brandy.

She looked in her mirror now and saw a deeply lined face of forty-six, a wrinkled neck and sagging breasts, dimpling thighs and drooping buttocks when she hoisted her dressing gown. It was hard to remember a time when her face was as smooth as ivory and her body was so firm she never needed a corset. Her thick hair was turning gray and that red dye she ordered from New York only made her look like a circus clown.

"Damn it, Rose," she whispered, draining her glass, unable to take her eyes from her reflection, "you've gotten too old and it's time to get out of this lousy business." She poured another generous drink and consumed half, examining laugh lines around her mouth and crow's feet around her eyes. "You let yourself get old," she said sadly, as though it was her fault.

She thought back to her meeting with Belle. The girl was so pretty, flawlessly pretty with the kind of appeal men would want at almost any cost. "She has no idea how beautiful she is," Rose said quietly, "how beautiful she can be, if she'll only listen to me."

The first time they met, Rose had had her doubts that a girl from a strict religious upbringing would come to work for her at the Lady, even to earn money to help her dying mother. But at this second meeting, Belle revealed the beginnings of desire to escape her life of poverty as a laundress. Wanting some of life's finer things would do more to bring Belle to the Lady than anything an outsider might do. Poverty and ambition had driven many a young girl to prostitution. Belle Green wouldn't be all that different . . . Rose knew from personal experience.

15

Cody's room was not much larger than a closet, roughly eight feet long and so narrow he had to squeeze past his cot to get to a door leading to rows of cells. Six iron cages, three on each side of a hallway, held the city of Fort Worth's prisoners while a much larger jail across from the courthouse was home to those who violated state or county laws. Sheriff Homer Casey and four deputies took care of county affairs while Marshal Hull and two deputies enforced city ordinances and ruled over most troubles in Hell's Half Acre. Soon after he stowed his gear in the back room, Cody was introduced to Dave Watkins, a second deputy serving with Cole Webb. Watkins was a quiet, brooding man with rope-like arms and an angry set to his jaw that never seemed to change. After introductions Marshal Hull left the office with Dave while it was handed to Cole to instruct Cody as to his duties.

"This here's the ring of cell keys," Cole said. "You never open no cell door 'less the marshal tells you. It don't matter if the jail's on fire, you let the sorry sons of bitches back there turn to pitch before you open a cell door. You give 'em their food through those openin's at the bottom of the bars an' pass water tins through the same way. You only clean out the slop pots when one of us is around to keep a shotgun on whoever's inside, 'specially if it's one of our bad boys, like Curry or Ketchum."

George Curry was in a cell on the left, while Cody remembered seeing Jake Ketchum asleep on an iron cot to the right of the hallway. Another man occupied a cell next to Curry. Cody nodded when he heard Cole's instructions. "I understand. Never open a cell door without you or the marshal bein' here.''

Cole tossed the ring of keys into a desk drawer. ''Or if ol' Dave's around; only don't stand between Dave an' a prisoner for no reason, on account of Dave's liable to shoot just because he feels like it or because the rheumatiz in his knee hurts, or for no reason at all. Back in the spring he blowed Hank Starr plumb to pieces in one of them cells—we had to use a shovel to pick up what was left of Hank so the undertaker'd have somethin' to bury. Dave claimed it was an accident, that his gun just went off, but any fool knows a shotgun don't go off accidental if it ain't been cocked. Dave never did like Hank. They had some trouble over a woman a few years back.''

''What did Marshal Hull say?'' Cody asked, trying not to think about what it would be like to use a shovel to gather up pieces of a corpse.

Cole grinned knowingly. ''He told Dave to be more careful, only Dave knew he didn't mean it all that much. The marshal an' Watkins been friends a long time. Dave is a mean bastard. Don't ever cross him, if you want some advice. He's good with a gun or his fists an' he ain't above shootin' a feller in the back now an' then. One time he ran across this wanted owlhoot by the name of Tommy Potter down by the railroad station. Potter was passed out drunk under a tree. Dave took a new axe handle from a barrel of 'em over at Simmons General Store an' beat Potter plumb to death afore he ever woke up. His head was all mushy, like he never had no skullbone. When Dave gets on a mad, he ain't to be trifled with. Hank Starr shouldn't have never messed with one of Dave's women, 'cause Dave killed him intentional, sure as a pinch of snuff makes spit.''

Cody was still puzzled over the way the law worked in Fort Worth. ''How did the marshal explain what happened?''

Again, Cole gave him a one-sided grin. ''Marshal Hull told the city attorney Starr was tryin' to escape. Ol' Hank was gonna hang anyway, so it saved the city some expense. A public hangin' costs money. Dave got it done for the price of a shotgun shell. Same for Tommy Potter. Dave claimed he was reachin' for a gun.''

Cody walked to an office window, wanting to forget about how Dave got rid of Hank Starr and Potter. "Marshal Hull said I was to get the prisoner's food across the street.''

"Over yonder at Mary's Café. You tell her how many prisoners we got and she'll give you that many plates. Twice a day you go over for the grub, about noon, an' after five o'clock. Mary's got a contract with the city to feed 'em, only I wouldn't advise you eat none of it yourself. There's been times when Mary's home cookin' has made some of our guests mighty sick.''

"I'll remember not to eat there.''

"Another thing,'' Cole continued, "sometimes folks come just to see Marshal Hull on business, like he told you. That's when you find somethin' else to do in the back.''

"Mind if I ask what sort of business it is?''

At that, Cole chuckled. "You'll learn soon enough; only if I was you, I'd forget everything I heard or seen round here. You don't ask no questions an' you keep your mouth shut.''

Was something dishonest going on in the marshal's office? Despite Cole's warnings, Cody wondered what it was. "I was just curious. It don't matter what it is, I don't reckon. He's the law in this town an' I'm only a jailer. Don't seem it would have anything to do with me.''

"It won't if you keep your nose out of it. Now, over yonder is a storeroom where we keep the prisoner's guns an' such. Also a dead man's personal stuff, until somebody comes to claim it, or when a corpse ain't got no kin. Then we throw it out, 'cept for a gun, or maybe a good pair of spurs. That feller's gear Curry killed is in there now . . . undertaker brought it over this mornin'. Said his name was Buford Davis. There's a letter from some woman up in Denver addressed to Davis. Marshal Hull will be askin' you to send his belongings to that Denver woman, if you can read an' write an' spell good enough. Davis was wanted up in Laramie for some kind of robbery, so his body'll be sent up to Wyoming on the train.''

"I get by," Cody said. "I can write the woman's name on a package, if you'll show me that letter."

Cole opened a door to a small room, hardly more than a broom closet. A pile of boots and hats and assorted clothing lay in a heap on the floor, some stained with dried blood. Cole rummaged through a pair of worn denims until he found a crumpled envelope. "Here it is," he muttered, handing the letter to Cody.

The envelope was addressed to Buford R. Davis in care of the Miller Ranch at Muleshoe, Texas. A return address showed it came from Alice Evans at 12 Porter Street, Denver, in Colorado Territory.

"I'll wrap up his things," Cody offered.

Cole wagged his head. "Not till the marshal says so. You don't do nothin', not even take a piss around here, unless Cordel says it's okay."

Cody put the letter in his shirt pocket. He glanced up at a clock atop the marshal's desk. "It's nearly eleven. You want me to go over to Mary's an' tell her we're needin' three plates?"

"The marshal said we ain't gonna feed Curry. I figure he'll be released as soon as Marshal Hull an' Dave get back from the judge's court. Curry killed Davis in self-defense, accordin' to what witnesses say."

"It's true," Cody agreed. "I saw what happened."

Cole slumped on the bench, eyeing Cody strangely. "So did I, an' if you'll remember, I was standin' right behind you. I come real close to shootin' you that night, figurin' you might be one of Curry's friends aimin' to take his side. For bein' so young you've got a hell of a lot of nerve, drawin' a gun on Curry like that, even if his back was turned. Marshal Hull told me you've got the makin's of a deputy marshal, he thinks. He also told me you faced right up to Jake Ketchum like you'd draw on him if he wanted." Cole examined Cody's holster. "Are you any good with a six-shooter?"

"I can shoot."

The deputy's eyes narrowed. "That ain't enough in the Acre. You'd better be fast or you'll wind up on Boot Hill. We had us a young deputy last year . . . name was Bobby Devine. He got shot near the end of his first week. Bullet went plumb through his liver.''

"Who shot him?" Cody asked, wondering if a deputy's job was what he really wanted, especially if something crooked might be going on in Marshal Hull's office.

"Nobody knew for sure. Judge Warren ordered a hangin' for a regular troublemaker from Maddox Flats by the name of Sharpe. We couldn't prove he done it, but he couldn't prove he didn't do it, so Marshal Hull arrested him an' charged him with murder. Sharpe was hanged, an' that satisfied everybody at City Hall.''

"Sounds like a different brand of justice to me. Maybe you hanged an innocent man.''

"Maybe. Maybe he didn't kill Bobby Devine, but odds were he did kill somebody, livin' in the Flats. Don't get no high-minded notions about how the law works in the Acre, Cody. This place is worse'n a den of rattlesnakes. A peace officer who works in this part of town had better be ready to close his eyes to some things if he aims to stay alive.''

Again, Cody's notion of the law's workings didn't quite fit what went on in Fort Worth. "Sounds like they give the marshal a mighty free rein.''

"He's got powerful friends at City Hall. Him'n Mayor Frank Tompkins see eye to eye on most things, an' Judge Warren believes in usin' plenty of rope on tough customers. Marshal Hull usually gets his way, so long as he keeps the Acre's troubles down here where they belong.''

Cody still wondered what the marshal's occasional visitors did or said that couldn't be talked about. But he needed a job and now he had one, paying fifty dollars a month, with prospects of making a deputy's rank later on.

Across the street a tiny café bore a sign, "Mary's Eatery,'' above the door. The café was in a clapboard building sandwiched between a saloon and a saddle shop. "I'll tell Mary to fix two plates,'' Cody said as he turned away from the window, thinking he was hungry himself, but not hungry enough to risk Mary's offering after what Cole had said.

Cole shook his head. "Just tell her you're the new jailer. She'll have the slop ready shortly."

Cole walked outside, noting how empty the street was. Hull's office was at the northern edge of the Acre, away from most larger saloons. To the west lay Fort Worth's legitimate businesses, its banks and stores, barbershops, better places to eat, and City Hall. The north side of town was devoted almost entirely to the livestock trade, cattle pens and buyers' offices, stores dealing in supplies needed by cowherd chuck wagons for long crossings of Indian Territory above the Red River. East of the Acre and much farther west, quiet residential sections of the city were spread along both sides of the Trinity River. In summer Fort Worth was in a lull, awaiting the arrival of huge herds of longhorns later in the fall and early spring. But when cattle drives began to form on the prairies north and west of town, city streets became jammed with cowboys and camp cooks and horse wranglers preparing for the arduous journey to Kansas. For four years, beginning at the age of sixteen, Cody had gone up the Chisholm with them. But at the ripe old age of twenty he'd seen enough of swollen rivers and stampedes to last a lifetime. Surveying Fort Worth's haphazard collection of buildings now, he felt better about trying to survive its dangers than risking even one more cattle drive into what was called "the Nations" by seasoned trail hands. There was no future herding cattle, and the chances of dying were too great for so little pay. If he had to choose another risky profession even on a temporary basis, it might as well be for more money.

He crossed the road and entered Mary's, finding he was her only customer at that time of day. An elderly woman with puffy cheeks beading sweat turned from a wood stove at the back, wiping her hands on a greasy apron.

"What'll you have, cowboy?" she asked, walking behind a row of stools facing a counter.

"I'm the new jailer. Deputy Webb said I was to come over here an' tell you we've got two prisoners to feed today."

The woman nodded, giving Cody a brief examination. "You're a bit on the young side to be workin' for Cordel, ain't you?"

"I'm twenty. The marshal must figure that's old enough."

She grunted and said, "Beans'll be ready in a wink. Might as well have a seat till I'm done. Coffee's free for the law, so help yourself to what's in that pot yonder," she added, pointing to a blackened coffeepot as she made her way back to her stove.

Cody ambled over to the coffee and poured a tin cup of what appeared to be black syrup while Mary banged tin plates on the stovetop. The place smelled of bacon grease and something else slightly stale he couldn't identify. He sat on a stool at the counter. Passing time, he took from his pocket the letter sent to Buford Davis, deciding it wouldn't matter much to a dead man if he read his mail.

The paper was so badly wrinkled he had trouble spreading it flat. He started reading after taking a taste of Mary's scorched coffee.

> Dear Bufe,
> See a woman named Miss Allene Wright in Fort Worth. She's a crib girl in the Acre. Ask around. She has a map to where the money is hid. Keep eyes open for George. He knows it was us double-crossed him.
> Alice

Cody read the letter again very carefully, until he was sure he understood every word. A woman named Miss Allene Wright had a map to where some money was hidden. Unexplained was the message that somehow Buford Davis and Alice Evans had double-crossed Curry over this money and George knew about it. Miss Allene Wright was a whore in Hell's Half Acre, explaining Davis's presence in Fort Worth— to look for her. Curry must have trailed Davis here, Cody thought, and as soon as Davis saw him, he went for Curry with a gun.

Cody wondered what to do with the information contained in the letter. He decided there was really only one choice— give it to Marshal Hull.

16

Jake Ketchum stiffened when Cody shoved a plate of beans through the opening in his cell. He was seated on the edge of his iron-frame cot, watching Cody through hooded eyelids.

"I'll get even with you, boy," he said, sounding hoarse, as though his throat had something caught in it.

Cody stood up, ignoring Ketchum, to put a second plate into a cell across the hallway.

Another voice came from the back of the jail. "Not if I get to him first," Curry said. "You pulled a gun on me, mister, and nobody does that without paying for it."

Cody glanced into Curry's cell. Curry came to the bars and held one in each fist, glaring between them.

"The marshal said I wasn't supposed to feed you on account of you'll be let out pretty soon." He meant to ignore Curry's threat the way he had Ketchum's.

"I don't give a damn about your jail food!" Curry hissed as his jaw clenched. "I'm warning you—you'll pay for throwing down on me when my back was turned."

Cody met Curry's look, finding no hint of fear or doubt in the gunman's eyes. "I was doin' my job," he explained, leaving out the fact he wasn't working for Marshal Hull that night. "You had him cold an' I couldn't just let you gun him down without it was a fair fight."

"You're a yellow son of a bitch for drawing on me from the back side."

Cody's temper flashed before he could contain it. He moved closer to Curry's cell, not quite within easy reaching distance.

"There's two things I ain't, Mr. Curry," he said just above a whisper. "One's yellow, an' the other's a son of a bitch of any kind." He looked squarely into Curry's dark pupils for a moment. "But if you think otherwise, you're welcome to try your hand against me anytime you're ready. It'll be settled after that an' there won't be no doubt about who's yellow or who's the son of a bitch."

Curry blinked, making it plain he hadn't expected to hear an invitation to a fight from Cody. His hands tightened around the bars. "Maybe I'll do that," he said, quieter than before. "I'll look you up when my business here is finished."

Cody knew what he meant—his business was finding the whore named Miss Allene Wright, and a map. "You do that," Cody replied, not backing down an inch. He had swung around to leave when he saw a figure blocking the doorway into Marshal Hull's office. With a bright sun coming through the office windows, right at first he couldn't make out who it was, nor could he recall hearing anyone come through the outer door while he was occupied feeding prisoners.

Deputy Watkins slumped against the door frame, hooking his thumbs in his gunbelt. "That was a mighty fine speech," he said to Cody. "Don't never let one of these so-called tough guys say they'll get you for puttin' 'em in jail. We've got us a special treatment for talk like that." He reached behind him, hefting a sawed-off double-barrel shotgun he'd leaned against the wall. "I heard what both those gents said to you." He began walking down the row of cells, resting the butt of his shotgun against his hip as he cocked both hammers, the sound of his boots and the click of iron echoing off the jail walls. He stopped in front of Ketchum's cell, aiming his gun between the bars at Jake. "No need to worry about this one," he said, grinning crookedly. "We get to watch him dance a jig at the end of a brand new rope. No sense wastin' time on him, 'cause he's as good as dead already. On the other hand, I could kill him and save the city some expense."

"Sweet Jesus," Jake whispered, drawing back against the wall, showing the whites of his eyes. "You wouldn't just shoot me like you done to Hank Starr that time . . ."

Dave's grin widened some. "Hank was tryin' to make a jailbreak. Hell, everybody knows he made a grab for this scattergun. It just went off. I reckon you'd say ol' Hank killed himself."

Cody couldn't quite believe Dave would taunt a prisoner so openly, threatening to shoot him to save expenses. Cody understood now why Cole said to be careful around Watkins. Dave was enjoying himself—he had to be half-crazy, not just mean in an ordinary way.

But when Dave removed his gun barrels from Jake's cell, he made a turn toward the back of the jail rather than ending with Ketchum. He came toward Cody, but his eyes were on Curry's cell. He walked to the bars Curry was holding before he stopped, not giving Cody even a passing glance. Very slowly, with a mixture of amusement and fascination on his face, he raised his shotgun until both muzzles were only inches below Curry's chin. Curry didn't move so much as a muscle.

"You've got a real ugly nose," Dave said. "You'd be a hell of a lot easier to look at if I blowed it off your face. All you gotta do is make a grab for this gun and I'll change your looks. Won't be no extra charge for doin' it, either." The grin left Dave's face entirely now. "Go ahead, Mr. Flatnose George Curry. Reach for my gun. Talk is, you're a real bad man, fast with a gun, not scared of nobody. Show me you ain't scared to make your play right now. Show me how tough you are . . ."

Curry's expression remained unchanged when he said, "I'm no fool. Give me a gun so things'll be square."

Dave's eyes rounded slightly. With the shotgun in his right hand, he reached across his belly and took out his pistol, a Colt .44 with smooth walnut grips. Butt-first, his lips drawn into a savage snarl, he held his revolver out to Curry. "I'd be real happy to oblige you," he said quietly, menacingly, offering up the gun so that all Curry had to do was take it.

Curry looked at Dave's pistol, only a glance.

Cody started to object—Marshal Hull would never allow such a thing to happen inside his jail if he knew about it. Dave was baiting Curry. He'd kill him the moment he reached for that gun and Curry knew it.

"I'd be dead before I had a chance to shoot," Curry said, sounding as calm as could be, without moving either hand. "In a fair fight things would be even."

Cody wasn't going to allow Dave to kill Curry in cold blood this way. He had made a move to step between them, when a voice from the end of the hallway halted him.

"That's enough, Dave. Holster your pistol and unlock his cell. Judge Warren said to let him go."

Marshal Hull stood in the door frame, outlined by sunlight shining through windows behind him. Dave's eyes flickered to the marshal, then back to Curry. He put his revolver away without a word of protest.

"I still claim you've got the ugliest nose I ever saw," he remarked, lowering his shotgun, then both hammers. "If Marshal Hull hadn't come along when he did, you'd look a hell of a lot different after today."

Cody took a breath. He wondered how long the marshal had stood there listening before he intervened. Or had Marshal Hull sent Dave back here to throw a scare into Curry before letting him out of jail? "I'll fetch the keys," Cody offered, speaking to Dave.

Dave merely nodded, then he gave Cody a sideways look. "You got balls," he said, as Cody started up the hall. "Gotta hand it to you for that. Just remember you ain't gotta take no shit off a prisoner. If one opens his mouth, you tell me about it."

Cody wanted to say he could handle his own affairs, yet he let it drop for the time being, not wanting to get on Dave's bad side.

When he walked up to the marshal, Hull held up a palm that was meant to stop him from going into the office.

"Don't pay too much attention to what Dave says. Every now and then he sees himself as a one-man vigilante committee. He's a good deputy. From time to time he lets his temper get the best of him."

Cody was tempted to ask if that was what had happened

when Hank Starr was blown to bits, or when Tommy Potter had his head turned to mush. It was better not to say anything. "I'll get him those keys" was all he said, heading for the desk drawer as quickly as he could.

When he unlocked Curry's cell, he avoided the looks Curry was giving him, taking note of where Dave stood, and the angle of his shotgun pointed at Curry. Curry sauntered out as calm as could be, like he'd known all along no one would harm him and that he'd be free as a bird in no time.

Marshal Hull was waiting for Curry near the front door with Curry's gunbelt. Dave followed him out with his twelve-gauge leveled.

"Here's your gun," Hull said evenly. "Take my advice and be real sure you don't use it again while you're in Fort Worth. I'd hate like hell to see your neck stretched, but you've got my word that's what'll happen next time . . . if there is a next time."

Curry strapped on his cartridge belt silently, then he tied down his holster to his right leg the way Cody's pa had shown him a long time ago, when he first learned how to draw and shoot with a pistol.

Curry reached for the doorknob. "I figure that piece of advice is worth what it cost me," he said. "I've got business here in town and until it's finished there's no need to discuss what might happen between you and me, or your halfwit deputy, or the boy yonder who's trying to sound like a man. But I've got a long memory, Cordel. We'll be seeing each other again, after I talk to the undertaker. Buford Davis had something that belonged to me and I want it back."

He let himself out, and to Cody's surprise, Marshal Hull did not say anything else. It was Dave who made a move like he meant to follow Curry outside.

"He called me a halfwit," Dave said hotly.

The marshal stopped him. "Let it rest for now. There'll be plenty of time to take care of George if he makes trouble. Wait until something happens. I'm sure it will . . ."

A bearlike man sporting a black beard came to the front door, dressed in a business suit and bow tie. His arrival ended the discussion between Dave and Marshal Hull. He came in and closed the door behind him, glancing through a window, perspiring in summer heat like he'd walked a long way.

"Howdy, Luther," the marshal said. "Have a seat over at the desk." He gave Dave and Cody a look. Deputy Webb walked out as soon as Luther headed for a chair, as though he knew he wasn't supposed to be there now.

Cody had been waiting for the opportunity to tell Marshal Hull what was in that letter in his pocket, but he remembered he had been told not to hang around when there were visitors. "I'll get that chamber pot from Curry's cell an' toss it out," he said, as Dave crossed the office to go outside.

As he was going back to empty the pot, he heard Luther say, "That was Flatnose Curry. I thought I recognized him. Rose is worried he'll cause trouble for us at the Lady by runnin' off our good customers."

Cody didn't hear Marshal Hull's reply because the sounds of spoons raking across tin plates drowned out voices. Ketchum and the other prisoner were wolfing down their beans, making enough noise to wake the dead. As he went in Curry's cell to pick up the pot, Cody remembered something Curry had said—he was headed to the undertaker's parlor because Buford Davis had something that was his.

"It's this letter he wants," Cody whispered to himself, the letter and the map it described. "He'll be back when he finds out Davis's things are in that closet."

Being careful not to spill any of the pot's yellow contents, he carried it to a rear door made of heavy oak planking. An iron bolt squeaked when he slid it back, and the door's hinges made a similar protest when he opened it.

The alley behind the jail reeked of garbage and sewer tanks dug into earth behind rows of buildings. He dumped the pot into one of the holes quickly, without breathing through his nose. As he was about to go back inside, he saw a man dressed in rags near a garbage heap, picking through it as though he was looking for something. When the man saw Cody, he straightened and hurried off with a bundle of rags under his arm.

After he bolted the jail door shut, Cody happened to glance up toward the front office. He saw Luther give Marshal Hull a fat envelope before he departed.

He wasn't thinking about what might be in the envelope when he walked up front—he needed to tell the marshal what was in the letter before Curry got back. But when he entered the office, he found Marshal Hull counting a fistful of money silently, with his back turned.

"I need to tell you somethin' real quick," Cody began, with Davis's letter in his hand.

Hull whirled around. "You were told to find something else to do when I had visitors," he snapped.

Cody glanced at the money again. "But I saw him leave an' I need to show you why Curry's in Fort Worth," he explained.

"I don't give a damn why he's here. Just make real sure you forget what you see right now. Understood?"

"Yessir. I never saw no money, or nobody named Luther who brung it here."

Hull stuffed the currency into an inside coat pocket. "So tell me what's so all-fired important about why Curry's here."

Cody handed over the envelope. "Read what's in this letter. It'll explain. There's a map showin' where some money is hid an' that's what Curry wanted from Buford Davis. That's how come he came all this way on the train."

The marshal took Davis's letter, opened it, and started to read slowly. A moment later his gray eyes lifted to Cody's face. "Well, I'll be damned," he said softly.

17

All afternoon there had been an uneasy silence between them, and as evening approached, every now and then Annabelle caught a glimpse of her ma wiping tears from her cheeks, when she thought Annabelle wasn't looking. No more had been said about the money put in Sunday collection plates or blasphemy on Annabelle's part, even though the uneasiness was still there, like a barrier they erected to keep more angry words from being exchanged. Heaps of laundry lay everywhere, as was usual on Mondays, requiring them to double their efforts to get all of it done. When a kettle of clothing was finished boiling in soap, it had to be rinsed in clean water, which meant Annabelle spent more time at a pump jack in the center of the campground, filling buckets of fresh water to carry back to their kettles. With dusk darkening the prairies west of town, she did her best to hurry back and forth with enough water to get finished doing the last of the rinsing so the clothes could be hung up to dry. As she carried heavy pails with aching arms, sweating in the late day heat, she thought about her visit to see Miss Rose, what they'd talked about, the older gentleman she said was a peace officer with whom she could get her first actual experience being poked for money, if only she could work up the nerve to do it at all.

I'd be so embarrassed, she thought. There were oil lamps in the rooms at the Lady and she wondered if they were put out during a gentleman's call. Otherwise, a man would see her completely naked the way Tommy Joe had, only it had been dark that night and he was just a boy. Would it be different if there were light? Was she too bashful to let a man see her naked? So many unanswered questions filled her mind as she went about carrying the last pails of water. The one thing she knew now was that being poked didn't hurt the way she had thought it might. In fact, it felt rather good in a wicked way, which was all the more evidence the devil had taken over her thoughts and actions. She was possessed by demons like some scriptures said happened to those who didn't fear God. Annabelle wasn't afraid of God anymore, the way her ma said she should be. Being God-fearing had done hardly anything for them, as far back as she could remember. And if it meant being poor all her life, she wasn't so sure it was as good as other choices, which allowed her to have money.

She thought about the five dollars Miss Rose had given her. It felt so nice, having five whole dollars nobody else knew about, to spend on a whim. The money made her feel rich in a silly sort of way. It wasn't that five dollars was all that much, but it was hers to spend however she wanted.

Carrying pails and slopping water on her skirt, she cast a look at a bright orange sunset, pink clouds above it, and lengthening shadows inching across the campground. Down deep, she knew what she had to do with the money. Her ma needed another bottle of medicine very soon and her conscience wouldn't let her spend the five dollars on anything else, although she had no idea how much laudanum actually cost.

When she got back to their wagon, she discovered her mother was nowhere in sight. "Ma?" she called out, resting her buckets near a rinsing kettle and searching the surrounding trees and clotheslines half-hidden by darkness, but finding no sign of her.

Then she saw a form resting on a blanket under their canvas lean-to. Hurrying over, she knelt down when she reached her ma's side. "What's wrong, Ma?" she asked softly.

A wet cough was her only answer at first.

"You feelin' okay?"

"There's a burnin' in my chest, child, worst it's ever been. I had to lie down for a spell."

"Take some of the medicine."

"Ain't hardly any left . . ." She coughed again.

"Take the rest of it. I'll get more tomorrow. I just know that nice lady will give us another bottle if I ask her to."

"She'll want money. We need every cent we got to git on to the next town. We shoulda left this place a long time ago. It's a breedin' ground for sin an' evil temptation. We shoulda never stopped here. I can see a change comin' over you, Annabelle, an' it's purely the work of Satan. You speak blasphemy like it was no more'n empty words. I never heard such talk comin' from you. It all started right here in this evil place."

She put her hand on Doris's shoulder. "I was only questionin' how come the Lord wants us to stay so poor. You're always prayin' real hard an' it don't seem to do no good, like when Pa died. It don't appear the Lord is listenin' to none of our best prayin', and now you're dyin' of this awful sickness an' He don't pay no attention, even when you put money in a preacher's plate. I was just wonderin' how come God don't act like He cares about us."

Doris began to sob quietly—Annabelle could feel her body shaking between ragged breaths.

"He cares 'bout you, Annabelle. It's me He's out to punish, for my sins."

She thought back to something her ma had said. "Maybe it's time you told me what you done, Ma. Maybe it'll help if you talked to me about it. It can't be nothin' so terrible bad."

"I can't hardly make myself say them words to you, child. I never wanted you to know . . ."

"Know what, Ma?"

Her silence lasted almost a minute. "What I done when I was a girl. I was a sinner, before I met your pa. Your pa forgave me, only it don't look like the Lord is done with me yet. I prayed every single day for forgiveness, but it weren't enough. God took Chester from me, from us, an' now He's out to punish me with the consumption pains until I die."

"I can't hardly believe you was a sinner. You never done a wrongful thing your whole life that I knowed of. You was always so gentle an' kind with me, like I was the most special girl in the world.''

Doris reached for her hand. ''You are the most special child on this earth, Annabelle. Don't you ever forget that. Don't let temptation take you down the wrong path like it done to me. I'll be payin' for my sinfulness the rest of my days.''

''What was it you done that was so awful?''

Another silence came between them, until Doris started to cry again. ''I became a fallen women,'' she sobbed. ''I worked in the cribs up in Saint Louis for nearly a year, till I met the finest man God ever created. Chester took me away with him to Texas an' I repented all my sins. Went to church every Sunday. Prayed as hard as I could for forgiveness for what I done in the past. I read from the Bible every night an' took the scriptures to heart. I learned to fear God an' wanted to live accordin' to scriptures every single day after that. Only God's wrath came down upon me an' He took Chester away. Now I'm dyin', too. It's God's punishment for sellin' myself to strangers over money. Along with the sin of drunkenness, fornication is the worst sin there is.''

Annabelle was too shocked to speak. She squeezed her ma's hand while she tried to think of something to say. She couldn't even begin to tell her that she was thinking of selling herself to men for money. Had her ma also been tired of being poor when she made her choice? ''That was such a long time ago, Ma. Looks like the Lord would have forgiven you after all this time, after so much prayin'. Maybe there was circumstances. What made you decide to do somethin' like that in the first place?''

Doris took her hand away to cover her eyes. ''I run off from home when I was thirteen, but that weren't no excuse. I met this drummer back in Kentucky who took me with him to Saint Louis. He was the devil's own disciple, only I was too young to know what it was he wanted then. He put the first taste of liquor inside my mouth an' that's when the devil took hold of my soul. I did whatever he wanted, so I could have more bottled spirits. Then he left me in Saint Louis with Satan's own cravin' for strong drink inside me. I became a tool of the devil, sellin' myself to men who had the price of whiskey. I was overcome by drunkenness an' fornication. I surely would have died without God sendin' a good man to preach me the gospel. Chester Green showed me the way to righteousness an' took me for his bride. We moved off to East Texas to start a farm, an' that's when the Lord blessed me with you, Annabelle. I believed I was forgiven for my sins. I didn't know nothin' 'bout how the wrath of God works until He took Chester from me an' gave me the sickness.''

Again, Annabelle was almost speechless. Her ma had been a crib girl and was given over to drunkenness until Chester Green found her and saved her. ''I ain't rightly sure just what to say to you, Ma. You was always the sweetest person to me an' that oughta matter to the Lord, seems like. You been goin' to church since I can remember. You worked hard with Pa in the fields all day an' raised the best garden in the county. You never let nary a drop of liquor touch your lips that I ever knew, nor said not one cussword out loud. The Lord should take into account how you changed.''

A bit later Doris stopped crying.

''Take the rest of that medicine,'' Annabelle said. ''You'll feel better. We'll figure a way to get some extra money so you can have more of it. Don't worry.''

A quiet spread over the campground as night came. Down near the creek crickets began to chirp. Doris pushed herself up on unsteady arms and touched Annabelle's cheek, searching her face. ''Do you still love me, child, after what I told you?''

''Of course I do, Ma. Nothin' can change that. It don't matter what you done way back then. All that matters is that you're my ma. We'll find some way to get by. You take the rest of your medicine an' lie down. I'll finish puttin' laundry on lines so it can dry before mornin'.''

''You're a good girl, Annabelle. Don't never let the devil git hold of you with temptation an' you'll do just fine.''

Of course, she couldn't tell her how the devil had already gotten inside her . . .

•   •   •

The hour was late, around midnight, when she took her bath standing in the back of their covered wagon, getting ready to see Cody—if he came tonight like he'd said he would. Doris was sound asleep after doses of laudanum had made her drowsy. The last of the laundry was hung out to dry. Annabelle could scarcely contain her excitement over prospects of Cody's visit. Her fingers shook with anticipation when she buttoned the front of a clean dress, a yellow one with patches on the elbows she'd owned for a number of years. In the dark she hoped he wouldn't notice the patches or a threadbare spot here and there. While she pumped rinse water, she took petals from a honeysuckle vine and ground them into a pulp to make scent for her skin. When she was dressed she climbed out of the wagon and fixed her hair, combing and brushing until it was just the way she wanted. Her dress, she noticed, was a bit too tight around her hips, and when she opened a button at the top, her breasts were pushed together, making them seem larger.

"He won't come," she whispered, more to prepare herself for disappointment than because she truly believed it. She gazed across a flat to a stand of trees running along the creek where he'd said he'd whistle for her. Her heart fluttered at the thought of kissing him again, a real kiss this time, not just a peck.

That same warm feeling returned to her groin and she was so sure now it was something evil. Had the same feeling driven her ma to work cribs in Saint Louis? Or was it a craving for strong drink, like she said it was. Both were surely the work of Satan.

She walked slowly among their clotheslines when impatience wouldn't allow her to stand still any longer, inspecting a wood pin here and there, a damp skirt or a blouse. Anticipation made her hands and feet tingle. Would Cody come? She dared not let herself count on it too much. Things never seemed to work out like they should when she wanted them badly.

She came to a gnarled mesquite trunk and leaned against it, gazing thoughtfully back toward the wagon. She still found it hard to believe her mother was ever a scarlet woman, or that she could be guilty of drunkenness. No matter how hard she

tried to imagine it, she couldn't. Her childhood memories of
her ma were sweet things, times of tenderness and understanding, of comfort in her arms when a thunderstorm awakened
her or a nightmare sent her scurrying from her bed to lie beside
her. When other kids at school teased her about her flour-sack
dresses or her worn-out shoes, her mother had always been
there to reassure her and dry her tears. "There's no shame in
bein' poor," Ma would say, "only shame upon them that's
too dumb to know how pretty a new sackcloth dress can be.
Don't let words from the mouths of the ignorant make you
ashamed of what we got. We've got more'n plenty other folks
in this valley."

And it was true—they were not as poor as some and there
was always enough to eat. Her pa was a good farmer and Ma's
garden grew the best tomatoes and corn in the county, and
snap beans so good they tasted sweet and cucumbers nearly
as big as watermelons, as well as acorn squash and sweet
potatoes. It wasn't until after Pa died that things turned hard.

She watched fires turn to embers below their kettles as a
cool breeze drifted in from the south. It was best to forget
about life on the farm while Pa was alive—it made no sense
to waste time remembering the past. In her immediate future
she faced a difficult choice, to give in to the devil's urges and
work for Miss Rose, or continue in the laundry business and
go west as soon as Ma was able to travel.

The outline of their old wagon rose against a backdrop of
night sky and twinkling stars. The wagon was a sad sight,
dilapidated and needing paint, a new canvas top, several wheel
spokes. This wagon and an old mule were all they had, along
with a few dollars left over from laundry profits, after expenses. A wagon and a laundry business was her future . . .
unless she accepted Miss Rose's offer to work at the Pink
Lady. One choice represented a future her ma wanted for her,
the other a life of sin. But along with sin came an end to years
of poverty.

A sharp whistle coming from the creek startled her. When
she heard it, she smiled and walked slowly away from the
tree.

18

She saw his silhouette in a clearing and almost ran the rest of the way, until she thought about how it would look, being too eager. His hat was pushed back on his head at a jaunty angle, so light from the stars shone on his face.

"Hi there, pretty lady," he said, wearing a grin so wide she saw his teeth gleam in the dark. "I didn't figure you'd come, bein' as you said Monday was a busy day."

She stopped in front of him, close enough to reach out and touch him. "Ma went to sleep. She was hurtin' real bad so she took laudanum. It helps her rest." She was blushing after he told her she was pretty, but it was night and he wouldn't know.

Cody aimed a thumb over his shoulder. "Let's sit on that creek bank for a spell so we can talk, if you ain't got a better idea."

"That sounds nice. It's cooler down there, where so many trees don't cut off the wind."

He took her hand to lead her to the stream and it happened so suddenly that his touch surprised her.

"I started that new job at the marshal's office today," he said, holding her arm to assist her while she sat down with her feet dangling over the creek bank. "Another deputy's watchin' the jail for me while I took a few hours time off. We had two real ornery types locked up in jail, a killer by the name of Flatnose George Curry, an' another murderer named Jake Ketchum."

"What a funny name, bein' called Flatnose," she said as he sat beside her, not too close. "Is it flat?"

"Somebody broke his nose an' it never healed right."

"You said he was a killer . . ."

"He killed a man over at Maude's the other night, only it was self-defense on account of the other feller drew first. I saw him draw—he's one of the fastest I ever seen."

"It sounds real dangerous, your new job."

"Not really. They're locked up without their guns. All I do is feed 'em twice a day an' open the cells when Marshal Hull tells me to. It ain't all that dangerous."

"Do you like workin' for the marshal?"

Cody thought a minute. "So far. Only I've got a feelin' there's somethin' not quite straight about him. Can't say for sure just what it is."

"A marshal oughta be real honest, don't you think? If he's the law, he oughta be somebody you can trust."

"That's true. Like I said, it's only a feelin'." He gave her a look and it seemed his eyes had their own light, making it so they appeared to glow. "You look real pretty tonight. That's a pretty dress an' I like the way you fix your hair." He let his gaze wander down to the opening where she'd left a button unfastened. "You're one mighty fine figure of a woman, Annabelle, if I ain't bein' too forward by sayin' so."

She averted her eyes, watching the surface of the stream for a moment. "It's okay if you say it, so long as you mean it."

"I mean every word. Why, you're so darned pretty I had to keep from thinkin' about you nearly all day."

She couldn't help smiling. "You know just how to make a girl feel good, don't you?" She wanted to tell him he was a handsome man, only this wasn't the proper time.

He chuckled. "To tell the truth, I ain't all that much when it comes to words."

"Sounds to me like you're doin' right well tonight."

He seemed to be preoccupied a moment.

"Have you got somethin' on your mind, Cody?" she asked.

He shrugged. "It has to do with jail business. You see, I found this letter in a dead man's pockets. The letter said there was this map showin' where some money is hid, only a woman who works in the Acre by the name of Miss Allene

Wright has it now. Flatnose Curry wants that map, an' I've got the feelin' there'll be more trouble over it, soon as Curry finds that woman.''

Annabelle recalled the name of a girl at the Pink Lady who let Tommy Joe poke her for five dollars. "There's a woman named Miss Allene down at the Pink Lady. I never heard her last name from the boy who told me about her."

Cody sounded excited when he said, "That could be the same one. I need to tell the marshal right away."

"What sort of map would show where money is hid?"

"Marshal Hull figures it's stolen money. Curry is a bad man an' a robber. So was the owlhoot he killed. That letter made it sound like the two of 'em was in on the money together, only now this Miss Allene Wright has a map showin' where it's buried, I reckon."

"You mean like a bank robbery?"

"Or maybe a train robbery," Cody remarked. "Curry wanted it bad enough to come all the way down from Laramie lookin' for it, an' the dead man's letter was from Denver, so it must be a real sizable pile of money."

"How exciting," Annabelle said. "Only it could get dangerous if this Flatnose Curry shows up before the marshal finds the map. I've been worryin' if you took that job you might get hurt."

Cody leaned a little closer to her. "I think it's nice you would worry about me."

"I did. A little." She felt him watching her and it wasn't unpleasant to be stared at by him.

"I reckon I'll admit I've been worryin' a little about what you'll do if somethin' happens to your ma. You've got no place of your own, only that wagon."

"I've been thinkin' about it, too. Seems like Ma's gettin' worse every single day. She ain't hardly strong enough to hang wet clothes on a line." Annabelle swung her feet back and forth while gazing absently across the creek, thinking out loud. "I'd need to find work . . . if somethin' happens."

"Work is hard to find these days. Maybe you could get a job over at the Emporium sellin' pies an' soda water."

She didn't dare tell him what she was thinking of doing, for he might think less of her if he knew she was considering becoming a scarlet woman. "I haven't decided yet what I'll do. If Ma gets any sicker, she'll have to go to a hospital an' that costs a world of money. I'd need lots of money to keep her in a hospital even for a little while."

"It'll be hard for a young woman to find work payin' lots of money," Cody said, "even as pretty a girl as you."

She turned to him. "You say the sweetest things, Cody. You make me feel pretty."

He put his arm around her shoulder and drew her close so his lips almost touched hers. "The other night you kissed me at the Emporium, only it wasn't much of a kiss, really." He bent down and kissed her gently, pulling her against his chest, although the pressure was slight behind her back, not enough to seem insistent or demanding. His lips lingered across her mouth for just a few seconds, then he backed away. "That's more what I had in mind," he said.

She was sorry it ended so quickly. "You can do it again if you'd like," she whispered.

He placed his hands around her waist and pressed his palms into the small of her back, kissing her harder this time, holding her longer. She laced her arms behind his neck. A tiny shiver of excitement raced through her. Parting her lips, she returned the pressure of his mouth. Something fluttered inside her chest like a butterfly's wings, and she held her breath. She was inexperienced when it came to tender kisses, uncertain how it was done when she felt as though her lungs would burst needing air. Her heart was beating so fast she was positive he could feel it hammering.

Just when it seemed she would surely faint, Cody pulled back and sighed. "Your lips are so soft," he said.

Exhaling, she blurted out, "I thought I'd die for wantin' a breath of air."

He grinned. "You're supposed to breathe through your nose, only you do it real slow. That way, a kiss can last longer."

"I never kissed anybody like that before. Not nearly so long, anyways."

"Takes some time to learn." His grin grew larger. "I'll be glad to give you a few lessons."

"You're makin' fun of me."

"No, I ain't. I don't reckon nobody's born knowin' how to kiss the right way."

"Seems like it oughta come natural."

"It does. Takes practice."

"You're only sayin' that so you can kiss me lots of times."

He chuckled. "Why, Annabelle, what made you say a thing like that?"

She smiled. "Because I think it's true."

He kissed her again. She still held her breath right at the beginning, until she tried breathing slowly through her nose. At the same time she became aware of warmth growing inside her, that same feeling of heat that had awakened her so many times lately.

"That's much better," he told her quietly, looking into her eyes, "only I'd still recommend more practice."

She hoped it wouldn't sound too naughty when she told him, "We can practice as long as you like."

He tightened his embrace, pulling her to his chest, kissing her even more passionately than before. When she wrapped both arms around his neck her breasts were flattened against his ribs, producing a tingling sensation in her nipples.

Very slowly, he pushed her down on the grass, lying beside her, their lips locked together in a kiss. In spite of herself she began to breathe harder, her nostrils flaring gently while the warmth increased between her thighs and the tingling became stronger in her nipples. She wondered if he intended to do more than kiss her, the way he was carrying on, kissing her so hard, rubbing his chest against her breasts. Things were happening so fast and the heat building inside her was only making it harder to think.

He took his mouth away, then he kissed her lightly on the tip of her nose.

"You're so sweet, Annabelle," he whispered, "just about the sweetest girl I ever met."

She tried to control her rapid breathing as best she could. "I figured a handsome cowboy like you would have sweethearts in nearly every town."

"It ain't like that. A drover has to stay on the move an' he don't hardly ever get to stay in one place long enough to meet a girl. At the end of the trail in places like Abilene there's mostly just women who hire themselves out. A man can't develop no real feelin's for that kind of girl."

"Why's that, Cody?" She really wanted to know, although a dose of common sense told her the answer.

"It's real simple. Women like that ain't capable of lovin' a man. They get hard as nails. They get paid to smile an' act friendly towards any cowboy who's got their price, but I never met one who gave a hoot about no special man. They feel the same way 'bout all of 'em. All they're after is money."

She thought about what he'd said. It was true, most of it, including the part about being after money. "I wonder how come they can't find nobody special to care about. Seems like they could if they wanted."

"That sorta life makes 'em hard, like I said. If they ever was to meet somebody they liked, I reckon they'd quit bein' hired women, only I don't see how a man could love a women who sold her charms to every cowpoke who came along."

Annabelle recalled what her mother had said. Chester Green had fallen in love with a scarlet woman and made her his wife. "I'll bet there's exceptions. If a man loves a woman strong enough, he could forget what she done in the past. If she really wanted to change."

"I couldn't never. Not me. I'd be thinkin' about all them drovers she'd been with. It wouldn't set right inside my head."

"Have you been with . . . hired women, Cody?"

He grinned a little. "A few. Three months on a cow trail is a long time to be without a woman. I never made it a regular habit." Lowering his face, he kissed her again.

As his lips touched hers, his words echoed back and forth in her mind, how he'd said he couldn't see how a man could love a girl who'd sold her charms to every cowpoke who came along. He'd made it plain he could never fall in love with her if she went to work at the Pink Lady.

The passion in his kiss emptied her thoughts and she gave in to the desire growing inside her.

19

Cordel sat up in bed when he heard repeated knocking on his front door. He reached for the heavy Remington .44 he kept on a nightstand and swung his feet to the floor, blinking away sleep fog.

"Who the hell is it?" he shouted, resting his thumb on the pistol's hammer. He hadn't heard boots on the porch steps and it angered him that he'd been sleeping so soundly. He'd been able to stay alive in a high-risk profession by practicing caution in everything he did, which included learning to sleep lightly. Was forty-six too old to be a lawman? he wondered, shaking his head.

"It's me—Cole!"

He sighed and tossed his gun on the bed, guessing what was wrong. Cole wouldn't come out to the house to wake him up unless it was something serious. Padding across his tiny living room in bare feet, he told himself there must have been another killing. Experience with men of Curry's ilk convinced him Curry would be involved in whatever had gone awry tonight, although the Acre was visited by so many ruthless types there could be dozens of other possibilities for trouble.

When he opened the door wearing only a nightshirt, his deputy began by blurting out an apology.

"I'm real sorry to wake you up, Marshal, but there's gonna be trouble down at the Pink Lady an' you know how much Miss Rose hates trouble at her place."

Cordel was sure now it had to be Curry, since only today a request had come from Rose by way of Luther Pierce to keep Curry away from her customers. "What kind of trouble?'' he asked, even though it really didn't matter all that much, since facing Curry again would mean there would be shooting this time.

"Two things," Cole said, out of breath from hurrying to the quieter part of town where Cordel lived. "First off, Flat-nose Curry is at the Lady askin' questions 'bout a particular woman. Him an' Luther nearly got into it a while ago, until Miss Rose got between 'em.''

"He was asking for a woman named Allene Wright," Cordel said tonelessly, remembering the letter Cody had shown him. He glanced at a clock on his fireplace mantel, trying to see what time it was in starlight coming through his front windows. It was past three in the morning, late for difficulties on a Monday night in the Acre during summer. "I should have looked for her myself and not waited till tomorrow. What's the other thing?''

"Cody said to tell you that same woman Curry wants is at the Lady workin' for Miss Rose—he found out tonight from some girl he went off to see while I was keepin' an eye on the jail. Cody said you'd recall what that letter said about a map.''

"I'll get dressed," Cordel sighed. "Meet me at the office, and fetch down my shotgun.''

"You want I should go wake up Dave?''

"No need. We'll handle this ourselves. Tell Cody he can go along. Might as well show him what's in store for my deputies if he takes a shine to the job.''

"He's got steady nerves for a kid.''

Cordel had begun to close the door as Cole spoke. "It may be just a bluff," the marshal said. "He ain't been tested yet.''

Cordel entered the office at ten minutes to four filled with a mixture of anger and dread, mad over being robbed of sleep and dreading an encounter with George Curry. As the years passed, he'd learned several things about wearing a badge and trying to keep peace in the Acre—one was that a certain amount of any lawman's success came as a result of luck. Being careful wasn't enough. There were always circumstances under which the most cautious man could be killed, given the wrong twist of fate. This was one reason he'd begun accepting bribes from some saloon owners, so he could quit the business with a grubstake sufficient to put him in a small ranching enterprise before a bullet in the back or a faster gun took him down.

Cody and Cole were waiting for him. Cole carried a shotgun balanced in his left hand, while the boy only wore his revolver tied down. "Any news?" Cordel asked, striding over to his desk to check the loads for his shortened twelve-gauge.

"Curry won't leave the Lady till he talks to that girl," Cole said, sweat glistening on his face like he was worried.

Cordel nodded, glancing over at Cody. "I told Cole to bring you along. You might as well get your feet wet tonight if you aim to make a deputy here. All you're expected to do is back us up if anything goes wrong. Take a shotgun if you're inclined."

The boy grinned, looking younger than Cordel remembered. "I never was much with a squirrel gun, Marshal. If it's the same to you, I'll do without."

"Suit yourself," he said, closing the breech with a flip of a wrist. "Let's go." He pocketed two extra shells and went to the door, saying, "Lock up behind us. Somebody bring a pair of irons, just in case. My money says Curry won't come peaceable."

They walked out into the darkness, heading down Tenth Street after Cole locked the door. Farther down the road a banjo played in a saloon somewhere, an odd accompaniment for three men facing a duel for their lives with a notorious killer. Cordel had made this same walk hundreds of times, not ever knowing whether it was his last. Fort Worth city councilmen were utter fools to think anyone would brave this kind of danger over and over again for a paltry two hundred dollars a month. Only by taking payments to look the other way from time to time was he able to take risks equal to the odds against surviving them. During nine years in office he'd lost three deputies to bullets and five to outright resignations, clear evidence the pay was not up to the task at the city marshal's office. Twice, voters gave him big votes of confidence at the polls while councilmen refused to budge over an increase in his salary, thus the need to supplement his income by other means.

He looked sideways at Cody as they neared the Lady, to see if the boy showed any fear. Fear was a healthy thing for a lawman in the Acre, and in Cordel's opinion, Cody didn't evidence nearly enough of it to stay alive for long. It was one thing to stand your ground when somebody pushed you, but a time came when it paid to avoid a head-on confrontation. Cody had too much in the way of confidence, probably a result of having a father like John Wade who had a reputation. Reputations with a gun were made by winning gunfights. Soon, perhaps tonight, the boy would get a chance to show what he was made of.

At a cross street Cordel signaled a halt, counting horses and buggies in front of saloons and gambling houses. "Cole, you take the back way," he said, tucking his coat behind the butt of his Remington, keeping his shotgun in his left hand. "We'll give you a minute or two to get inside, then we'll come in the front door as quiet as we can. If he reaches for a gun, kill him. Try not to shoot anybody else if you can help it, or shoot holes in any of Rose's expensive furniture. Aim high. I told Judge Warren it was a mistake letting him go. We could have trumped up some kind of charge to hold him."

"You shoulda let Dave kill him when we had him jailed. We'd have all swore he was tryin' to escape," Cole said. "Dave was itchin' to pull that trigger, only you made him stop just when he was ready."

"There were witnesses," Cordel reminded him, examining the front of the Pink Lady half a block away. "Get going. The sooner we get this over, the sooner I can get back to bed."

Cole took off at a trot, turning down an alley running in back of the Lady. The banjo and a piano played farther down the street, at the Stockmen's Retreat. Cordel's grip tightened on his shotgun, as he thought about the moment when he faced Curry.

"Anythin' special you want me to do?" Cody asked. In

spite of his size, better than six feet, he sounded boyish tonight and Cordel wondered if he should have brought him after all. He was a good-natured kid and willing to work, but this wasn't part of his jailer's job.

"Stay back out of the way, to the left of the door. If he starts shooting, which I figure he will, see how many holes you can put in his hide without killing anybody else."

Cody shrugged. "Whatever you say, Marshal, but it don't take but one hole in the right place to finish him."

He wondered if the boy was that good with a pistol. "Just kill the son of a bitch any way you can if he goes for his gun. I don't give a damn how you do it. Let's go. Cole's had enough time to get inside by now."

They walked side by side toward the Lady and it seemed their boots were keeping time to the melody coming from the Stockmen's. Cordel rested a thumb on one hammer of his shotgun, ready for all hell to break loose as soon as he opened the Lady's front door.

Climbing wood steps to the boardwalk, he took a deep breath and reached for the doorknob, ignoring a pair of cowboys idling on benches beside the door. One of them said, "Be careful goin' in there, Marshal. Miss Rose is on the prod over some jasper who won't clear out of her place. He's got a gun."

Cordel nodded, a silent acknowledgement of the warning. He'd faced down dozens of men like Curry before, yet tonight he was uneasy. Were the fates about to give him a losing hand? Or was he simply getting older, more cautious when it came to risking his life? Without an answer he shouldered the door open and spread his feet apart, sweeping the parlor for a glimpse of his adversary.

He saw Rose first, standing in front of a staircase leading to the second floor. The place was quiet, too quiet. Luther Pierce was at the bar, scowling, with a trace of blood trickling from his lower lip. Three of Rose's girls sat alone on love seats or sofas. One held a bloody cloth to her cheek but there was no sign of Curry.

"Where is he?" Cordel asked aloud, stepping into the room.

Too late, he saw a figure to the right of the door with his back to the wall. Cordel swung his shotgun, thumbing the hammer back as he wheeled toward Curry. A woman screamed. Cordel's finger had curled around the trigger when suddenly a flash of bright light came at him from Curry's direction, accompanied by a loud bang. Something struck his chest—it felt like he'd been kicked by a mule.

He was thrown backward amid the roar of a gun blast, and as he fell, he knew he'd been shot. His head slammed into the door with enough force to knock him senseless. In a daze he watched Curry crouch down and fire another shot at the back of the room. A cry of pain sounded at almost the same time—Cole Webb slumped against a door frame, clutching his abdomen, dropping his shotgun to the floor.

Curry spun around and fired point-blank into Luther Pierce's forehead just as Luther was pulling a gun from his coat. The top of Luther's skull ruptured, sending blood and bone fragments all over a mirror in back of Rose's bar. Luther was slammed into the mirror, shattering it while a chorus of screams came from every direction, then he fell out of sight, leaving a red smear on the remnants of glass behind him.

Searing pain radiated through Cordel's chest, rendering him unable to move, and he was sure he was dying when a voice behind him shouted, "Drop the gun!"

Curry made a half turn, bringing his gun up, just as Cody stepped over Cordel to plant his feet. Cody's pistol thundered, ending a fleeting moment of silence.

Curry was lifted off the floor. He staggered backward with his face twisted in pain, trying to regain his footing on one of the Lady's imported rugs. Blood squirted from his right shoulder as he fell heavily against the bar, sliding down to his rump.

"Drop the gun or I'll blow your arm off!" Cody warned, even before the echo of gunfire died down.

Curry's dark eyes beheld the man who'd shot him, and in back of his stare Cordel saw the fires of hell burning. For a second or two neither man moved.

"I said drop it!" Cody demanded, "or I'll kill you deader'n

pig shit!'' He cocked his single-action pistol and aimed down at Curry's head.

Greater waves of pain brought tears to Cordel's eyes. With all his might he tried to sit up so he could help the boy cover Curry, and yet his muscles refused to move. Tears almost blinded him, although he didn't need good vision to hear the dull thud of Curry's gun as it dropped to the floor.

Through a watery haze he saw Cody walk over and bend down to take Curry's pistol.

''If it matters,'' he heard Cody say, ''I coulda put that slug through your heart, if I'd wanted. The marshal said to kill you if I got the chance. You gave me plenty of chances. Now hold still while I put these wrist irons on.''

Cordel began to lose consciousness when the room started to spin. He saw Rose bending over him.

''How bad is it?'' he hissed, clenching his teeth.

She opened his coat and frowned. ''It's high, so it likely missed your heart. I'm sending for my carriage. I'll take you to the hospital.'' She put a handkerchief inside his shirt and pressed it against his chest to slow down the bleeding. ''Luther is dead. Your deputy is badly wounded. We'll take him with us to the hospital.''

''What about . . . Curry?'' His voice was growing weaker.

''Your new deputy has him cuffed.''

''He . . . ain't . . . a deputy yet. Today . . . was his first day as my jailer.''

''Lie still, Cordel. Save your strength. That bullet could be in a bad place.''

''I had . . . this bad feeling . . . about tonight.''

''I never knew you were superstitious.''

He didn't think he was, but it pained him too much to deny it. He remembered Curry was hit in the shoulder and that meant he would probably survive. Unless . . . In spite of his wound he wanted vengeance.

''Tell Cody . . . to come . . . over here. Get everybody . . . else out of the place.''

''Why's that, Cordel?''

"Just do like I asked you." He was gasping for air now and time might be running short.

He heard Rose telling her girls to go upstairs. Fighting to remain conscious, a moment later he saw Cody hovering over him.

"Listen . . . to . . . me, Cody. Make . . . sure Curry . . . don't leave this place . . . alive. Shoot him. Say he . . . was trying . . . to run."

"I couldn't do that, Marshal," the boy said. "He ain't even armed an' he's wearin' those wrist irons."

He tried to focus on Cody's face. "You can't . . . let him get away . . . with this."

"I can't shoot no unarmed man like that. I just plain can't do it."

Cordel could feel blood pooling underneath him. His surroundings looked dim, like someone had turned down the lamps. "All you . . . gotta do . . . is say . . . he was . . . trying to run."

"Sorry, Marshal Hull, but I ain't made that way."

A black fog crept over Cordel and he felt nothing more.

20

Cody felt sick to his stomach. His wonderful evening with Annabelle was entirely forgotten now. Seeing Marshal Hull with a mortal wound, and Cole lying gut-shot in a pool of blood ended his sweet recollections of time spent with the girl. And the sight of Rose Denadale's business manager sprawled behind the bar with the back of his head blown away left his belly churning. Quite suddenly, the calm of a summer night had erupted into a deadly exchange of gunfire in which he was the only participant without a bullet wound.

He stuck his pistol into Flatnose Curry's back as Marshal Hull and Cole were being carried outside. "Walk in front of me. Don't try nothin' stupid. I can't miss when I'm this close."

"I'm bleeding real bad," Curry protested. "I need a doctor or I'll bleed to death." He hadn't taken a step toward the door.

"I'll bring a doctor to the jail. Right now, you're more likely to die from a busted spine unless you start walkin' out of this place." He prodded Curry's backbone with his gun muzzle.

Curry started away from the bar, favoring his right shoulder in such a way that he leaned to one side. Cody knew he was still dangerous, and as a precaution, he cocked his revolver a second time, and the sound made Curry flinch. There was so much blood near the door they couldn't avoid stepping in it as they crossed the room and went outside.

The street was packed with curious spectators watching the marshal and Cole being loaded in Rose's carriage, but when they saw Cody holding a gun on Curry, all eyes turned and someone on the boardwalk said, "That's the feller who shot Flatnose George Curry right there!"

Curry started down the steps and people gave him plenty of room even though his wrists were manacled and he didn't have his gun. There was no more music coming from down the street, for it seemed everyone had been drawn outside by the series of gunshots. Cody heard whispered questions from the crowd—"Who is that guy? What's his name? Did Cordel hire a new deputy?"

Then a voice Cody recognized said, "His name's Cody Wade an' he's one bad hombre to tangle with. He's Marshal Hull's jailer. First day on the job an' he's already arrested somebody. Don't go for no gun against him or he's liable to blow you plumb out of your socks."

Newt was grinning at him from the edge of the crowd. Faces were turned to Newt, listening, as Cody herded his prisoner up Tenth Street toward jail.

"He's from down around Waco," Newt continued, enjoying all the attention. "His pappy was Big John Wade, a shootist of some reputation a few years back. Cody's real gentle-natured unless you push him . . . then he gets meaner'n a two-headed diamondback."

Cody wished Newt wouldn't say so much, but with a dangerous man like Curry to keep an eye on, he couldn't risk a distraction. If Curry felt he had any advantage before they got to jail, he was sure to try something.

"I know what's runnin' through your mind," Cody told Curry when they were out of listening distance by onlookers. "You're thinkin' about swingin' around when we get to a dark stretch of this road, makin' a play for my gun. Just so you'll know ahead of time, this hammer drops real easy, hardly a touch to send it down."

"I'm hurt," Curry groaned, limping even though his wound was in a shoulder. "Get me a doctor quick before I bleed to death."

"I'll do that, just as soon as we get to the office." Cody swallowed bitter bile, remembering their short fight and how much blood was shed. In the blink of an eye three men were down. One was dead. Cole would probably die as a result of being gut-shot. Marshal Hull's wound looked serious. Had he given Curry another split second to turn around, he might also be dead.

Some job, he thought. For fifty dollars a month he'd almost been killed the first day.

It was when they reached the office that Cody realized he didn't have a key to the door—it was in Cole's pocket. "I'll have to bust out a window," he said, shoving Curry up the steps. "Ain't got my own key yet."

He broke a window with his gun muzzle and reached around to unlock the door as soon as tinkling glass stopped falling inside. Curry stood quiet as a lamb, hunkered over like his shoulder gave him plenty of pain.

"March to the back," Cody ordered, waving his gun barrel in the same direction. "The quicker you get it done, the quicker I can get you a sawbones."

His prisoner seemed uncharacteristically agreeable, moving across the office obediently with a grimmace on his face. As Cody turned up a lamp and got cell keys from a desk drawer, he couldn't help but wonder why Curry was so meek and mild tonight, with only a flesh wound. He'd seemed fearless before.

When Curry was locked behind bars, Cody holstered his gun.

"What was all that busted glass about?" Jake Ketchum asked from the darkness of his cell.

Cody ignored his question and hurried to the front, returning the keys to Marshal Hull's desk before he went off to find a doctor. He closed the door, but couldn't lock it. It wouldn't have mattered anyway, since a windowpane was broken.

He was surprised to find Newt waiting for him outside, with that same grin on his face like he'd been eating a persimmon.

"You're makin' quite a name for yourself already, pardner," Newt said, "outshootin' the likes of Flatnose Curry."

"I didn't outshoot him. The odds were against him, is all it was. He shot three men before I hit him. He bit off more'n he could chew."

Newt joined him as he headed for the center of town, where

a former Confederate Army hospital served citizens of Fort Worth, as well as injured trail hands passing through in late fall and early spring. Cody walked as rapidly as he could.

"Word is, the marshal's wound is mighty bad, Cody. What'll you do if he dies?"

"I hadn't thought about it. Things have been happenin' real fast. Too fast."

"I sure as hell hope you don't get yourself killed."

"I'm tryin' hard to avoid it, Newt. You won't see me jump in front of no bullet if I can help it. If Marshal Hull dies, I reckon they'll make Cole the city marshal. But if I'm any judge of things, Cole won't make it. He's gut-shot, an' hardly anybody lives through a bullet in the belly. That don't leave but one deputy, Dave Watkins, an' he's crazy as a sackful of loons. He killed a prisoner—blew him to bits while he was in his cell on account of he'd messed with Dave's girl. Another time, he beat a drunk to death with an axe handle. If they make Dave the marshal, I'll quit this job, before I take orders from him."

"Maybe then we'll go into business together like we planned to all along." Newt sounded real hopeful about it.

"We'll see. Right now I've gotta find a doctor who'll come to the jail to tend to Curry. He's bleedin' like a stuck hog an' complainin' about it. He don't act like no bad man when he's got a hole in him. Took the fight right out of his craw."

"By mornin' you'll be near as famous as Abe Lincoln, after folks hear what you did."

"Lincoln's dead. That ain't the kind of famous I aim to be if I have a say in it."

They came to a gaslit street and turned for the hospital. Newt matched Cody's longer legs stride for stride across a city block lined with better stores and a bank, reaching a corner where the three-story brick hospital stood, its lower windows ablaze with lamplight.

An elderly nurse stopped Cody a few feet inside the building.

"I'm Marshal Hull's jailer," he began, "an' we've got a

bad-wounded prisoner locked up in city jail. He needs a doctor real soon.''

She gave him a look of reproach. ''Marshal Hull is having a bullet taken out of his chest right now, young man. The only doctor we have tonight is trying to save his life. Then there's a wounded deputy who needs attention. After that, I'll ask Dr. Roberts if he'll visit your prisoner. First things must come first. Saving the lives of good policemen is far more important than saving a criminal.''

He couldn't argue. ''How's the marshal doin'?'' At the end of a hall he saw a sign above a door reading ''Surgery'' and he supposed that was where Cordel and Cole were now.

''It's too soon to tell. Dr. Roberts is doing everything he can.''

Cody thought a minute. ''If he asks, tell him I locked up our prisoner, that I'll stand guard there until Dave comes to tell me what to do. I'm kinda new at this, ma'am. First day on a new job, an' there wasn't time for him to explain everything.''

''I'll tell him if he asks,'' she said. ''It's almost dawn, and before too long, other doctors will arrive. As soon as we can, I'll see that a doctor visits your jail. Until then, tie a cloth around his wound so he'll bleed less and keep him comfortable.''

Cody didn't like a part of her instructions. ''I'll tie that cloth, ma'am, but as to seein' that he's comfortable, I ain't so inclined to do it. He shot three men tonight an' it seems to me we hadn't oughta do anythin' extra for him.'' He swung around for the door with Newt at his heels, before the woman could give him any more suggestions about how Curry should be treated.

Outside, Newt strode up beside him.

''I could fetch that veterinarian for you,'' he said. ''They call him Doc Grimes. He has a little shack down in the Flats.''

''He'd be better'n nothin', I reckon. If you don't mind, I'd be obliged if you brung him to the jail.''

''He's liable to be drunk this time of night.''

"It won't matter much. If he can walk, he can fix a bandage for Curry's shoulder. Bring him, if he'll come."

Newt swung off in the direction of Maddox Flats while Cody hurried back toward the jail. So much had happened tonight and he couldn't sort all of it out quite yet. There was a chance the marshal and Cole would die from their wounds, leaving only Dave and himself running the office. He supposed the city would hold elections for a new marshal, but that would take time. Even if both men recovered, they would be laid up for a spell, and that meant he'd be working for Dave until Marshal Hull got back, if he decided to stay. Which he wouldn't. Dave wasn't in possession of his full senses. Cody had seen just how close he came to killing Flatnose Curry while he was in a cell. If it hadn't been for the marshal stepping in, Curry would be dead.

As soon as he rounded the corner at Tenth Street, he knew something was wrong. The office door was ajar. Slowing his gait to a careful walk, he drew his pistol and kept to the shadows of porch roofs and buildings until he came to the jail.

The door was open. Marshal Hull's desk lamp burned brightly and he could see the office was empty. Creeping up the steps, he covered his approach with his .44-.40 until he stood in the doorway.

"Damn," he whispered, when he saw cell doors open down the hallway. He inched forward, wary, noticing that a desk drawer was open, the one where keys were kept.

A few drops of blood shone wetly on the floor and now Cody was sure someone had come in to spring his prisoner. Advancing to a spot where he could see every cell, he found them empty. Curry was gone, and so was Jake Ketchum. A third prisoner whose name he didn't know was also missing.

"I'll get the blame for this," he said, lowering his gun to his side, then holstering it.

When Dave found out what happened, he would go on a rampage looking for Curry and Ketchum. It was very likely Cody would lose his job over it, leaving the office unlocked and unguarded to go for a doctor.

He cast a glance through the broken window, dreading what

Dave would say and do when he arrived for work. There would be hell to pay and Cody would be paying it as soon as Dave got to the office.

"I don't reckon I was cut out to be a lawman anyway," he said, thinking Curry and Ketchum couldn't have gotten very far. He noted that several gunbelts were missing from pegs on a wall to the right of Marshal Hull's desk. The escaped prisoners were armed.

He made up his mind to go after them. Curry was wounded. He needed a horse to get out of town, making a livery stable the most logical place to go.

21

He ran so hard he was wheezing by the time he got to Bud's Livery at the end of Dauphin Street. Dogs barked at him almost every step of the way, set off by someone running through sleepy neighborhoods just before daybreak. Gasping for air, he stumbled to a halt near a corral fence, searching shadows for any sign of movement close to the barn, listening for any sound. The stable was quiet.

He'd guessed wrong. Another livery sat east of the railroad station a half mile from where he was now, the place he and Newt stabled their horses when they came to town. Too far to run all the way, probably too far to make it before Curry and Ketchum got their hands on stolen mounts. Someone must have been watching the jail, waiting for a chance to help a prisoner escape. Either Curry or Ketchum had an associate waiting for the right opportunity. That same friend could have provided saddled horses.

Cursing his bad luck, Cody had wheeled away from the fence to make a dash toward the depot, when, from the corner of his eye, he saw a shape move below an eave of the barn. Thirty yards away, a man with a pistol took aim at him.

Cody dove to the ground, rolling, clawing his own gun free, losing his hat as he fell. An explosion accompanied a stabbing finger of orange flame from a corner of the stable. The whine of lead screamed past his left ear. But as light from a gun muzzle flickered and went out, he drew a quick bead and fired an answering shot, feeling his Mason Colt buck in his palm when its powder charge ignited, banging so loudly it hurt his ears.

He missed, and fired again, steadying the .44-.40 with both hands.

A thin voice cried out in pain. He saw someone spin away from the stable wall as though he'd been caught in a mighty gust of wind. Arms windmilling, he flung his pistol skyward and swung around a second time before he fell, landing on his back with a grunt. His gun skittered across a stretch of hardpan and disappeared into the darkness.

"What the hell's goin' on?" an angry voice shouted from a shack across the road, its windows brightening suddenly when a lantern was lit inside.

Cody kept his eyes on the man he'd shot, figuring two more men were somewhere in the barn. It made sense that the three escaped prisoners would stick together until they found horses.

"Who's doin' all the goddamn shootin'?" the same voice asked from an open window. Light from windows cast yellow squares on a narrow lane passing in front of the house.

The downed gunman lay still. Nothing moved near the stable or in any of the corrals. And still Cody waited, pressed flat on his belly, wondering where the other two might be. He was out in the open, making an easy target if he showed himself by attempting a run for the fence.

Suddenly, the door of the shack swung open. A man holding a shotgun peered around the door frame. "That's my stable you're shootin' holes in!" he shouted. "Just who the hell are you?"

Before Cody could warn him, a volley of gunfire blasted from the livery. Bullets splintered thin clapboard planking. Wood chips flew where lead slugs drilled through the stable owner's house, making a snapping noise. His shotgun discharged as he was driven backward by bullets riddling his chest. When his gun went off, it was aimed toward the ceiling, and it seemed the walls of his shack convulsed as an ear-splitting roar belched from windows and the doorway. He landed on his back, yelping for all he was worth, thrashing back and forth on the floor in his longjohns as his shotgun fell across his chest.

Cody had seen two muzzle flashes wink from the back of

the barn. Both guns were fired from the same spot. Scrambling
to his knees, he dove for a corral fence post and landed behind
it, gasping, his heart hammering. In the midst of this deadly
gun battle he suddenly realized he was truly afraid, afraid of
dying. For the first time in his life he was looking for a way
out of a fight instead of ways to win it.

Peering around the post, he tried to concentrate, doing his
best to ignore cries from the wounded man lying in his shack.
A chorus of neighborhood dogs had filled the darkness with
their sounds as soon as the guns went off, and they prevented
Cody from hearing noises in the stable—it seemed every dog
in Fort Worth had begun to bark when shots were fired.
Clamping the butt of his gun in a clammy fist, he waited,
frozen to the spot, battling an urge to crawl backward and
make a run for it before he was killed.

Is it because of the girl? he wondered. Were his developing
feelings toward Annabelle making him think twice? He hardly
knew her, and yet he seldom thought of anything else lately.
Since he met her, she'd been on his mind almost continually
and at night he dreamt about her.

The stableman shouted, "Help me! Somebody help me!"

Big black shadows began to whirl in a corral behind the
barn, and when Cody saw them, he knew what they meant.
The escaped men were boarding horses. His conscience demanded that he try to stop them, while another voice inside
his head warned him to lie still in order to save his own skin.

"Somebody . . . please . . . help me!" The cries were softer.

Cody hadn't been a firsthand witness to death since his pa
died, and that had come about peacefully, while he slept. Until
tonight he'd been so sure he wouldn't be afraid of it. But with
bloody scenes at the Pink Lady still fresh in his mind and the
bellow of gunshots ringing in his ears, he came to a new understanding of what dying violently was like. It was one thing
to think about it, and another to be there to smell the blood
and gunpowder, to see flesh torn to pieces by molten lead.

"Help . . . me." The voice was weakening.

Two figures, the outlines of men on horses, swirled away
from the back of the barn. Hooves pounded, then stopped, as

gate hinges squeaked. Cody had a clear shot at a rider's back for only an instant. For reasons he didn't fully understand, he did not raise his gun, but merely lay there on his belly like a spectator.

Drumming hooves raced away from the livery, down an alley behind a row of houses. Cody listened to them as his breathing began to slow. He'd let them get away without lifting a finger.

Dogs continued barking as horses galloped east through a part of Maddox Flats. When the hoofbeats faded, he came slowly to his feet, dusting off his pants and shirt before retrieving his hat. The stableman was moaning—he could see him in light from the lamp, resting on the floor of his house with bloodstains over his chest and stomach.

Before he went for help, Cody trudged over to the man he'd shot, to see if he might, by chance, be Flatnose Curry. The closer he came, the more certain he was that it was someone else. It had been a lucky shot, taken too quickly to be sure of his aim. He slowed his footsteps when he reached the body, tasting more bile rising in his throat.

Looking down, he recognized Jake Ketchum. Ketchum's sightless eyes gazed blankly at the heavens, his mouth agape, spittle drying on his lips. A dark stain on the front of his shirt was near a spot where a bullet would have pierced his heart.

Cody stared off into the darkness. Curry had gotten away, and he would have to answer for leaving the jail unguarded. But as he thought about the possible consequences of his neglect, he discovered he didn't mind all that much, no matter what happened. Becoming a lawman looked like a poor choice, after tonight. For so little money the risks were decidedly high, like riding herd on a group of longhorns all the way to Kansas. There had to be an easier way to make a living.

Once again, his eyes fell to the body. He'd killed a man tonight, and even though his victim had been a killer on his way to the gallows, the notion that he'd taken another man's life didn't sit all that well in his mind. Hundreds of times, as he practiced a fast draw under his pa's watchful eye, he'd said to himself that he could do it—kill a man if he had to, if he had no choice. But now, looking at Jake Ketchum, his chest stilled forever by Cody's bullet, something about it seemed wrong. In a fistfight there was a winner and a loser, yet both walked away after it was done. When a fight was made with guns the loser lost permanently and the winner had to bear the weight of it on his conscience for the rest of his days.

"Help." The stableman's feeble call reminded him that he needed to go for help quickly or the man might die of blood loss.

He strode away from the livery in a black mood, thankful to be alive. He'd learned a few things about himself the past few hours, not many of them good. In a tight spot he could shoot a moving target, but when the chips were down, he'd run out of nerve and the sight of death made him queasy. His first taste of fear left him feeling hollow, like a shell. After that bullet came so close to his ear, all the fight went out of him. Underneath his tough-talking exterior, he'd discovered more than a little bit of doubt. Unsettling, to find out he wasn't who he'd thought he was.

Dawn grayed skies to the east as he lengthened his strides back toward the center of town. The stable owner's wounds looked bad, which probably meant another death could be tallied to the account of Flatnose Curry. This was Cody's first real introduction to the handiwork of a genuine bad man, a killer, and now he began to wonder how much Curry was like his pa might have been in his wilder days. Had John Wade killed men in cold blood the way Curry did tonight at the Lady? Gunned them down without hardly any reason other than that they stood in his way? Cody had never thought of his pa as that kind of man before. Could John Wade have been anything like George Curry?

As he turned off Dauphin Street onto Tenth, Cody saw a group of men gathered in front of the office. Dave Watkins stood before a half dozen horsemen shouting instructions. Every rider was armed with a rifle or a shotgun.

"Gun the sons of bitches down on sight!" Dave yelled. "It don't make a damn where they're at or what they're doin', just be damn sure you kill 'em. The city'll pay a hundred-dollar reward to whoever gets Flatnose Curry, dead or alive, an' fifty dollars to whoever gets Ketchum.''

Cody broke into a trot to reach Dave's posse before any of them rode off. Another man, wearing a split-tail frock coat and bowler, stood on the porch alongside Dave. He spoke as Cody was running up.

"Don't forget you've been deputized. You're actin' with all the legal authority you need. Don't hesitate to bring those men in full of bullet holes, boys. Sheriff Casey's men are gettin' mounted to help us track them down.''

Cody reached the back of the group out of wind. Dave saw him and said, ''There's the kid! Tell us what happened, boy. I heard shootin' comin' from the east side. We'd better get a good explanation for how come this jailhouse is empty . . .''

All eyes were on Cody—some were unfriendly stares. ''They rode east, Curry and the other prisoner. I killed Jake Ketchum. Curry is wounded in a shoulder, bleedin' like hell, but he can still shoot. They shot the feller who owns the livery over on Dauphin Street an' he needs a doctor right away. They stole two of his horses an' headed east through Maddox Flats.''

''Let's ride!'' a horseman shouted, waving his rifle above his head as he spurred his horse up Tenth Street. The others wheeled their mounts and galloped after him, readying their guns.

Dave was staring at Cody. The man in the bowler was also giving him a questioning look.

''You killed Ketchum?'' Dave asked, like he couldn't quite believe it.

''Yessir, I did.''

''Somebody said you was the one who winged Curry down at the Lady. How come you didn't kill him?''

He had to think about it while he caught his breath. ''It was happenin' real fast, but since I wasn't no regular deputy I guess I was afraid it wouldn't be legal if I shot him dead, so I put a bullet in his shoulder. I warned him if he made another move I'd put the next one through his heart. That's when he gave up his gun. I put irons on him an' brung him here to the jail, only I didn't have no key to the door, so I had to break out a window so I could get in. I went to fetch a doctor for him, on account of he was bleedin' so bad. Somebody must have come in while me an' Newt was at the hospital askin' for a sawbones. When I got back, every cell was empty, so I ran for the closest livery, figurin' they'd need horses to get clear of town.''

''And you found them?'' the man in the bowler asked, stepping off the porch to approach Cody. ''You shot it out with them, with three of them, and you got Jake Ketchum before the others rode away?''

''Yessir.'' He didn't know who the man was, but it was clear he was someone with authority. ''It was dark an' I was afoot, so I came back here to tell Deputy Watkins about it, seein' as I'm not a regular lawman, only a jailer. Today was my first full day on the job.''

''I'm Mayor Frank Tompkins.'' He stuck out his hand.

''Cody Wade, sir.'' He shook with the mayor, finding his palm soft, unaccustomed to hard labor.

''You'll be a full-fledged deputy soon enough,'' Tompkins said as he gave Cody a closer look. ''From what I've heard, you're a very brave young man. You were there, so you know Marshal Hull is in serious condition and he may not live out the day. Deputy Webb has grave internal injuries. I just came from the hospital, after speaking with Dr. Roberts. We're seriously short-handed at this office now. Come to City Hall later this morning. I'll see that you're sworn in as a peace officer.''

Cody started to speak, to tell the mayor he didn't want any more of being a peace officer.

Dave said, ''I'll send a doctor down to Bud's Livery, and the undertaker for Ketchum. Appears you just earned yourself a fifty-dollar reward, Cody.''

''That's right,'' Mayor Tompkins agreed. ''I'll fill out the papers while you're at my office. I'm sure you could use fifty dollars.''

Cody nodded, keeping silent about his wish to get out of the lawman's profession. Fifty dollars was a lot of money and he did not want to sour the mayor's willingness to pay it by crawfishing at the wrong time.

Dave came off the porch to clap Cody on the shoulder. "You did right well tonight, son. You've got the makin's of a deputy, just like Cordel said. You showed you had backbone." He walked off in the direction of the hospital with his shotgun under his arm, glancing east every now and then, listening for noises that might mean the posse was hard on Curry's trail.

Mayor Tompkins was giving him a thorough appraisal, running his eyes up and down Cody's frame. "How old are you, Mr. Wade?" He asked like he believed he was too young for the job.

"I'm twenty, sir."

Tompkins nodded. "And you killed Jake Ketchum, besides the fact you winged George Curry in the shoulder. That's mighty good shooting. Jake needed killing. He was a back alley character in this part of town for years, robbing honest people, most likely doing a killing or two we didn't know about. You have done this city a favor, ridding us of Jake. It sounds like George Curry is cut from the same cloth. It's quite clear you have good instincts when it comes to men of their breed. Although you're young, you seem perfectly suited for a peace officer's job here. I assure you, your age will not prejudice me against you. Come over to my office later today and I'll swear you in." He lowered his voice. "Deputy Watkins is a bit too hotheaded to assume the marshal's job if anything should happen to Cordel Hull. Watkins has a few black marks on his record. The city council would never vote him in even as a temporary replacement. Dave would turn this part of town into a slaughterhouse, I'm afraid. Under certain conditions, with the right restraints, you might be just the candidate we'll need. We can talk it over, after I speak with a few of our councilmen. Of course, we'd have to check out your background to make sure there's nothing in your past that might rule you out."

It was time to tell the mayor he didn't want the marshal's job, yet he didn't right then, promising himself he'd decline the offer later. "I reckon I'd better saddle my horse so I can help look for Curry. I'll stop by City Hall so we can talk as soon as we get back, whenever that'll be."

Tompkins smiled. His fleshy face was a sickly shade of gray in dawn's early light. "I'll be looking forward to it." He made a turn on his heel and sauntered off toward the middle of town.

Cody shook his head, climbing the porch steps to take a long gun from the rifle rack. About the last thing on earth he wanted was Marshal Hull's job . . .

22

A gentle rain came from the south on feathery gusts of wind while Annabelle was preparing black-eyed peas. The sky darkened rapidly. As raindrops struck flames underneath their kettles, a hissing sound announced an end to laundering. Before the ground grew wet, windswept dust clouds encircled clean clothes drying on lines, so that no matter how quickly she hurried to take them down, most of their customers' apparel was dirty again, coated with a gritty layer of sand and dust. Doris did what she could to help out, until a coughing spell doubled her over at the back of the wagon. By the time Annabelle was finished bringing in the clothes, most were soiled and in need of washing again.

She helped her ma to the lean-to after dropping a canvas tail piece from the rear wagon bow. Smoke from extinguishing fires drifted under their shelter, worsening Doris's cough while making Annabelle's eyes burn. The smell of damp coals and smoke and dust filled her nose, and before she knew it, thinking about all the work they faced cleaning the same clothes twice, she began to cry.

"It ain't fair!" she whimpered, stamping her foot, balling her hands.

Doris sat on her stool, coughing again and again, unable to catch her breath. Distant thunder rumbled. Soon every fire was out, smoldering, giving off steam. The patter of rain drummed on their roof and against the wagon sheet, forming little puddles in low spots across the campground.

"We'll have to do it all over!" Annabelle cried, overcome by despair and fatigue. Made restless by Cody's visit, she hadn't gone to bed until four in the morning. His touch had given her the greatest pleasure she could ever imagine. His lips covering her mouth made her feel weak, shaky, wanting more. The experience was all the more evidence she'd been overtaken by Satan's desires, which she had no wish to control.

"Now, now, child," Doris whispered, wiping her mouth. "You must be patient. The Lord has willed it to rain, an' so it has."

She caught herself quickly before she said anything against the Lord's will. Rain poured off their lean-to in sheets as she sobbed quietly, exhausted, turning her back on Doris so she did not see her crying. Then she remembered her peas and stepped out into the rain to put a lid on them. Raindrops pelted her, making a mess of her hair, her yellow dress, her shoes. She smelled the peas and found she wasn't hungry; she was too weary and dejected to eat.

By the time she got back to the shelter, she was soaked. At once she noticed Doris had fallen off her stool, and was lying in the dirt on her side.

"Ma!" she cried, rushing over to her.

Blood trickled from Doris's mouth and it appeared she was asleep. Annabelle shook her.

"Wake up, Ma! What's wrong?"

She got no response, only more blood as it seeped from her mother's mouth and nose.

Fear twisted her stomach. Was her ma dying? Or was it only exhaustion making her sleep so deeply?

Summoning all her strength, she lifted Doris's shoulders and pulled her to her pallet, covering her with a moth-eaten blanket.

"She's gotta have a doctor," Annabelle whispered, talking to herself. "It'll have to be mighty soon, too."

Gradually the summer shower ended, slowing to a few drops at first, then ending completely. Everything smelled damp when wind blew in behind the vanishing clouds, sweeping across the flats and making tiny ripples on the surface of puddles. Wind made their canvas roof flutter, popping it,

straining the tie-down ropes. Annabelle sat beside her ma as
though she were in a trance, staring off at the tops of trees
swaying in the wind, thinking about what she had to do in
order to make enough money to afford a hospital room and a
doctor's visits. Working for Miss Rose, she could make plenty
of money to do that.

Remembering what Cody had said, the way he felt about
crib girls for hire, she knew she would lose his attentions if
she became a scarlet woman. He couldn't love her—he'd
made that plain as day when he talked about hired women up
in Kansas.

"I wish I didn't have to choose," she said, no longer crying
over wet clothes, saddened now by the thought of losing her
chance to be loved by Cody. She couldn't remember ever feeling so completely alone. Choosing to work at the Pink Lady
meant never seeing Cody again, denying them the opportunity
to see if they might fall in love. But what else was she to do?
There was only one way to get enough money for a hospital
and a doctor.

"It just ain't fair," she said into the wind, resisting the urge
to cry again.

Doris coughed in her deep sleep, a wet sound. Phlegm
turned pink by blood dribbled from her lips. Annabelle took
the handkerchief and wiped it away gently. Watching her ma
while she slept, it was still hard to believe she'd ever worked
the cribs or gotten drunk on whiskey. Annabelle had only
known her as a mother, a sweet-natured woman who gave her
kindness and compassion and all of her understanding. How
could she be two people so completely different?

It happened when she was young, Annabelle thought, before
she knew better. Or had Chester Green come along at exactly
the right time, in time to save her from a lifetime of sin? Was
this the reason she believed so strongly in the scriptures?

And what of Annabelle's own choice? If she went to work
at the Pink Lady, would she suffer some terrible illness like
her ma? Or was it only coincidence that she came down with
the consumption? How was Annabelle to know? The money
was so very tempting.

An hour passed, an hour of quiet deliberations during which she got no answers. Annabelle was distracted when a man came to pick up his laundry, an older gentleman who'd gotten off the noon train on Saturday.

"I'm sorry, mister, but your clothes got dirty when that big rain blowed in. We can have 'em for you tomorrow mornin' if it don't rain again."

He accepted the news graciously enough. "I'll be leaving on tomorrow's train, missy, if I don't get myself killed before then in this hellhole. Be sure they're ready before noon. There've been so many killings lately I can't be sure I'll be alive to get my laundry."

"Was somebody killed last night?" she asked. She had this vague recollection of hearing gunshots sometime after Cody left.

He nodded. "At least two, and the city marshal may die as a result of the shootings, as well as his deputy."

"Was his deputy hurt? An' do you recall his name?" She was thinking of Cody as soon as he said it, worrying, her mouth gone suddenly dry.

"The newspaper said his name was Coleman Webb, I believe."

"Wasn't no mention of Cody Wade, was there?"

"Why yes, he's the young man who killed one of the escaping prisoners, and I believe he also shot the famous gunfighter named Flatnose Curry. Curry and another man got away. The story's in this afternoon's special edition of the paper, if you care to read about it. It's big news, that Marshal Cordel Hull was shot in a saloon last night. He's clinging to his life by a thread."

Annabelle calmed her fears, although she wondered how Cody could have done so much after he'd stayed so long with her last night. "I'll sure read it," she promised. "An' I'm real sorry 'bout your clothes, only I can't help it if it rained. Ma says it was the Lord's will . . ."

"I'll be back tomorrow morning, miss. Please be sure they are ready in time."

"You got my promise, mister, if the Lord'll just hold off with another one of them cloudbursts."

He chuckled and walked away, whistling a tune with his hands in his pants pockets.

She was still stunned by the news, that Cody had killed an escaping prisoner and wounded a bad man everyone called Flatnose. Cody didn't seem the type to perform killings. When he was with her, he was gentle, soft-spoken, almost bashful at times. Could the old man be mistaken? And it was almost as shocking to learn the shootings happened only a few blocks away while she slept.

"I hope he's okay," she said quietly, gazing across rooftops in the Acre. She wanted a copy of the newspaper, but papers cost money. She decided to spare a nickle from the five dollars Miss Rose had given her, so she could read about Cody.

She hurried to the back of the wagon and took a dollar from her hidden money, stopping long enough to check on her ma before she took off at a run for the newspaper office on Main Street. A few people gave her curious stares because of her haste when she raced past, dodging mud puddles left in the road by the storm.

With her change in her pocket and a newspaper under her arm, she trotted back to the campground, making sure no one was there awaiting their laundry before she sat down to read the headlines and the following story.

CRAZED KILLER GUNS DOWN CITY MARSHAL

More blood has been shed in the city's infamous Acre as our courageous city marshal, Cordel Hull, again put his life on the line for Fort Worth citizens in order to keep the peace. We are saddened to report the marshal was gunned down by a man of most foul reputation, George "Flatnose" Curry, lately of Wyoming and other federal territories west. A deputy marshal, Coleman Webb, was also mortally wounded by Curry. The manager of an establishment in the Acre was killed outright by a bullet to his brain in the melee, again by Curry. Luther M. Pierce, formerly a resident of New Orleans, reportedly died instantly.

Marshal Hull, a veteran of nine years in public office, is in critical condition from a bullet in the chest. Deputy Webb was felled by a bullet through his abdomen and is not expected to survive, according to noted Fort Worth surgeon Dr. Louis Roberts. At presstime, both policemen were still alive.

Mayor Frank Tompkins deplored the actions of Curry and gave high praise to the city's new jailer, Cody Wade, until recently a resident of Waco. Wade shot and wounded Curry by virtue of his quick-handedness with a pistol, although during a subsequent jail escape, Curry and two more prisoners managed to get away. One of the fleeing prisoners, a murderer named Jake Ketchum, had the sad misfortune of running across twenty-year-old jailer Cody Wade in the dark of night at Bud Adams's Livery Stable on Dauphin Street as the prisoners were trying to steal horses. Wade killed Ketchum in an exchange of hot lead, with a bullet through his heart, but not before stable owner Ansel "Bud" Adams was felled by a hail of bullets fired by the fleeing outlaws. Adams, a longtime Fort Worth businessman, died at 10 A.M. this morning. Funeral services are pending at Wilkins Funeral Home.

An all-out manhunt has been launched for George Curry and an accomplice by Tarrant County Sheriff Homer Casey. Deputized men are combing every inch of the city and county with orders to kill Curry on sight. A one-hundred-dollar reward for Curry, dead or alive, has been posted by Mayor Tompkins. As of this writing the outlaw is still at large.

A prayer vigil for Marshal Hull and his deputy will be held at the Tarrant County Hospital, led by Reverend Clarence Baugh of Trinity River Baptist Church. Concerned citizens are urged to attend and offer prayers for both of the city's dedicated police officers.

She read the part about Cody again, pressing the newspaper flat on her lap to keep wind from rustling it. As she was about to put it away, she heard footsteps.

"Afternoon, Annabelle," Tommy Joe said, keeping his voice low when he saw Doris sleeping. He walked up from the creek in a pair of overalls, wearing his battered cowboy hat with a crow's feather stuck in the crown. "I reckon you jus' read 'bout all of the excitement at the Lady last night . . ."

"The paper didn't say where it happened," she replied. "I didn't know it happened at Miss Rose's place." She hadn't seen Tommy Joe since the night he poked her, and for some reason she was deeply embarrassed to see him now.

"I seen the whole thing . . . right afterwards, after all the shootin' stopped. I was one helpin' to carry Deputy Webb out to Miss Rose's carriage."

She folded her paper and got up, sticking it in the back of the wagon along with her silver money, two 10-cent pieces and three quarters. "Did you see that new jailer who shot all the bad men?" she asked, making her interest sound casual.

"Sure did. I seen him take Flatnose Curry to jail, an' I seen him here a time or two. One time he fixed up your ol' wagon hubs. 'Nother time I seen the two of you down at the creek an' you was kissin'."

"Be quiet or Ma'll hear you!" Her embarrassment deepened when she learned Tommy Joe had been watching. "What were you doin' spyin' on us?"

"Wasn't spyin'. Only walkin' by on my way home."

"Go away, Tommy Joe! Can't you see I'm busy?"

"You was readin' a newspaper . . ."

"I was fixin' to start more fires. The rain drowned 'em out an' ruined all our laundry business. You hadn't oughta spied on me like that. Ain't you got nothin' better to do?"

"How come you're so all-fired mad about it, Annabelle?"

She looked down at her shoes. "Please go away," she said to him softly, not meaning to sound angry. "It ain't been much of a good day. Ma's been real sick an' the rain ruined everything we had hung up to dry. Leave us alone. Please. I've got a lot of thinkin' to do. Ma's needin' a doctor real bad. She ain't woke up in several hours an' she's bleedin' somethin' fierce, coughin' up more blood than she ever did. She don't eat hardly at all. I have to think real hard 'bout what I'm gonna do.''

"You can work for Miss Rose. Why, you'll be rich in no time an' you won't have no more worries.''

"I know,'' she whispered, glancing over to her ma's pallet. "I need to think about it. Now, please leave me alone so I can get this laundry done. I gotta have time to think . . .''

23

Stirring bubbling kettles, sleeving sweat and smoke from her eyes, by sundown she was exhausted. She'd eaten a bowl of salty peas without really tasting them an hour earlier, out of necessity when she felt weak rather than hunger. Doris slept soundly throughout the afternoon, too soundly it seemed. Annabelle tried to wake her several times without success. It was clear she was in some kind of stupor from which she couldn't return on her own, worrying Annabelle that much more. She made up her mind to ask someone at the hospital tomorrow how much a doctor's visit would be, and the cost of a hospital room. But first she had to wash clothes soiled by the rainstorm.

Several times she saw groups of heavily armed men riding to the depot, or along side streets and alleys, searching for the escaped prisoners she'd read about in the newspaper. When a five o'clock train came from the east, more than a dozen men surrounded the train station, making sure no one boarded without a ticket. Each time she saw a mounted posse, she looked for Cody among them. She still found it hard to believe he'd been the one who shot it out with those bad men last night. She wondered how he could be so gentle with her and have a mean streak when it came to chasing outlaws. In the paper it said he'd killed a man—she couldn't fit Cody into the mold of a killer, no matter what the reason.

When the last kettle was thoroughly stirred, she went over to their lean-to. Doris was still asleep.

"Wake up, Ma," she said, shaking her shoulder gently.

No amount of coaxing did any good. She slept like she never intended to wake up again.

"What's wrong, Ma? How come you can't hear me?"

She remembered how her pa died, finally slipping into a long sleep from which he never awakened. One morning, Ma said he was gone to heaven, that he'd just stopped breathing during the night to be with the angels because he was suffering so much and could not get well on his own.

"You'll be with the angels, too," Annabelle whispered, stroking her mother's forehead. "You won't be hurtin' no more up yonder. You'll be forgiven for what you done before. The Lord ain't gonna hold it against you when you get to them pearly gates. Just you wait an' see . . ."

Rays of crimson sun bathed the campground as she got up to begin carrying rinse water. With a pail in each hand she walked back and forth from the well, too exhausted to think, going about her chores mechanically. In the back of her mind she knew there was a decision to be made—whether or not to work for Miss Rose. Putting it off only made it loom larger in her thoughts as night came to Fort Worth.

When the last bucket of water had been poured, she sat down to collect herself, staring into a bed of red coals below a pot full of shirts and blouses. Working alone further convinced her she couldn't do laundry by herself. Her back ached and her arms felt like lead weights. Every article of rinsed clothing still had to be hung up to dry before she could rest.

She glanced over her shoulder. Doris slept as she had all day.

She's dying, Annabelle thought. Then what'll I do?

She remembered what she'd looked like in a borrowed silk dress when she stood before Miss Rose's mirror. Instead of carrying a water bucket she could be wearing a lacy gown and new shoes, if she agreed to Rose Denadale's proposition. She would own perfume and silk stockings, live in a nice room and have plenty of money.

"It would be so good not to be poor," she said, after taking a long look at their wagon, and the piece of canvas tied to one side that was now the only home she had. "I'll lose Cody if I do it, but I wouldn't have no more worries."

Then she told herself she didn't care, that having money

was more important for selfish reasons, as well as giving her a way to provide for herself and her mother. "We wouldn't need nobody or have to take no charity. Cody's just a cowboy. He's liable to up an' ride off anyday. Can't count on him for nothin' much because he's a drifter, like Ma said."

Annabelle closed her eyes, seeing Miss Rose's fancy room in her mind. "There'd be no more sleepin' on hard ground. No more black-eyed peas an' frybread day after day." Miss Rose had mentioned that a glass of wine helped to calm upset nerves. She wondered what wine tasted like and how it could calm someone. "I could ask her for a little taste . . . just to see if I liked it." Fear of nervousness when she let a gentleman caller see her naked made her wonder if wine might help. "I could make myself do it, for enough money," she whispered, pushing away any notions that it was either right or wrong. She wouldn't have to do it forever if she saved most of the money she made.

Facing several hours hanging up wet garments, she stood and stretched her sore muscles. "I can make myself do it," she said with a deep sigh. "Cody don't care nothin' about me or he'd have come by to tell me what happened last night."

A nighthawk flew above her as she began taking garments to clotheslines. The bird screeched once and soared off on a gust of wind, hunting alone in the darkness.

A bearded man aboard a rawboned mule rode to the campground from the south. He appeared to watch Annabelle's fires for some time before he selected a campsite near the stream, not far from where their mule was tethered on a grazing rope. As she hung wet clothes out to dry, she noticed him staring at her and it gave her a case of the shivers. The stranger was dressed in rags and his gear had a makeshift look, only a piece of a saddle without any stirrups and a few personal items in a dirty warbag tied over his mule's withers.

Annabelle made a show of ignoring him, keeping her back to him while she finished hanging clothes. When the last shirt was pinned to a line, she carried her baskets back to the wagon as a fire began to flicker where the newcomer camped. She felt his eyes on her and wouldn't look that way. She'd become accustomed to stares as they moved from town to town. Two women traveling alone in a broken-down wagon usually drew more than a few curious looks, although she often felt it was folks feeling sorry for a half-starved mule pulling a heavy load who stared at them most of the time.

The stranger was boiling coffee . . . She could smell it on wind blowing from the south. And in the fire's yellow light she could see him watching her while his coffee proved up, making her all the more uncomfortable. She kept busy putting baskets and water pails away, wishing Doris would awaken so the newcomer would see she wasn't alone. But when she looked in on her ma, she found her sleeping soundly, as before, and that began to worry her.

"How come you can't wake up?" she asked, touching her cheek with her fingertips. "Please don't die, Ma. Soon as I can, I'll run to the hospital an' find out how much a doctor costs, maybe a room there, too. You'll only get worse unless you get treatments right away . . ." Annabelle had no idea what sort of treatments a doctor could offer. Doc Collins back in San Augustine had said there wasn't a cure for consumption, only a dry climate. But he hadn't been able to do anything for her pa either, and sometimes she wondered if Doc Collins knew much of anything at all about doctoring folks.

She adjusted Doris's pillow so she'd be more comfortable and sat beside her in the darkness, keeping an eye on the stranger as the hour approached midnight. Annabelle was so sleepy she wasn't able to think clearly, and she dozed off from time to time. While she dozed, she dreamed about pretty dresses and a room with a bed and a canopy. In her dream she wore red leather shoes and stockings made of silk. A crystal goblet in her hand was brimming with red wine, although when she tasted it, it had no taste at all. She saw herself coming down the stairs at the Pink Lady, being stared at by a parlor full of smiling gentlemen. There was some polite applause and a man in a derby hat raised his glass in a toast and said, "To the most beautiful gal in town! Real nice to meet

you, Belle, and I'm looking forward to seeing you again sometime.''

She awoke with a start and sat up, blinking in the glare of
a brilliant morning sunrise. Rubbing her eyes, she looked
across the campground to find that the worrysome stranger was
gone. She had slept so soundly she hadn't heard him leave.
Only the blackened remains of his fire showed where he'd
been before she dropped off to sleep.

Doris was still sleeping. A trace of fresh blood lay on her
pillow and on her lips. Annabelle wiped her mother's mouth
with a clean handerkerchief and got up, noticing a stiffness in
her lower back and her shoulders. A breeze fluttered dry clothing on the lines, a reminder that she needed to take them down
and begin folding in order to be on time for the noon train.
The sky was clear above her and she was grateful another
shower hadn't come along to ruin everything again.

When she went to get her clothes baskets, she saw that the
canvas tail piece at the back of the wagon had been pushed
aside. And when she peered in, everything had been tossed
here and there in haphazard fashion. She gasped and put a
hand over her mouth.

''Someone's been here!'' she cried.

A quick search of her belongings revealed her money was
gone from its hiding place in the little jewelry box. And the
baking soda tin where Doris kept her money was open, empty,
lying at the bottom of the wagon bed.

''We've been robbed!'' Annabelle screamed, tears of frus-
tration and anger brimming in her eyes.

She turned quickly toward the spot where the stranger had
made his fire last night.

''He robbed us while I was asleep.'' For a moment she
could not catch her breath, and was not quite able to believe
their misfortune. While it wasn't all that much money, it was
all they had, and now they were penniless. ''Why would somebody . . . ?'' She broke down and cried, covering her face with
her palms, weeping bitter tears while her body shook from

head to toe. She sat down on her rump in the dirt and wept softly for several minutes.

She heard trotting horses and looked up a moment later, when a posse swung around the corner from Rusk Street. Scrambling to her feet, she waved and shouted, "Over here! Somebody help me!"

Six men carrying shotguns and rifles aimed their horses for her wagon. They wore badges on their shirts. She recognized one of them, a friend of Cody's who'd brought his laundry with him the first time they met. She recalled that his name was Newt Sims. As they came toward her, she dried her eyes and walked away from the wagon to meet them.

"Howdy, Miss Annabelle," Newt said, sifting a double-barrel shotgun to his left hand, resting the stock against his thigh the moment his horse stopped. "Is somethin' wrong?"

"We was robbed last night," she began, trying not to start crying again when she talked about it. "This man on a skinny ol' mule made a fire down by the creek. He robbed our wagon while we was asleep an' took off with our money."

Newt appeared concerned. "What'd he look like?" He gazed past her to the creek bank where she'd been pointing.

"He had a black beard. He had holes in his britches an' the elbows of his shirt. I seen him real good when he rode in, an' the whole time he kept starin' at us."

"I'll keep my eyes open for him, ma'am, but right now we've got orders to look for George Curry an' another feller who broke jail with him. Sheriff Casey an' the mayor want 'em brought in before sundown. They deputized better'n fifty men to cover the whole county lookin' for 'em. There's a hundred-dollar reward been posted for Curry."

She nodded. "It was in the newspaper. I saw where Cody had to shoot somebody . . ."

"He killed Jake Ketchum an' wounded Curry. Mayor Tompkins swore Cody in as a regular deputy this afternoon an' he's leadin' one of the search parties just now east of town." Newt shifted a plug of tobacco to his other cheek and spat loudly. "We'll be glad to keep an eye out for this feller on the mule, but fact is we've got to hunt down them two escaped prisoners. If we see a man on a mule, we'll question him real close an' haul him over to the sheriff. That's nearly all I can promise you.''

"I'd be obliged if you told Cody about it, when you see him. If it wouldn't trouble you none.''

"No trouble at all," Newt said, glancing over his shoulder. "I reckon we'd better be goin'. Sorry to hear 'bout your run of bad luck.'' He looked past her. "How's your ma doin'?''

"She can't wake up. I was gonna take her to the hospital as soon as I could, only now we ain't got any money.''

Newt wagged his head sympathetically. "Wish there was some way I could help, but I ain't got no regular job yet. I'll make mention of it when I see Cody. Maybe he's got some ideas. Nice seein' you again, Miss Annabelle. If we find that bearded feller ridin' a mule, we'll bring him in for questionin' by the sheriff.''

"We'd be mighty grateful, Mr. Sims.''

He touched the brim of his hat politely and swung his horse toward the depot. The posse men flanking him turned off and rode in the same direction. As soon as their backs were turned, she felt more tears coming and bowed her head, struggling to control her emotions. It seemed she'd done more crying the past few days than she had the rest of her life. Most all her troubles were a result of being poor, she told herself.

She'd been offered a way to end it, yet she couldn't quite summon the nerve. Only now, things were much worse. Their mule was out of corn and their firewood was almost gone. They had a few black-eyed peas and a little bit of flour to eat, and Doris needed a doctor.

"I'll go talk to Miss Rose soon as Ma wakes up," she said in a tight voice, determined not to cry again. "I reckon it's time I done a bit of growin' up. I'm nearly seventeen . . .''

24

Rose listened to the girl blurt out her story about her sick mother and the robbery. Belle was the only bright spot in recent events, and particularly today, after making funeral arrangements for Luther, she needed cheering up. Dealing with Allene was just as unpleasant this morning . . . She'd been too shocked by Luther's death to talk to her right after the shooting, even though Allene was the reason Flatnose Curry had come there in the first place. Now, with Cordel lying near death at the hospital, something had to be done to bring business back. Word of this kind spread like a prairie fire among well-heeled customers who didn't care to be shot at while enjoying a game of cards or a girl.

"So you see," Belle explained, the corners of her mouth turning down as though she could cry, "I gotta do somethin' real soon. Ma can't hardly keep her eyes open. We ain't got a cent left for food or medicine or corn for our mule. She needs to go to the hospital. Even if I do decide to come to work for you, I can't up an' leave her alone at that wagon, the shape she's in. She can't hardly see after herself an' she won't eat."

Rose let a moment pass, not wanting to seem too anxious to help. "If I agree to let you work here, I might be willing to let you borrow some money. That way, you could see that your mother got the care she needed right away. I suppose I could loan you some dresses until you got on your feet, but I wouldn't want to do it unless we had an understanding."

"What sorta understanding?"

"That you'd work for me until the loan was repaid, and

you'd never go to work for anyone else here. If I trusted you enough to get you started in the business, I'd expect loyalty from you in return.''

She chewed her bottom lip thoughtfully. "I've just nearly made up my mind that I can do it, Miss Rose. You see, Ma says when a woman sells herself for money, it's wrong. I was brought up to be God-fearin', an' the Bible says fornication is a real bad sin, only Ma done it herself a long time ago. She was given over to wickedness back then, drinkin' whiskey an' workin' a crib in Saint Louis. She'd nearly die if she knew what I was fixin' to do, only she's dyin' anyway, looks like. I reckon I like the idea of havin' money, too. It's terrible, bein' so poor. Maybe notions like that are the work of the devil, like Ma claims it is. Seems like just lately the devil's gotten hold of me in the worst way, because I'm always thinkin' about what it would be like to have a nice room like this, an' fancy dresses like the ones you wear. Can't say I ain't nervous about doin' it, though. You told me once a glass of wine might help, only right then I'd promised Ma I'd live by the scriptures . . .''

Rose surprised herself when she felt a tiny twinge of guilt. Belle was a good girl at heart, merely looking for a way to end a lifelong cycle of poverty. In many ways she reminded Rose of her own dilemma so long ago, when being poor seemed worse than giving a stranger a few minutes of intimacy. "I don't believe a glass or two of wine is wrong, Belle. When I was young, I was so very poor, just like you. I got tired of being hungry, of not having a place to sleep. I'm not sorry for what I did to have a better life. I don't believe I've ever harmed anyone by giving some gentlemen a few moments of pleasure, or drinking a modest amount of bottled spirits from time to time. No one was ever harmed by what I did and that's what counts.''

Belle nodded, like she agreed. "Right at first, when I was only thinkin' about workin' for you, I told myself I'd be doin' it for my ma, if I done it at all. Only that ain't exactly the truth. I'd be doin' it for me, same as for her. Lately, there's this funny feelin' inside me, like a voice tellin' me it's okay to consort with a man if I wanted. I reckon it's the devil's own voice. That's what Ma would say.''

Rose opened a dresser drawer, taking out a bottle of French red wine and a glass she kept for occasions such as this. ''Take a small glass of wine, to see how it tastes. If we can reach an agreement, I'll have my carriage sent for your mother so she can be taken to the hospital. Perhaps someone there can arrange for a boardinghouse room where someone can care for her, after she's seen a doctor. I'll advance you the money you need against your future earnings and loan you a dress. You'll have a room here, so you won't be without anything.'' She uncorked the wine and poured Belle a drink. ''Try this while you're thinking it over.''

Belle took the glass and sniffed its contents warily. ''It has a sweet smell, don't it? Like fruit, only sweeter.'' She put it to her mouth and took a tentative sip. ''It kinda burns goin' down,'' she added, frowning a little.

''You'll get used to it.'' Leaning back in her chair, waiting for the wine to relax her, Rose smiled.

Belle sampled another swallow. ''I've got one more thing to think about, Miss Rose. There's this cowboy. I like him a lot, only we hardly more'n just met. He's got a job down at the city jail. His name's Cody Wade, an' he told me he couldn't ever have feelin's for a hired woman.''

Rose stiffened. Cody Wade was the boy who'd wounded Flatnose Curry in her parlor last night. He was big and good-looking, and quick with a gun. ''I've seen him. He was with Marshal Hull when the shooting started. Peace officers don't make very much money. Cordel is a friend of mine and he's always having trouble making ends meet. He has a few . . . paying investments on the side. You have to choose, Belle, between having a sweetheart and earning a good living here. I won't allow you to have suitors paying you social calls while you're working. It's just good business. You can see him anywhere you wish, but not here, nor during working hours.''

''He wouldn't anyways, not after he found out,'' she told her quietly. She drank more wine, resting comfortably on the edge of the bed. ''I suppose I'll do it, what you want me to do. If I'm nervous the first few times, I hope it don't matter. I ain't all that used to nobody starin' at me, 'specially not without havin' any clothes on. I'll agree to work for you until all the money is paid back, an' you got my word I won't never work for nobody else.'' She sighed, looking down at her glass. ''Maybe there's a part of me who's just like my ma was back then. She told me she done it when she was young, before she knowed better. I got an itch to have some money for a change. If that's sinful, then I guess I'm inclined toward bein' a sinner.''

''I prefer to call it ambition, Belle. Finish your wine and I'll have my driver bring the carriage around back. We'll take your mother to the hospital and while we're there, I'll visit Cordel a moment. Then we'll get you fitted for a dress, some stockings and shoes. The gentleman I'd planned to have for your first caller won't be . . . available. But I do know someone down at City Hall who'll be very interested in you. We can talk about it later, after we get back from the hospital.''

''That'll be just fine, Miss Rose,'' she said, calmed by the wine so quickly she appeared to be sleepy. ''I'll need to take a bath an' fix my hair some.'' Belle drained her glass and licked her lips.

''I can help you with your hair.'' Rose got up slowly, taking note of Belle's smooth skin, a flawless olive complexion flattering her dark eyes.

She'll be the talk of this town, Rose thought, crossing the room to her back door. Maybe the topic of conversation along the entire Chisholm Trail when cowhands got together to reminisce on lonely nights. Belle would command top money from better customers, cattle buyers and ranchers and businessmen who could pay for the best. All she needed was a little polish with her manners and speech, things Rose could teach her, and the best clothing money could buy, an investment in her future, which was also part of the future of the Pink Lady.

She opened the door and called downstairs, ''Have Riggs bring my carriage around to the back.''

What had begun as a gloomy day was starting to look considerably better. Belle Green had come like a ray of sunshine just when things seemed to be at their worst.

Riggs lifted the frail woman gently and carried her to the rear buggy seat. Rose sat in front, saying nothing to the girl when she saw how sad and forlorn the old wagon looked, and their canvas-covered shelter, rows of smoke-blackened pots resting in heaps of ashes, drooping clotheslines that were empty now. This was where Belle lived and it was no wonder she wanted something better.

Belle got in first. Riggs placed Belle's mother across the girl's lap so that her head rested comfortably. By the look on Riggs's face, he was worried. He adjusted the angle on his silk top hat, dusting off his black suit coat and trousers.

"She hasn't opened her eyes," he said, glancing up at Rose before he climbed in. "She's breathing okay, but there's a lot of blood . . ." He didn't finish when Rose gave him a stern look.

"Take us to the hospital," Rose said quietly, keeping sun off her face with a parasol. She wore a modest green dress that covered her bosom. Judging by the appearance of Doris Green, she wouldn't be alive much longer, although her illness did serve a purpose, giving Belle a push in the right direction, a reason she needed to make good money.

They wheeled away from the public campground in a swirl of chalky dust, heading into the middle of town, driving past a bank where Rose kept most of her money. Now and then she made sizable charitable contributions to an orphan's fund or a needy cause in the name of the Pink Lady, which endeared her to a good many city officials and some of the town's leading citizens. It helped to silence critics' voices after a disturbance in the Acre, when the bank announced Miss Rose Denadale was giving money to some worthy charity. It was necessary politics, as necessary to staying in business as weekly payments made to Cordel Hull.

Riggs drove to a side hospital door and halted the carriage under the shade of a slanting roof above the driveway. He got

down to assist Rose from her seat before he lifted Doris in his
arms.

Rose walked in first, holding a door open for Riggs until
he carried the woman inside. Belle followed them in, seemingly a bit frightened by a hospital's strange sights and smells.
Odors mingled together, ether and rubbing alcohol and euca-
lyptus oil in a room made stifling by midday heat.

A nurse left her desk as soon as the door was closed, coming
over quickly, examining the woman in Riggs's arms. "What
is wrong with her?" she asked.

"She's got the consumption," Belle said, her voice so soft
it was hard to hear. "She needs a doctor real bad. She ain't
able to wake up."

The nurse, an older woman dressed in a dark blue gown,
with a white nurse's cap pinned in her hair, pointed to a row
of single beds against a wall. "Put her over there. A doctor
will be down to look at her shortly, although I'm afraid if she
has consumption there is precious little anyone can do . . ."

Riggs took Doris to a bed. Belle kept her hands clasped
tightly behind her, looking as if she were about to cry.

"Her name is Doris Green," Rose began, "and all her expenses will be paid by me. I'm Rose Denadale, and you'll
only have to present a bill for charges to the Cattlemen's Bank.
Ask for the president of the bank, Mr. Longley. I want this
woman to have the best care you can give her." She looked
down a hall. "And now, if you'll be so kind as to direct me
to Marshal Hull's room, I'll look in on him."

Before the nurse responded, Belle turned to Rose with tears
in her eyes.

"I won't ever forget how nice you're bein' to us," Belle
said, sniffling once.

Rose put an arm around her, patting her gently on the back.
"There, there, Belle. Don't cry. I'm sure they'll do as much
as they can for her."

The girl buried her face in Rose's neck. "I promise I'll try
real hard to make money so I can pay you back," she whispered so no one else could hear.

"I know you will, my dear. Wait here for me while I see

how Cordel is doing. Don't worry so much. Everything will turn out for the best . . . for both of us.''

"The marshal's upstairs,'' their nurse said, with just a hint of disgust in her voice—something Rose was accustomed to, when other women knew who she was.

"Thank you,'' she replied, hugging Belle one more time before she walked down the hallway to a staircase.

She was directed to Cordel's room by another nurse, who told her Cordel was sleeping.

"He's been given morphine for his pain, so he don't wake up all that often,'' she said, opening a door to a private room with a view of the city.

Rose walked to the foot of his bed. Cordel's face was the color of his white pillowcase. "What do the doctors have to say about his chances?'' A blood-encrusted bandage covered his left shoulder. He was sound asleep.

"It can go either way,'' the nurse said. "His deputy wasn't quite so lucky. He died a few hours ago.''

Rose forced herself to think of all possible consequences if Cordel didn't make it. Shaved cards would have to be taken from her dealers' tables and no more loaded dice could be used late at night when a gambler was too drunk to notice. An honest lawman would find the brake on her roulette wheel soon enough and that would change the odds considerably in her customers' favor.

"Too bad,'' she said absently, not really thinking about the deputy now. Unless Cordel returned to his duties before the fall cattle drives began, the Pink Lady and a few other establishments like hers faced lost revenues.

I'll still have my girls, she thought. Belle would bring men flocking to her doors. It was time to get Belle ready for a select group of wealthy men. The girl was a godsend, coming at a perfect time. A shooting like the one at the Lady could bring an establishment down, unless something was done to lure customers back. A beautiful girl was the answer. And now she had one . . .

25

Cody was mad at himself when he lost their tracks. Where a pair of horses entered the Trinity River, dim hoofprints were easy to read, but no matter how carefully he combed both sides of the river, he couldn't find where Curry and a swindler wanted in Ohio named Jimmy Foster had ridden out. Ten posse men rode back and forth on the north riverbank looking for tracks, and no one found anything at all, not a single print. Curry and Foster couldn't have kept to the water very far, since horses weren't much as swimmers, yet somehow they had left it without a trace.

A posse man named Leland Sikes rode over on a winded bay. "I can't find no sign of 'em," he said, watching the riverbank with a frown puckering his leathery face. He'd told Cody about going up the Chisholm dozens of times, and that because of it he'd be a good tracker, having chased stray steers all over Indian territory and parts of Kansas.

"Me either. It's damn near like their horses sprouted wings so they could fly outa here."

"I figure they rode the shallows fer a few miles downstream till they found a stretch of rock someplace. They'd head north fer Injun territory soon as they could, so the law couldn't touch 'em after they crossed the Red."

"That's as good a guess as any," Cody agreed, gazing north. "We'll never catch up to 'em now if they're well mounted. Might just as well go back an' give Mayor Tompkins the bad news. Only thing in our favor is that Curry's wounded. He might stop to see after that bullet hole sometime. Can't say if there'd be much of a chance we'd find him. I reckon it kinda depends on how sickly he's feelin'.''

"I could sure use a piece of that hundred-dollar reward,'' Sikes said. "If it's all the same to you, I believe I'll keep on lookin'.''

"Suit yourself. I'll ride back to town to tell the mayor we lost their tracks. I'll tell him that some of you are gonna keep searchin' for hoofprints.''

"There's four of us who'll stick together,'' Sikes promised. "If any of the others care to ride along, they'll do it on their own, I s'pose.''

Cody reined his dun for the river. "Be real careful if you happen to run across Curry. He's still dangerous, even with a hole in him. It didn't appear him'n Foster took any rifles from the marshal's office, but I wouldn't count on 'em bein' without a long gun.'' He heeled his gelding down to the water and urged it into muddy shallows, wondering how angry Mayor Tompkins would be when he heard they'd lost both fugitives. When Tompkins swore him in as a full-fledged deputy, he hadn't said anything about not wanting the job. The mayor knew about Dave's craziness, calling it "black marks'' on his record. If someone else took over as the city marshal, Cody thought he might stay on for a spell, needing money the way he did.

His dun began to swim and he slid out of his saddle to free it of a load. A good river horse was worth its weight in gold to a cowboy who couldn't swim. Clinging to his saddle horn, he let his horse do the work, floating beside it across a short stretch of deep water, too tired after a night without rest to think of anything other than sleep.

It was dark when he got to the office. Newt and another man wearing a tin star were sitting on the front porch. Cody swung down from his saddle and tested his legs, finding them stiff from long hours aboard a horse.

"I take it you didn't find 'em,'' Newt said offhandedly, with a wad of tobacco balled in his cheek.

"Just tracks, an' then we couldn't find where they come out of the river.'' He tied off his dun and sat down beside Newt with sleep tugging his eyelids. "We figure they headed north to cross the Red. Curry knows there'll be a bunch of men lookin' for him, so he'll keep movin'."

Newt shook his head. "We just got word that Marshal Hull's deputy passed away this mornin'. Makes Curry two times a killer. The marshal ain't doin' so good hisself."

Cody took off his hat, sleeving sweat from his forehead, and then he leaned against a porch post. "At least he's still alive. It's a shame Cole had to die. This job sure as hell don't allow a man no carelessness."

Newt spat into the dust. "I was supposed to tell you 'bout what happened to Miss Annabelle. She an' her ma got robbed by a gent on a mule last night. Took every cent of their money. She asked me to mention it to you. We looked for that feller whilst we was lookin' for Curry. Never saw nobody fit the description she gave us. She was mighty upset by it. Said her ma was real sickly, needin' to go to the hospital."

He'd been thinking about her off and on all day, and when he heard what Newt said, he sat upright. "I can let her have part of that fifty-dollar reward money, I reckon. I feel sorry for her." He got up and slipped the knot in his reins. "I'll ride over to their wagon. If you see Deputy Watkins, tell him we lost Curry's tracks at the river. After I talk to Annabelle, I'll look him up so I can tell him about it."

Newt stood up, dusting off the seat of his pants. He looked so different, wearing a badge. "Dave's talkin' to the mayor down at City Hall. He's madder'n hell 'cause Mayor Tomp-kins won't let him be the actin' city marshal until Cordel Hull gets better. He stomped off like he was fixin' to quit his job unless they gave him what he wanted."

Cody stepped in a stirrup and pulled himself slowly over his saddle. "Don't get in Dave's way while he's mad," he said as he gathered his reins to ride off.

"That's a natural fact," the cowboy seated beside Newt said quickly, like he knew all about Dave's bad temper. "Dave ain't got a lick of sense when anybody gets his tail feathers ruffled an' he's sure as hell liable to explode. The only feller he'd listen to was Marshal Hull, an' with him laid up there's

no way to stop what he'll do next. Unless somebody kills him
first.''

Too tired to continue the discussion, Cody waved to Newt
and headed for the campground. He wouldn't let himself think
about Dave right now, not until he found out how Annabelle
was doing. Without any money, she and her mother faced
mighty tough times. By offering her some of his reward earnings, he could help them get by for a spell, and maybe soften
Mrs. Green's objections to his interest in her daughter.

Before he reached their wagon, he knew something was
amiss. No fires burned underneath any of the kettles. He found
no one there and sat his horse for a time, puzzling over what
had become of them, where they might be. He remembered
Newt said the woman needed to see a doctor, and about the
only place they'd find one tonight was the hospital. Reining
north, he set out to make an inquiry there, before he told
Mayor Tompkins what had happened in the search for Curry
and Foster.

Riding through the center of town, he gave in to fatigue and
slumped in his saddle, resting his palms on the saddle horn.
He'd been without sleep for forty hours or more, and unless
he got some shuteye soon, he risked falling off his horse.

The route he followed took him past City Hall. When he
came to the square, he saw a group of men gathered around
Mayor Tompkins, some carrying flaming torches or lanterns.
He could hear a few angry voices before he rode up. County
Sheriff Homer Casey was there on the steps beside Tompkins,
trying to calm a mob of thirty or forty citizens.

''Something's gotta be done!'' someone shouted.

''This bloodshed has to be stopped!'' another cried.

Cody reined to a halt at one of several hitching posts where
dozens more horses were tied; he listened to what was being
said as he swung down to tie his dun.

''This town ain't no decent place to live, Sheriff!'' a man
holding a torch insisted. ''Our wives and children won't be
safe on city streets until those desperados are caught and
hung.''

A murmur of agreement spread through the crowd while

Cody walked toward Tompkins and Casey. Sheriff Casey held up both hands for quiet.

"We're doin' everything we can," he said. "We've got posses scourin' the countryside, an' men ridin' regular patrols throughout the city. George Curry is badly wounded, an' Foster ain't a danger, just a small-time thief wanted up north for sellin' phony shares in a gold mine. Jake Ketchum is dead, so there ain't a thing to worry about, most likely. Curry's on the run. If he's got any sense, he won't come back."

Cody wasn't so sure, hearing the sheriff's predictions. If Curry wanted that map to the buried money, he might make another try at reaching Allene Wright sometime soon. Edging his way up to Mayor Tompkins, Cody wondered if keeping an eye on Allene was a way to recapture Curry.

Tompkins saw him and quickly beckoned Cody to the top step beside him.

"Here's the deputy who shot Curry and killed Jake Ketchum, boys. Let's listen to what he has to say."

It was evident the mayor wanted attention on someone else at the moment. All eyes fell on Cody now and the crowd quieted down a bit. He felt edgy with so many people watching him, listening to what he was about to tell them.

He cleared his throat, suddenly wide awake. "Flatnose Curry is hurt pretty serious, so I don't figure he'll look for any more trouble . . ."

"Then how come he killed Bud Adams?" someone demanded.

Cody thought about it. "He was cornered, tryin' to steal a horse so he could get away. He was shootin' his way out of that stable when Adams got hit. It was mostly bad luck for Adams."

A man standing at the edge of the crowd pointed to Cody and said, "I seen this feller marchin' Curry to jail last night. He paraded him right past me with a gun against his backbone. I'll give him his due, boys. He handled himself right well."

A few whispered voices asked who Cody was, before the mayor spoke again. "I'm asking you to go back home and let us handle this the proper way. Raising a ruckus now serves no purpose, and if you'll be patient, Deputy Wade and Sheriff Casey can do their jobs. We'll find George Curry sooner or later, and when we do, I give you my word we'll hang him for what he's done. I've spoken with Judge Warren and he has assured me a speedy trial for Curry and whoever helped him escape. Go home, so our peace officers can get on with their business.''

Slowly, by twos and threes, men began leaving. The man who'd spoken for Cody came over and shook his hand before he left, saying, ''You done yourself proud, mister.''

Cody thanked him while the others moved away. When no one else was in listening distance, he turned to Mayor Tompkins and the sheriff. ''We lost their tracks at the river. We tracked 'em to the east side of town, where they made it look like they meant to cross over, only we never found where they rode out or horse tracks of any kind. It's pretty certain they'll head north to Indian territory so Texas lawmen can't come after 'em. Curry is bleedin' real bad, so I don't look for him to be no more of the same kind of trouble. He was lookin' for a woman here, an' now I know where to find her. Maybe if I talked to her, she'd tell me somethin' that might help us.''

Tompkins nodded. ''Handle it any way you see fit, Mr. Wade. As of today, you're empowered to conduct an investigation into this matter, so long as you act within the law.''

He grinned self-consciously. ''I'm not all that well acquainted with the law, Mayor Tompkins. Truth is, I hadn't made no plans to learn about it, really. But I reckon I can ask the sheriff if I need to know anything special.''

Sheriff Casey agreed, saying, ''You can count on my help if you need it. Tell me about this woman . . .''

He decided to fill Casey in on everything he knew. ''A woman named Allene Wright is someone Curry was lookin' for, on account of she's supposed to have this map showin' where some money was hid. Marshal Hull an' me figured it was stolen money, maybe from a bank robbery. I found Allene Wright workin' at the Pink Lady, only Curry found out, too. That's what he was doin' there last night, when me an' the

marshal and Cole Webb showed up. It was a bad coincidence
for Marshal Hull an' Cole.''

"Where's the woman now?'' Casey asked.

"I never got around to findin' out. Those three broke jail
an' I've been chasin' Curry ever since.''

"I'll ask Rose Denadale about her,'' Casey said, rubbing
his unshaven chin like he was thinking. "In the mornin' I'll
send a few of my deputies to scout the river for tracks, just
to see if you overlooked anything.''

"I'd call myself a decent tracker, Sheriff,'' he said, a bit
put off by Casey's remark. "We combed every inch of that
river best we could.''

Casey gave him a steely look. "You look young. Sometimes a man with experience is called for. Besides that, outside
of town this falls under my jurisdiction.'' He nodded to Mayor
Tompkins and went down the steps without saying another
word.

Cody shrugged, speaking to the mayor. "I don't know much
of anything 'bout jurisdiction, but I know how to read sign.
Can't see how it matters how old I am.''

Tompkins watched the sheriff walk across Main Street in
the dark. "Don't take offense, Mr. Wade. Homer came real
close to losing an election the last time he ran for office. He
never got along with Cordel, making it a rivalry, so to speak,
between the sheriff's job and the city marshal's. Take whatever steps you feel are necessary to find George Curry. Getting
him caught is all that matters.''

"I'll start lookin' at first light,'' Cody said. "Right now
I've gotta get some sleep. I'll question that woman tomorrow.
I think she'll know somethin' about where Curry aims to hide
until his shoulder heals.''

Tompkins merely grunted and pursed his lips as he went
back up the steps, leaving Cody alone in front of City Hall to
collect his horse before he went to bed. He'd meant to inquire
as to the whereabouts of Annabelle and her mother tonight,
but as tired as he was now, he decided it would have to wait
until morning.

As he mounted up and rode east to put his horse away for

the night, he thought about Jake Ketchum, that he'd killed him, and what Jake looked like lying there with a hole through his chest. It was bothering him more than he wished it would, facing up to the idea he was a killer now. It should have mattered that Jake didn't give him a choice, shooting at him first, trying to kill him in the dark with a coward's shot from hiding. But no matter how Cody examined what happened, there was something about being a killer he didn't cotton to at all.

26

Her reflection seemed a bit fuzzy, indistinct, and she felt
dizzy when she moved her head too quickly. She stood before
the mirror wearing Miss Rose's red dress, stockings, and red
leather shoes, looking for all the world like someone else, a
much older woman with large breasts and painted lips and hair
done up in a fan of ringlets held in place by red ribbon. Under
the dress she had on a corset drawn tight around her middle
so that it squeezed her bosom, showing more cleavage where
the gown was cut low in front.

"I look different," she said. Her voice sounded husky, not
like her own.

"You look pretty." Miss Rose said it like she meant every
word.

A hot bath and two more glasses of wine had made her
arms and legs feel like licorice sticks, sort of wobbly and loose
so they didn't work just right.

"Thank you, ma'am," she said, turning a bit so she could
see the rounding of her buttocks, and high heel, lace-up shoes
making her much taller. "It's this dress . . ."

"It isn't the dress, my dear. You are a beautiful woman, so
very beautiful even without the dress."

She remembered seeing herself in the mirror wearing only
a corset and stockings, and how naughty she felt while looking
at her reflection when she was only half-dressed. Miss Rose
was so right about how wine helped her get past being anxious
over her first time with a paying customer. "I don't feel nervous hardly at all. I ain't nearly as scared as I was."

"A proper lady doesn't say ain't, Belle. I'm going to teach

you how to speak correctly, like a lady should. I'll show you how to sit in a chair so a gentleman can see a little bit of your legs without showing too much. These are things you'll need to learn.''

"I'll try to remember. I never did think I could learn to act like a proper lady, seein' as I didn't know how a real lady is supposed to act.''

"It will take time. Do you think you're ready to see your first gentleman caller?''

She took a deep breath, still gazing at her image in soft lamplight. She'd pushed Cody from her thoughts earlier in the evening, but just now he was there again even though she didn't want to think about him, about what she was doing. "I sure hope he's a nice man, Miss Rose. I hope he'll understand when I ain't all that sure what to do right at first.''

"He's a gentleman. I'm quite sure he'll be patient with you from the beginning. He's a very important man in this town, but you'll only be told his first name. His name is Frank, and he's an older gentleman. When he comes to your room, you let him in, and remember to smile. Be friendly and your callers will be the same with you. Ask him to sit on the edge of the bed, and offer him a glass of wine. Turn down the lamp a little and then begin taking off your dress. He may want you to help him out of his clothes. After that, just do what comes naturally. Remember to take your time . . . don't rush things. And don't ask him for any money. I'll take care of that part before he comes to see you.''

"I reckon you can show me that room now, Miss Rose. I'm as ready as I'm ever gonna be, I suppose.''

Rose smiled and got up from her dressing table. "You'll like the room, Belle. I'm giving you a special room, reserved for our very best customers. It will be yours from now on.''

Annabelle turned away from the mirror, having some trouble walking in high heels as she followed Rose into the hallway, then to a door marked number 5.

Sipping wine while sitting at her own dressing table, complete with hairbrush and comb and a tin of rouge, she heard a soft knock. She glanced in the mirror and got up, unsteady in her borrowed heels, feeling dizzy from another glass of sweet port. She'd been thinking about her ma just then, how a doctor said there was nothing he could do for her besides making her as comfortable as possible, and giving her pain-killers. Tomorrow she would be taken by ambulance to Fitsimmons Rooming House in a quiet part of town, where a woman named Ruth would see after her. Doris wouldn't be in any more pain and she'd never be hungry or sleeping out in the weather or doing another kettle of someone else's dirty laundry on a rub board.

Annabelle paused near the door, admiring a canopied bed, a cast iron bathtub, a satin dressing screen, and the dark purple rug that matched her bedspread. Her room was every bit as beautiful as the one Miss Rose had.

It's mine, she thought, feeling a rush of pleasure, steadying herself with the doorknob when she felt dizzy.

Someone knocked again.

"It'll be Frank," she whispered, driving every other thought from her mind, reminding herself not to say "ain't" if she could help it. Smiling, she opened the door a crack.

An overfed man in a vested suit held out a small box wrapped in white paper with a bow made of golden ribbon around it. He offered her the box and bowed politely. "My name is Frank and I was told you're expecting me," he said. "This is for you, Belle. I was told you liked perfume . . ."

She took his present, still holding on to the door when it felt as though she might fall off her high heels. "Why, thank you, Frank," she whispered. "Please do come in." Her heart was beating rapidly now in spite of the wine.

He came through her door quickly and took out his handkerchief to mop his sweating brow. "Hot out tonight," he told her. His eyes fell to her bosom, remaining there a moment as she was closing the door. "Rose was right about you. Quite right indeed if you don't mind my saying so. You are a gorgeous young woman if ever I saw one. So feminine, so dainty. That's a beautiful dress you're wearing, and you have lovely hair."

"Thank you," Annabelle said, trying not to pay much attention to Frank's large stomach, his fleshy jowls or the gray pallor of his wrinkled skin. She looked at her present. "May I open it now?" she asked.

"Of course, my dear." He took off his coat and tossed in on the bed, unfastening his bow tie, then a top button on his wilted white shirt collar. "It isn't much, but Rose told me you wanted something with a nice scent."

She walked to her dressing table, being careful not to fall. She removed the bright ribbon and placed it gently with her brush and comb, thinking how nice the ribbon would look in her hair. A moment was needed to open the tiny box, where she found a bottle of lilac water. After opening it, she placed a dab behind each ear. "That's very nice of you, Frank," she said. "Would it be the right time to offer you a glass of wine?"

He nodded, watching her with interest. "I'd like some wine on a night like this, being it's so awfully hot." He sat down on the edge of her mattress without ever taking his eyes off her.

"It is hot," she agreed, walking uncertain steps to a table beside her bed where port and a clean glass sat next to a lamp. She turned down the lamp's wick and poured wine for him without spilling any of it.

She'd forgotten to smile and did so quickly. Now that the room was darker, she felt better, less concerned about how she was expected to act. "Are you ready for me to take off my dress?" she asked, standing in front of him, feeling as though he'd begun to undress her with his eyes.

"That would be . . . nice," he said quietly, staring at the tops of her breasts where they showed above her gown.

Reaching for fasteners in back, she opened them slowly, one at a time until the dress fell down on her hips. She wriggled it off and stepped out of it while her heart continued to race. That warm feeling began in her groin, spreading, filling her with excitement the way it always did, although at the same time she hoped Frank was not disappointed when he saw her, how slender she was.

"Let me open your corset," he breathed, gulping down wine as he reached for her corset strings, his hands trembling.

She stepped a little closer, smiling down at him. "You can do might' near whatever you want, Frank, only I ain't . . . I never done this before, not for money."

He flashed a quick grin. "That's real special, Belle, being I'm your first one. I won't forget it. I'll be generous when I come to see you every week."

"You'll come every week?" It sounded like a lot of visits, but he would also be spending a great deal of money if he came to see her so often.

He loosened her laces, his eyes rounding when he saw more of her breasts where her corset opened in front. Using two fingers, he pulled it down so her nipples were exposed. "I'd like to see you every week if that's okay, Belle. If you'd want me to."

She wasn't prepared for it when he leaned closer and put his lips over a nipple, sucking it gently. A tingling sensation went from her breast to the pit of her stomach. "That feels so good, Frank," she sighed, telling herself the devil inside her made her say it.

Seconds later he drew back. "Lie down on the bed, Belle, so I can lie beside you," he told her hoarsely, breathing a little faster than he was before.

She did as he asked, pulling back her bedspread so they had clean linen sheets beneath them. She sat down and untied laces on both shoes before she took them off. Frank opened his shirt in a bit of a hurry and tossed it carelessly to the floor. He kept staring at her breasts like he'd never seen anything like them before. His chest and stomach were flabby, quivering when he moved about, and his white skin had a sweaty sheen to it that made him look like he'd been out in the rain naked.

Annabelle smiled, raising her slender legs to the mattress. "You seem like a real nice man, Frank," she said, stretching out so he could see her white silk stockings—he wasn't paying much attention to anything but her bosom and that came as a surprise.

He pulled off his shoes and lay down next to her, resting

on an elbow with his belly sagging grotesquely. "You're quite the beautiful one," he said, "and I'm always nice to beautiful ladies. I can be very generous, too, to a lady who's somebody special to me."

As he cupped one breast in a quivering palm, Annabelle felt herself shivering. "Maybe I can be that special lady, Frank. I promise I'll try real hard to be somebody special, only I ain't sure I know how." She'd forgotten again not to say "ain't" in a gentleman caller's presence, but Frank didn't seem to mind. Her heart was beating so rapidly it felt as if it would burst inside her chest and she was sure Frank could feel it hammering with the hand covering her nipple.

Without any warning he reached for her corset and pulled it down roughly, frightening her when he did it so suddenly. He had a glassy look in his eyes, staring at her stomach and the swirl of dark hair between her thighs.

"I can't wait any longer," he said, breathing harder as he opened the front of his pants.

She hadn't expected things to happen so quickly. Frank was panting, pulling her legs apart before she realized he was about to enter her. His weight threatened to crush her when he lay on her rib cage, probing her soft inner parts with his member while shaking from head to toe, sweating profusely. He grunted a few times, moving back and forth and making bedsprings squeak, then he stiffened, closing his eyes so tightly he had the look of someone who was in terrible pain.

Annabelle struggled to breathe, feeling something warm and wet inside. "Are you okay, Frank?" she gasped, wondering why he was grimacing, why his eyes were closed.

He relaxed, taking several deep breaths. "I'm fine, my darling," he murmured, smiling now. "That was wonderful. You made me feel so good. You're everything Rose said you would be."

She couldn't imagine what she'd done that was so wonderful, since he'd hardly got started before it was over. "I'm so glad you ain't disappointed, seein' it was my first time an' all."

Pushing up on his palms, he gazed down at her. "You were

absolutely splendid, Belle.'' Malodorous perspiration dripped
off him onto her chest, her neck and face while he spoke. ''I
could not have asked for anything more.'' He withdrew from
her and then rolled to one side of the bed, still having difficulty
breathing.

Sticky fluid seeped down her inner thighs. There had been
no pain, only a growing feeling of humiliation. ''I'm real glad
you liked me,'' she whispered, glancing over to the washstand
and a pitcher of water, remembering what Miss Rose told her
to do as soon as a caller finished. She willed herself to think
about the money and nothing else, not the fat man's jelly running out of her or how it got there.

Frank got up and donned his shoes and shirt as though he
was in something of a hurry. Annabelle covered herself with
a towel and lay there watching him dress, controlling an urge
to cry.

''I'll be seeing you again soon, Belle,'' he said, coming over
to the bed, kissing her lightly on the cheek. He took a five-
dollar banknote from his pocket and placed it on her washstand. ''Here's a little something extra for you, my darling,
because you were so sweet.'' He smiled and went to the door,
letting himself out.

As soon as the door closed, tears began rolling down her
face before she could do anything to halt them. Swinging her
legs off the bed, she covered her eyes with her hands, sobbing
softly in the room's heavy silence. Her thoughts were a confused maze of contradictions, wanting Cody now more than
she ever had before, and at the same time thinking how her
ma wasn't suffering the way she had before the doctor gave
her painkillers. She wanted to live in this beautiful room, own
nice dresses and shoes, have money to spend. But was all that
worth what she'd had to do in order to get it?

When a breeze gently lifted the curtains away from a win-
dow beside her bed, she got up and looked out at the night.
Somewhere in the Acre a piano kept time to the beat of a
drum, banging out a fast melody. Staring across dark rooftops,
Annabelle dried her eyes, feeling the breeze dry her skin where
Frank's sweat had fallen on her body, listening to the music

play without really hearing it. Her mind was on other things, on the decision she'd made.

"It's done," she said to a sky full of stars, as though she thought someone up there might be listening.

27

He was sleeping soundly in his tiny room in back of the jail when voices awakened him. Almost as a reflex he reached for the pistol hanging from a bedpost before he got up. Creeping forward cautiously, he made his way between empty cells in the dark until he could see what was going on outside. Four men, one holding a lantern, gathered around someone on the back of a horse—he had a rag tied over his mouth and his wrists were bound, although he bore no resemblance to Flat-nose Curry. Wearing nothing but his denims, Cody crossed the office floor, avoiding pieces of broken glass on his way to the door, padding softly in bare feet so that no one noticed him until he came out on the porch with his gun leveled.

When he got a closer look, he recognized Jimmy Foster as the man who was bound and gagged. Four cowboys wearing tin stars surrounded Foster as he was pulled off his horse by Leland Sikes. Sikes saw Cody and said, "Look what we found in this ol' barn north of the river, hidin' up in the loft like he was a treed possum."

Cody lowered his gun. Foster's head was bloody and he had bruises on his cheeks where a bandanna let them show. He was a man of slight stature, shivering in spite of the heat of a summer night, and Cody guessed he'd been given rough treatment by Sikes and his men. "Bring him inside," he told them. "Was there any sign of Curry?"

Sikes grinned a bit sheepishly. "We asked him, only he was hard to convince right at first. He claims Curry doubled back in the direction of town after they made the river. He swore on his mammy's grave he's tellin' the truth."

Cody knew where Curry would go if he got back to town. He'd find Allene Wright if he could. "That means he'll be headed over to the Pink Lady sooner or later. Soon as I lock Foster away an' get dressed, we'd better have a look."

Sikes ushered Foster up the steps at gunpoint, although it was easy to see a gun wasn't needed. Foster went willingly into the office, completely subdued by his ordeal at the hands of the four deputized cowboys. A young cowboy carrying a lantern came inside, waiting until Cody got a desk lamp lit before he extinguished his, resting it on the bench where Cole Webb used to sit.

"I'll untie his ropes," Sikes offered, giving Foster a cold stare. "He ain't goin' no place now, don't reckon."

Cody took cell keys from the desk drawer. "I'll lock him up an' take the keys with me, seein' as I can't lock that front door till we get a new windowpane. I've got this hunch Curry's gonna show up at the Pink Lady after a bit. He's in town lookin' for a particular woman . . ."

Sikes chuckled, shoving Foster toward the rows of cells. "He'd have to be plumb loco to risk his neck for a pretty gal after all the troubles he's had. Bein' lovesick's liable to put his neck in a noose this time."

Cody didn't bother explaining why Curry would come back. He wasn't loco or anything of the kind, merely determined to get his hands on that map to the hidden money before someone else got to it ahead of him. It was downright meanness that would give Curry enough nerve to come back to a town swarming with armed men who would shoot him on sight if he showed himself.

He locked Jimmy Foster in a cell and hurried to the back to dress and strap on his gunbelt. He found he was torn by different feelings when it came to Curry, wanting to settle a score for what he'd done to Cole and for wounding Marshal Hull, but on another side of things recalling how he'd felt after killing Jake Ketchum. Cody didn't want any more dead men on his conscience. And there was a chance Curry was fast enough to get off the first shot.

As he was sleeving into his shirt, he noticed the glimmer

of his badge in the light coming from the front office. He touched it briefly and thought about what wearing a badge meant. Becoming a peace officer had been the farthest thing from his mind when he and Newt rode up from Waco. In a matter of days everything got turned around, and now he was in just about the last profession on earth he would have chosen for himself.

They ran into Newt and four more posse men as Cody led Sikes and his partners toward the Pink Lady. Newt's eyes were hooded and he looked as tired as Cody felt. Newt halted his horse in the middle of the road, waiting for Cody to walk up.

"There's trouble in the makin' over at the Stockmen's," Newt said, resting an elbow on his saddle horn, "only it ain't comin' from no outlaws. That deputy by the name of Watkins is gettin' hisself wall-eyed drunk down yonder, tellin' anybody who'll sit an' listen that he's fed up with this here town. He says Mayor Tompkins won't let him be the actin' marshal till Cordel Hull's well enough to come back. He swears he's gonna tell the mayor to stick the deputy's job up his ass."

"It's none of my affair," Cody said, his mind on what they had heard about Curry doubling back at the river. He aimed a thumb at Leland Sikes. "These boys found the other escaped prisoner, and he told 'em Flatnose Curry rode back this way. Curry's dead set on talkin' to a woman named Allene Wright at the Pink Lady. If we keep an eye on the place, maybe somebody'll spot him."

Newt counted men wearing badges. "Means that reward has to be split eight ways ... nine, countin' you. We was sorta figurin' on collectin' that money ourselves, if we could get it done an' not get our heads blowed off."

"Nobody's gonna collect it unless we find him, Newt. Some of you keep an eye on the alley in back. Stay out of sight an' maybe he'll show up, if he thinks we ain't watchin' the place."

"I'll climb on the roof," Sikes offered. "Shorty, you can get on a roof across that alley so we'll have him in a cross fire if he comes round to the back."

To end any further discussion, Cody stepped around Newt and the posse men, moving quickly toward the middle of the Acre with Sikes and the others hurrying to catch up. Almost as an afterthought he drew his .44-.40 and opened the loading gate, making sure he carried six unfired cartridges in the chambers before any shooting started. He wasn't looking for a shooting contest with George Curry—Curry was fast, as fast as the eye could follow.

At a cross street half a block from the Pink Lady, Sikes and his cowboys turned off to cover the alley. Newt rode to a hitchrail and swung down, looking about as nervous as a man could be as he tied off his horse. Cody felt a little uneasy himself when he thought about the likelihood of a run-in with Curry, but with so many deputies covering the place, Curry would have to be a fool to make his move now.

Near the front steps he hesitated a moment, passing a look up and down both sides of the road, examining shadows underneath dark porches, making sure of things. Farther down the street he heard music coming from the Stockmen's, and remembered what Newt had said about Dave being there. It was late, well past midnight, a time when business in the Acre began to slow down. If Curry was coming, he'd wait even longer, until most places closed, to keep from being spotted.

Newt and three deputies took up positions across the road on benches with a view of the Lady's front door. Cody mounted the steps, meaning to talk to Rose Denadale before he asked to speak to Allene, so that Rose would know Curry might be headed back this way. When he turned the doorknob, he had a flashback of what had happened the last time he came here—in a matter of seconds guns had begun exploding and there was no time to think about what he was doing; he'd acted on nothing but instinct when he saw Curry holding a smoking gun.

The parlor smelled of cigar smoke. Cody went inside, halting near the door. A few gamblers sat at poker tables. A few more stood around the roulette wheel placing bets. At the back a dice table stood empty. Over at the bar, where love seats were arranged so girls could sit with patrons, Cody's gaze came to rest on one particular young woman in a silky red dress. He saw her and yet for a second or two his mind went blank, until he recognized her. Seated beside a man wearing a dark brown suit with a handlebar mustache flowing from his upper lip, Annabelle Green drank from a crystal goblet, smiling over something the man said.

Cody couldn't believe his eyes, not trusting what he saw. The hum of conversation in a crowded room prevented him from hearing her voice, but he knew his eyes were not playing tricks on him after he gave her a second look. She didn't notice him, paying attention to what the man seated next to her was saying, looking more beautiful than Cody ever imagined she could. Her hair was done up differently and her dress showed so much that she appeared to be almost naked on top.

Not until a moment later did he realize what finding her in the Pink Lady meant.

"She's a whore," he whispered to himself, and the discovery entered his heart like the tip of a knife blade. He was dumbstruck, unable to grasp that she was the same bashful girl he'd met down by the creek, a girl who hadn't known how to kiss until he showed her the way it was done.

He watched her take a sip of dark wine. He couldn't move—it was as if his feet were nailed to the floor. Something Newt told him, that Annabelle and her mother had been robbed by a man riding a mule, echoed through his memory.

She laughed, and looked in Cody's direction. Their eyes met, and suddenly the smile left Annabelle's face.

Her mouth dropped open. She stared at him as though no one else was in the parlor. For several seconds they simply looked at each other, until Annabelle came quickly to her feet.

She wheeled toward a staircase and said something to the man on the love seat before she hurried to the stairs as fast as she could, holding onto a polished railing, her face turned away from him. When she went out of sight on the second floor, he noted how closely he was being watched by the stranger she had been sitting with.

Rose Denadale, wearing a low-cut black gown and high heels, came from behind the bar. She looked at Cody, then up the stairs, seemingly puzzled by Annabelle's hasty disappearance, before she came toward him. She stopped and spoke to the man on the love seat briefly, smiling. But when she turned to Cody again, there was no smile on her face as she crossed the parlor.

"Why are you here?" she asked in an unfriendly way, her brow pinched, eyes darting between Cody and the front door.

For the time being he forgot about Annabelle to answer her question. "I've reason to believe George Curry is comin' back to see a woman who works for you by the name of Allene Wright. Her name was in a letter havin' somethin' to do with a man Curry shot the other night."

"Allene isn't here anymore. I fired her this morning."

"Curry might not know that, Miss Denadale. He could cause you a lot of trouble if he shows up lookin' for her."

"That's your job, Deputy, but I want you to do it outside my place. You'll run off my customers, if you stay. Gentlemen get nervous having the law around, so please go away. I'm paying good money for protection . . ." Her voice trailed off unexpectedly before she finished.

"I just thought you oughta know, ma'am. I'm new at this job so I ain't real clear how it's done. Some men will be watchin' from across the street an' up on your roof, in case he shows up."

Her frown deepened. "Are you an acquaintance of Belle's?"

"I don't know anybody named Belle, ma'am, but if you mean a girl named Annabelle, the one who ran upstairs all of a sudden, I reckon you could say we're acquainted some."

"I see. That may explain why she's upset. I do wish you'd have found a better time to come. I'd only introduced her to Mr. Longabaugh a moment ago."

Cody noticed that Longabaugh was still watching him with a great deal of interest. "I heard Annabelle an' her ma got robbed last night. Didn't appear they had much to start with, makin' things worse if a thief took what little bit they had."

"I've taken care of everything," Rose told him. "Her mother is being well cared for."

"I reckon that means she's workin' here for you, don't it?" He hooked his thumbs in his gunbelt when he felt his hands begin to shake, after learning Annabelle was, indeed, a working girl at the Pink Lady now.

"It really isn't any of your business what she does, Deputy. Now, if you don't mind, please leave, so my customers and my girls can get back to having a pleasant evening here, without interference from the law."

Cody backed away, ready to walk off at once. "Didn't mean to interfere, Miss Denadale. I only wanted you to know 'bout Curry. I'd be obliged if you told me where Miss Allene Wright went."

"I have no idea. Nor do I care. She's probably sucking off some old man in an alley someplace. That's all she's good for, in my opinion. She's an opium smoker and I won't allow it here at my place. I warned her a number of times."

He nodded and reached for the door. "Good evenin', ma'am. I wonder if you'd mind givin' my best regards to Miss Annabelle for me?"

"I'll try to remember. What did you say your name was?"

"I didn't say, but my name's Cody Wade. She'll know who I am. She'll remember."

He went out and closed the door behind him before his real feelings showed. Finding Annabelle in the Pink Lady had been such a shock he hadn't been able to think straight. He believed he knew her well enough to judge she wasn't the type to work in a whorehouse, but there was no denying what he had just heard and seen with his own two eyes.

He turned toward the jail without speaking to Newt or any of the other posse men. Right then he wanted to be alone. Trudging through the dark, he shook his head, feeling sad and a little bit lonely. Annabelle had seemed so sweet and innocent, not like any of the hardened crib women he'd known.

"Won't be long till she's just like the rest of 'em," he said to himself, making up his mind to forget her as quickly as he could.

28

Gray skies above the cemetery warned of rain, a fitting day for Coleman Webb's funeral, and the color of Cody's dark mood that morning. A preacher stood at the foot of Cole's casket with his Bible open, reading in a sonorous voice to a small group of mourners gathered around the grave. A few raindrops began to fall, pattering gently on the pine coffin and mounds of earth piled on either side of a six-foot hole where the body lay. The smell of rain grew stronger as the preacher turned to another page.

Cody stood beside Mayor Tompkins with his head bowed as a gust of wind swept dust and loose soil over the gravesite. Prior to the funeral they had been talking about last night's events, the capture of Foster and what Sikes had learned regarding Curry's whereabouts. Mayor Tompkins related that Dave Watkins had stormed into his office early this morning to turn in his badge, leaving Cody as the only deputy city marshal. Tompkins asked Cody if he intended to stay on for a while, seeing as the city marshal's office was shorthanded. The way his question was worded made Cody feel a sense of obligation to Cordel Hull, who was reported to be improving slightly, with chances looking much better he'd recover. If it hadn't been for finding Annabelle at the Pink Lady last night, Cody might have felt a little better about things in general. But as he'd tossed and turned on his cot until dawn with memories of Annabelle wearing that revealing red dress floating through his light sleep, he'd awakened in a dreary mood and it followed him to Cole's funeral. Newt had stopped by before Cody rode out to the cemetery, to say Curry hadn't shown

himself in the Acre before daylight. Sikes and some of his
men were still watching the Lady, but no one believed Curry
would be so brazen as to come during the day. Newt had gone
to his boardinghouse to get some sleep, after asking Cody what
was wrong. Cody knew he wasn't doing a very good job of
hiding the way he felt after discovering Annabelle at Rose
Denadale's, although he didn't say anything to Newt about it.

"Ashes to ashes and dust to dust," the preacher said, as he
closed his Bible and tossed a handful of dirt into the hole
where Cole's coffin rested. "Amen."

A soft chorus of amens came from the mourners. Cody took
a last look at the grave and put on his Stetson, just as more
rain began to pelt leaves on a nearby pecan tree, rattling down
on his hat brim, splattering on the ground around his boots,
and making tiny puffs of dust arise where drops fell. He turned
away from the grave to find Mayor Tompkins watching him.

"I've asked the City Council to approve my request making
you acting city marshal until Cordel is better," Tompkins said.
"I sent a wire down to Waco inquiring about you. According
to the district attorney you have no criminal record, so that
clears you to act in any official capacity here."

"I hadn't thought about bein' city marshal. I hardly know
beans about the law. Seems like a marshal oughta know what's
legal an' what ain't."

Tompkins nodded, like he understood. "The main thing
we're after while Cordel is laid up is having someone who
can keep the peace, in particular down in the Acre. While I'll
admit you're a bit inexperienced, you've shown an uncanny
knack for handling the violent men who frequent those establishments. We need someone who isn't afraid of tough characters, someone who can handle a gun without shooting
everyone in sight. Dave Watkins has shown an incurable pen-
chant for killing which keeps us from considering him for the
position, even on a temporary basis. Cordel seems to be the
only man who can control him. We can't let Watkins turn our
streets into a shooting gallery. You'll be authorized to hire a
pair of deputies. Subject to City Council approval, of course.
Until Cordel is able to return to his duties, you'll be paid one

hundred and fifty dollars a month, plus necessary expenses while running the city jail. I assure you it's a generous offer, and come election time, who knows what might happen? If you ran for city marshal, you could get elected by thousands of this city's grateful citizens. On a permanent basis, that job will pay two hundred a month. I want you to think it over very carefully. Cordel was awake this morning when I went to see him and he asked if you'd stop by. I filled him in on what you've done while he was unconscious. He told me he knew all along you had the makings of a good peace officer.''

Cody tilted his hat into the wind while he thought about the mayor's proposition. Rain came down harder, soaking his shirt to his skin. "I suppose I can drop by to talk to the marshal about it, only it still seems like I oughta know somethin' about what's legal before I took on that kind of responsibility . . .''

"Let me put it to you this way, Cody," Tompkins explained as they started toward the cemetery fence. "It isn't so terribly important that you know the letter of the law in that job, only that you can handle . . . difficult situations when they arise. And as you know, they do arise fairly often in Hell's Half Acre. We need to be sure it's under control down there. Otherwise, some of our city fathers will raise a stink. The Acre is good for the city's business climate. It brings in outside money from passing cowherds, money our town wouldn't have if we didn't offer those cowboys what they're looking for. As mayor of Fort Worth I see it as my civic duty to do what's best for us. For businessmen who would suffer without the cattlemen's money.''

They had walked side by side to Cody's dun gelding tethered to a picket post before he said anything more. "I'll talk to Marshal Hull about it. Thanks for the offer. I'll think it over, like you said." He slipped the knot in his reins and mounted, giving the sky a quick look. "I'll let you know what I decide when I get done thinkin'." Swinging his horse away from the fence, he turned up his collar to keep out the rain and heeled his dun for the hospital.

"You'll be glad you accepted," Tompkins said as he rode off.

Right then, Cody wasn't quite so sure.

• • •

Cordel Hull looked more dead than alive. His face was the color of milk and his cheeks had a sunken look. He peered up at Cody through drooping eyelids as soon as a nurse showed Cody into his room.

"You're lookin' a sight better'n the last time," Cody said, holding his rain-soaked hat in his hand. Raindrops fell against a windowpane next to the marshal's bed. The hospital room was hot, stuffy, reeking of medicine smells.

"I hear Curry got away." Hull's voice was hoarse. "He'll need a doctor, bleeding like he was. Somebody'll have to take the bullet out. Keep an eye on that horse doctor's place. Doc Grimes don't ask many questions so long as he gets paid."

"I'll do that, Marshal. We found out Curry rode a circle back toward town. The feller who broke jail with him said Curry headed back this way. I figure he'll try an' talk to that woman mentioned in the letter we found on Davis, lookin' for her map."

"He's got balls, don't he?" Hull remarked, wincing when he raised his head off the pillow to watch it rain. He looked up at Cody. "Frank told me he's offering you the acting city marshal's job until I get back on the job."

"He did, only I ain't sure I'll take it. That's a big dose of responsibility. Worst is, I don't know a damn thing about the law. When I told him, he said it don't matter. He wants things kept quiet down in the Acre."

Hull's gaze drifted down to Cody's gun. "You can handle it. You've got nerve, and you can damn sure shoot straight. Besides that you aren't scared of trouble, and that's real important when you're dealing with men who think they're tough. The doc told me I'd be back on my feet in a couple of weeks. I'd consider it a personal favor if you'd take over till I'm able to make it down to the office."

Cody had hoped it wouldn't become personal, making it easier to decline the job. "I ain't all that sure I'm cut out to be a lawman, Marshal. To tell the truth it's kinda dangerous. I got shot at my first day, when I had Curry an' Ketchum cornered over at the livery. It sorta got me to thinkin' . . . ."

"You never ducked lead before?"

"Never did." He didn't want to admit he was frightened when a bullet flew past his ear, but it was better to come clean than to bite off more than he could chew. "Like I said, it got me to thinkin' maybe I ain't as fearless as I figured I was."

"Being scared of a bullet is natural, Cody. It's a healthy thing. The right amount of fear will help keep you alive in this profession. A man who don't respect a gun won't last long. You can hire a couple of deputies to even the odds against you. I'll have to approve them first, now that Cole's gone. Too bad about Cole. He shoulda been more careful. I suppose the same can be said about me. I stepped in that place before I knew what was on both sides of the door. It damn near cost me everything."

"Seems to me like, the way Mayor Tompkins put things, I'd be nearly the same as a hired gun for the city of Fort Worth, not a regular peace officer who knows about the law."

Hull cracked a weak grin. "That's about all any lawman is, when you get right down to it. You balance things. Gentler folk don't like getting their hands dirty, so they hire men like you and me to protect them from lawless types. In my opinion there's no shame attached to it, standing up for peaceful citizens when they aren't able to do it themselves. You can learn the law as time goes by."

Cody's eyes wandered to the window while he thought about it. He supposed he could study law books if he meant to stay on with the marshal's office. "I reckon I can give it a try for a week or two. I'd like to hire a pardner of mine, Newt Sims, as one of my deputies. I've known him for years an' I trust him."

"Suit yourself," Hull said quietly, resting his head on the pillow again. "I'm sure Frank told you Dave quit this morning. Dave's too hot-tempered to handle affairs by himself, so it's probably for the best. Take Sims to Frank's office so he can be sworn in. Tell Frank I approve of him."

"They already swore him in to hunt for Curry, but I'll take him by the mayor's office anyhow."

"The pay's eighty a month. Frank said you'll get a hundred and fifty until I get back."

"I can't promise I'll stay, Marshal. But I'll give it the best I've got."

Hull appeared to remember something. "Frank also said you killed Jake Ketchum that night, while they were trying to get out of town. That was a nice piece of work. Too bad you didn't get a clean shot at Curry."

Cody couldn't tell him he had that clean shot for a moment, that he'd been too scared to take it. "I'm not much on killin' somebody who ain't tryin' real hard to kill me."

"You had a chance to kill him down at Rose's that night, if you'd gotten everyone else out of the room . . ."

Cody remembered what the marshal had asked him to do. "He was wounded. Wasn't no fight left in him right then. I just ain't able to kill a man who's defenseless."

Hull's expression darkened. "Some men need killing. If you wear a badge long enough, you'll begin to see it my way. There comes a time when the law of the gun is the only law they understand."

He wasn't going to argue it now. "I reckon I'd best get to the office. I busted out a window when I didn't have a key so's I could lock Curry away. Somebody was watchin'. Soon as I went to get a doctor for Curry, they opened all the cells. That's how the jailbreak come about. I'll ask the mayor 'bout fixin' that window soon as I get back. I got a key to the door now, when I went to the undertaker's for Cole's personal things."

"I'm mighty glad you're staying on, Cody. I'll rest better knowing the job's in good hands."

"Hope you feel better real soon, Marshal." He put on his hat and walked out of the room, wondering if he'd done the right thing for all concerned. He wasn't quite convinced as he took the stairs two at a time to the ground floor.

His horse stood hipshot under an elm tree, its head lowered while rain continued to fall. Cody waited in a doorway of the hospital for the shower to end. With time on his hands, he thought about Annabelle, how much it hurt to find out she was working at the Lady. Leaning against a door frame, he wished things could have turned out differently for her. He concluded, after a bit of thinking on the subject, that she probably felt she had no choice. With a sick mother to care for and no money after being robbed by some stranger passing by on a mule, she took the only way out of the fix she was in. It would be wrong to blame her, but he knew he couldn't feel the same way toward her from now on.

She'll turn hard as nails, he thought. There was no point in thinking about her any longer, since no man could have feelings for a whore. She belonged to whoever could pay the price for a few moments of her company.

The rain slacked off a bit as skies brightened in the west. When he grew tired of thinking about Annabelle, Cody walked to his horse, and mounted a rain-slick saddle. If he aimed to be the city marshal for Fort Worth, he had work to do, a deputy to hire along with Newt, if Newt wanted the job. And there was a window to fix at the jail, besides an escaped killer to hunt down—plenty to keep him occupied.

He rode away from the elm tree, bent on giving the marshal's job his full attention, seeing as Annabelle Green was no longer a distraction. His first order of business was hiring Newt and one more man he could trust . . . Leland Sikes seemed like a capable gent for this line of work. As soon as he could, he had to track down the woman named Allene Wright—he was convinced she was the key to finding Flat-nose Curry, the only reason he'd come back to town even though he knew there was a price on his head.

29

She watched it rain from her open bedroom window, inhaling cool air while listening to water run down a gutter from a corner of the second-story roof. Her thoughts drifted aimlessly. She had awakened late this morning to a splitting headache and bitter memories of last night's introductions to two men—Frank, and a dapper gentleman from Wyoming Territory named Harry Longabaugh. Harry told her his friends called him the Sundance Kid, although he said it in a joking way, as if it had no special meaning. The time she spent with him was a blur in her memory, after drinking too much wine to soften the anguish she experienced after Cody came. When she happened to look up at Cody in the parlor last night, when she saw the expression on his face upon discovering her there, she'd run upstairs to hide her tears and calm herself with more wine. Too much wine, so that recollections of time she spent with Harry Longabaugh were dim, indistinct, like having a vague memory of some unpleasant dream.

I'm no different than my ma was back then, she thought, as she remembered the effects of strong drink, the dizziness and a curious settling of her nerves, the way it quieted the voice of her conscience. She'd sold herself to two men while under the spell of liquor, and today, thinking back on it in the harsh light of day, she felt unclean, soiled by what she'd done. More than anything else she regretted losing a chance to fall in love with Cody, to have him fall in love with her. He'd told her straight out that he could never have feelings for a hired woman, and a woman for hire was what she had become.

"No sense cryin' over it," she told herself quietly, gazing

out the window of room number 5, a room that was hers now, after Miss Rose sent Allene away for smoking something called opium in this very same room. It was a beautiful room, furnished not all that differently than the one belonging to Miss Rose.

Annabelle turned away from her window long enough to take a look at the bed, a dresser, the bathtub, a ruby carpet almost as large as the room itself. In exchange for these lovely surroundings, and a way to earn money, she'd given up several very important things, not the least of which was the way she used to feel about herself. In a dark corner of her brain was a nagging worry, that what she had done could never be erased.

"Ma won't ever have to know," she said, knowing how much it would hurt her if she learned what Annabelle was doing.

A gust of damp wind fluttered curtains away from her windowsill, drawing her attention back to the summer storm. "If we was still in the laundry business, everything would be ruined again," she remembered aloud, in some ways thankful not to be washing any more clothes for strangers or living out of a wagon, at the same time feeling a longing for the way things were before she became a scarlet woman, before she'd tasted wine, before the devil took hold of her. Before she made a choice that would cost her Cody's affections, if there ever had been any chance he might feel that way at all. He'd said so many things to her that night while she was in his arms beside the stream, but did he mean them? After what she'd done, she would never know . . .

She stood at her window several minutes more, until so many gloomy thoughts filled her head she didn't want to think of them any longer. There was only one escape from the way she felt now, and to ease her pain she crossed over to her dresser for a glass, pouring herself a generous amount of wine.

Sitting in front of her mirror wearing the corset Miss Rose had given her, she studied her reflection a moment while sipping dark red spirits, wondering what would become of her now. The woman staring back at her looked older, so very

different from the girl she thought she was before coming to
Fort Worth.

Sometime later a soft knock at her door startled her. She
put on a dressing gown she found in the clothes closet and
opened her door a crack, wondering if it might be Miss Rose.

A plump Negro woman said, "Afternoon, Miss Belle. My
name's Fannie Mae. Miss Rose say fer me to tell you when I
fix somethin' to eat downstairs in th' kitchen."

"Thank you, but I'm not really hungry," she said, feeling
a bit of dizziness from the wine. "If Miss Rose don't care,
I'd be grateful if I could have another bottle of wine. I ain't
feelin' too well today."

Fannie Mae nodded. "I'll fetch you a couple, Miss Belle. I
can bring 'em up, seein' as you're feelin' poorly. If you decide
you want somethin' to eat later on, it'll be on the stove. You
come down anytime you like."

The woman hurried off before Annabelle could say thank
you again. She closed her door and emptied her glass while
steadying herself with the corner of her dressing table. It was
easier to drink more wine than to think about what she'd become, how she had changed. She promised herself she
wouldn't think about Cody again, at least not now. There
would be plenty of time for that later, after the liquor made it
hurt less to remember him.

Thunder rumbled outside her window, awakening her from
deep sleep. She sat up in bed, listening to the drum of rain
against the roof. A dark sky the color of lead allowed very
little light into her room and for a moment she collected her
thoughts in the darkness, slowly blinking away sleep fog and
the aftermath of several more glasses of wine, before she
swung her feet off the mattress.

As she stood up, she heard a noise, a door opening.

"Who's there?" she asked softly, holding onto a bedpost
as she tried to clear her head.

A dark shape entered her room, a man dressed in wet oilskin
moving quickly, almost soundlessly. She couldn't see his face
in the shadow below his hat. He came toward her—she saw

a pistol in his hand and opened her mouth to scream.

A huge hand slapped across her cheek, spinning her away
from the bed. She collapsed on the floor with her mind reeling
while her face felt as though it had suddenly caught fire. When
she opened her eyes, she saw the barrel of a gun the intruder
was aiming down at her head.

"Where's the map?" he snarled.

In her confused state she couldn't think clearly. "What map
are you talkin' about, mister?" she stammered, tasting blood
on her lips.

He leaned closer. "You're the wrong woman. Where the
hell is Allene?"

Annabelle tried to sit up. "She don't work here no more. I
don't know where she's at . . ." She suddenly recalled something Cody had said about a map to some hidden money, stolen money he said he thought it was, and that Flatnose Curry
had come to Fort Worth looking for it. As Annabelle's eyes
slowly began to focus on the intruder's nose, she noticed how
misshapen it was, smashed against his face—this was Curry,
the dangerous escaped killer everyone was searching for.

"Don't lie to me! Where did she go?"

"I swear I don't know, mister. Miss Rose told her to leave
on account of she smoked opium. It's against the rules."

Curry stood a little straighter and lowered his gun to his
side. Water trickled off his slicker from being out in the rain
and Annabelle wondered how he could have gotten inside
without a posse seeing him; she guessed he'd come from the
alley out back, under cover of the storm.

"Damn the luck," he hissed, gritting his teeth, working his
hand around his pistol grips. He glanced out her window
briefly. "They quit looking for me in the rain. That bitch has
something belongs to me and I aim to find it." Curry glared
at her again. "You could be lying. If I smash that pretty face
of yours, maybe it'll help refresh your memory."

She inched backward on the rug, fearing another blow. "I'd
tell you if I knew where she was, mister. I swear I would . . ."

Curry seemed to be carrying one arm differently, dropping
a shoulder like he was in pain, and it was then she remembered

that Cody had shot him downstairs in the parlor when the marshal had been wounded and Miss Rose's manager got killed. Curry smelled of sweat and wet clothing. When pale light from the window showed his features, he looked so terrifying she could scarcely breathe—his disfigured nose made him look more frightening, like something evil from a storybook.

"I can't leave you here or you'll tell the law I'm back in town. Get dressed. You're coming with me. If you're a good girl and keep quiet until I find Allene, I'll let you go as soon as I get that map. Make it quick. Nobody's watching the back right now on account of the rain."

Fear tightened her throat so she could hardly speak. "I'm feelin' poorly, mister. Please don't make me go with you."

He reached down suddenly, seizing her by the hair, pulling her roughly to her feet, and it was all she could do to keep from screaming when he hurt her.

"Get dressed!" he growled, placing the muzzle of his pistol below her chin. "I'm taking you with me, just in case those law dogs get too close. Do like I say and you won't get hurt, but if you double-cross me, I'll blow a tunnel through your skull."

He shoved her toward the closet, keeping his gun against her bare back. She dressed quickly, donning her old yellow dress and worn shoes while her heart thumped wildly, wondering where he was taking her, and if he'd keep his promise not to hurt her if she did what he wanted her to do.

Curry prodded her at gunpoint into the hallway after he made sure it was empty, guiding her to a door leading down wood steps to a storeroom at the rear of the building. Another door stood ajar, opening into the alley. Rain had turned the alley into a river of mud, which clung to her shoes when he pushed her outside, with his gun touching her spine.

Darkness and steady rainfall obscured almost every feature along the rows of tiny shacks where he took her, pausing often to be sure streets were empty before he moved them cautiously toward the east side of town. No one ventured outside in the bad weather. Turning down a narrow lane crowded with one-room shacks built close together, Curry seemed to know where he was going, urging her onward with his gun barrel until they came to a clapboard house with a steeply slanted roof shedding rain around its foundation.

"Up those steps," he told her, looking both ways to be sure no one was watching.

Annabelle shivered, climbing slippery steps to a thin plank door where Curry rapped softly with his fist.

"Who's knockin'?" a creaky woman's voice asked from inside.

"It's me. Open up quick."

The door swung inward. A thin, elderly woman with hollow cheeks and broken, yellowed teeth motioned them in. She gave Annabelle a questioning look.

"Who's the girl?"

Curry shut the door, glancing over his shoulder. "I found her in Allene's room. She claims Allene got thrown out of the Pink Lady because she smoked opium." He pulled off his hat and sleeved out of his slicker gingerly, wincing when he moved his right arm to holster his pistol. A dark bloodstain covered the right side of his shirt. "I've got to find out where she went and I'm running out of time. I can feel the fever starting in my arm. I'll be laid up a few days till it heals if that goddamn horse doctor knows what he's talking about."

The woman's brow furrowed. "If she's a whore, she'll come to this part of town, so's she can work. I can ask around soon as this rain lets up."

"There isn't time to wait for it to stop raining, old woman. I paid you good money to help me out and I damn sure expect you to earn it now. Find out where she is. Make real sure you don't tell anybody why you're looking for her." Curry turned quickly to Annabelle, pointing to a rocking chair next to a side window. "Sit down and keep quiet over there."

Curry seated himself in a chair with a view of the road as the old woman opened a tattered parasol. She went out without a word to Curry, closing her door gently behind her.

Annabelle still shivered in her rain-soaked dress, with her

hair plastered wetly to her head and neck. She was sure Curry watched her from the corner of his eye every now and then, which only made her shivering worse. She harbored no doubts he would do as he'd promised if she tried to escape, thus she sat as still as she could despite chill bumps pimpling her skin.

I wish Cody knew where I was, she thought, until she remembered the look on his face when he saw her in the parlor at Miss Rose's last night. He knew what she'd become and now he wouldn't care what happened to her, being she was a whore.

Curry watched the road through a foggy windowpane, his eyes flickering nervously back and forth. The patter of rain was the only sound for several minutes. Curry rested his gun in his lap as the waiting continued.

As much to pass time as anything else, Annabelle thought of her mother, hoping those medicines they gave her stopped the hurt in her chest. Watching Curry through her eyelashes, she tried to calm herself. Today, more than ever before, she felt completely alone. The only friend she had left in the whole world was Tommy Joe Booker and he was just a boy who'd wanted to poke her. Her ma would probably die before spring and that would be the end of everything, leaving her without anyone special who cared. Miss Rose only cared for her because she made money for the Pink Lady, or so it seemed after last night.

She told herself she had to get used to being on her own, to not having anyone else to rely on. The time had come to grow up. She wasn't a little girl any longer.

30

With the coming of night, the storm showed no sign of lessening. Curry kept the house dark, focusing all his attention on a front windowpane, growing edgier as time passed. An hour after the woman left, he got up and began to prowl back and forth across the floor, peering out windows on all sides while holding his gun like he expected trouble.

"That old bitch better not double-cross me," he muttered to himself, halting at one front window to lean cautiously around the sill. He stiffened and hunkered down, bringing his pistol up quickly. "Somebody's coming." He turned to Annabelle. "Keep quiet."

For a moment Curry watched the window, then he relaxed and said, "It's Stella. Maybe she found Allene . . ."

The door opened. Stella closed her parasol and came inside. Curry shut the door behind her.

"She's stayin' at the Chinaman's place in the alley behind Dauphin Street." Stella's voice was little more than a whisper. "Go north till you see a sign sayin' 'Chang's Chinese Laundry' on the east side of the road. Turn down that alley. Chang's got a den fer opium smokers in the back. That's where Allene is right now, only you'd better watch out fer that young deputy marshal. I seen him walkin' down Tenth Street just now, an' he's carryin' a shotgun."

"I remember him," Curry said, holstering his gun, taking his slicker from a peg on Stella's wall. "Either he's plumb crazy or real good with a gun. If he gets in my way, I'll kill him. He's the one who put this bullet hole in my arm."

Annabelle watched Curry shoulder into his oilskin, and she

hoped he wouldn't run into Cody on his way to the Chang's laundry. Curry reached into a pocket with his good arm and handed Stella some money.

"I'm gonna tie this girl in your rocking chair. Don't let her loose until sunrise or she'll tell the law where I am. After I get that map from Allene, I'm pulling out of town. Just make damn sure the girl doesn't get loose before dawn. Bring me some cord, and be quick about it."

Stella disappeared into a small room off the back. A moment later she returned with a length of clothesline. Curry took the rope and came over to Annabelle's chair.

"Put your hands behind you," he demanded. "If you stay put and keep real quiet, nothing's gonna happen to you."

She did as he wanted, holding her hands behind the chair as he bound her wrists together—the rope was so tight it pinched her skin, yet she remained silent about it.

Curry buttoned his slicker after her wrists were tied. He went to the door and looked outside. "Remember what I said, old woman. Don't untie that rope until daybreak." He crept out on the stoop with his pistol drawn, and went softly down the steps in a steady rain.

Stella closed the door, making it dark in her shack, with only a small amount of light coming through the windows. She went to a windowpane. When Curry was out of sight, she struck a match to a candle and put it on a table at the back of the room before padding over to Annabelle.

"You heard what he said. I gotta keep you tied up till it gets light. Ain't nothin' personal, honey."

Annabelle's mind was racing to find a way to warn Cody about Curry's plans, that he'd shoot to kill if they ran across each other. "Please let me go," she begged, trying to read Stella's face in candlelight, looking for understanding. "The deputy is a friend of mine. He's lookin' for that same woman, Miss Allene, an' if he goes to that Chinaman's place, Flatnose Curry is liable to shoot him."

Stella wagged her head side to side. "Can't do that, girl, or George'll know I turned you loose. George ain't the sort to show no forgiveness. I took his money, fer fetchin' Doc

Grimes over to my place an' helpin' him stay hid out till he could sit a saddle. Your deputy friend will have to take care of his own self this time."

"Please! All I'll do is warn him not to go there. Curry will have plenty of time to find his map an' get out of town if you let me loose now. Cody's no killer like Curry is. He just turned twenty years old an' he ain't no bad man with a gun."

Stella pulled the empty chair over so she faced Annabelle. "You can save your breath, honey. I ain't lettin' you go till the sun comes up." She studied Annabelle's face. "You're young to be workin' a crib. Pretty, too. I was pretty once, before the pox overtook me. I'm dyin' real slow because of it. Havin' the pox is the worst kind of dyin' there is, 'cause it's slow an' you know you're dyin' from it. You can't hardly look in a mirror or you'll see what's come of you. A pretty young thing like you oughta think 'bout things like the pox before you take up workin' the cribs."

Pain from the ropes around Annabelle's wrists and worrying about Cody prevented her from listening too closely to Stella at first. "What's the pox?" she asked, turning her hands behind her back to see if she could work the ropes free herself.

"A whore's sickness," she said quietly, passing her fingers through thinning blond hair. "You git sores all over. Later on, your teeth start to fall out an' your hair drops off like you was a dog sheddin' its coat. Them sores fester, runnin' pus, an' you can't hardly eat nothin' at all. A doctor over at the hospital told me I'd go blind from it, towards the end. It's a hell of a miserable way to die."

"I'm sorry to hear 'bout your troubles. My ma is dyin', too, of the consumption. I don't figure she'll last till spring. She coughs up blood an' won't eat a bite to speak of. She hurts all the time. I don't reckon there's no such thing as a good way to die. Gettin' shot can't be no easier. If you'll just let me go, I can keep Cody from goin' near that Chinaman's place . . ."

Stella half smiled. "Is that deputy somebody real dear to you?"

Annabelle looked away. "Not anymore, I don't reckon. He

knows I went to work at Miss Rose's place, an' he told me plain he couldn't never have no feelin's for a scarlet woman. But that don't mean I wouldn't want to keep him from gettin' killed. I'd do that because I've still got special feelin's for him, even if he don't feel the same way 'bout me.''

Stella leaned a bit closer and in candlelight it appeared there was a trace of mist in her eyes. ''How long you been at the Pink Lady?'' She asked like the answer mattered to her.

''Only just last night. It was real hard to decide if I was gonna do it. The devil got inside me, makin' me think about how it would be nice to have so much money 'stead of bein' poor like we was. Miss Rose advanced me money so I could take my ma to the hospital, an' she gave me nice clothes to wear, an' a room with a big four-poster bed. We got this agreement, that I'll work for her till I get the money paid back. Only I couldn't hardly make myself do it last night. I drank so much wine it didn't hurt me no more to think about it, before I done it twice. She never told me there was somethin' called the pox to worry about. All she said was, I could make a lot of money.''

Stella nodded. ''You're makin' her a right smart of money, too. I doubt she mentioned things like havin' a baby you don't want, or gettin' a whore's sickness like the pox. There's other things, like drinkin' so much liquor you can't think straight or wantin' opium so bad you'll nearly die if you don't git none. I done it a long time ago . . . seems like a long time ago when I was pretty an' young.'' A tear trickled down one side of her nose as she talked. ''I had a baby, a baby boy, only he died a few weeks after he was borned. The doctor said it was my milk killed him, that smokin' opium ruined my milk for a baby. I was too young to know those things back then. Nobody told me.''

Annabelle stopped struggling with her ropes. She looked at Stella, remembering what her ma had told her. ''Ma said the consumption was God's punishment for bein' a scarlet woman when she was younger. She told me she worked the cribs in Saint Louis when she was a girl, an' how my pa saved her from it when he up an' married her. I never wanted to work in a place like the Pink Lady, but there don't hardly seem no other way to make money for somebody poor like me.''

"There's other ways. If I'd known what was in store for me, I'd have done without money. For a little while I was happy with what money could buy. Until I got sick. Until my baby died. I got nobody now, an' no money left. I rent this ol' shack an' do floor cleanin' for saloons to git by. I'm gonna die one of these days an' won't nobody notice after I'm gone.''

"You ain't got any family?''

"A brother someplace, only he don't write me no more after he found out I was a whore. Respectable folks don't want no kind of association with whores, 'cept for men who come to see you at night, so long as you're pretty.''

Hearing what Stella said only made Annabelle feel worse as she recalled her first night at the Lady. "Don't mean no disrespect by it, but I wouldn't want to end up like what's happened to you, bein' sick, not havin' anybody who cares. Sounds like you're terrible lonely an' sad . . .''

Stella wiped her cheek with a bony finger. For a moment she listened to the rain. "It ain't too late for you like it is for me. You can git yourself away from Hell's Half Acre an' never go back. There's been a thousand times I wish I had.''

Annabelle remained silent for a time—her thoughts were on Cody. "If you'd untie this rope, I'd always be mighty grateful. I could run tell Cody he oughta stay away from that Chinaman's place, if he'd listen. Might keep him from gettin' killed.''

"I promised George I'd help him. I took his money.''

"Curry's a bad man—he killed Miss Rose's manager an' killed a deputy named Coleman Webb, too. The marshal is wounded serious an' it's all because of him. If Cody finds him, he could wind up dead, same as the others.''

"He might not pay no attention to what you say, an' if he's lucky, maybe he won't run across George before he gits what he came after an' clears out of town.''

"Cody's lookin' for the same woman, Miss Allene Wright. He told me so the other night.''

Stella rested her hands on her lap, toying with a loose bit of thread from her skirt. "You got love for him, don't you?"

"I reckon maybe I do, even if it don't do no good to love him after what I done. He saw me workin' at the Pink Lady. He knows what I did last night, so he ain't gonna love me back. He told me how he feels 'bout hired women."

"Men can be bad to judge a woman when they ain't all that lily white themselves. If he's like most men, he's been with a few women by the time he's full grown."

"He told me he'd poked some up in Abilene while he was with a trail drive. That's how come he knew he couldn't have feelin's for no woman who sold herself. He said it made 'em hard-natured so all they wanted was money."

"Some do get hard," Stella agreed. "It ain't no easy life the way it looks. There's still time for you to change your mind about it . . . so you don't end up like me."

Listening to Stella, Annabelle was having second thoughts. "It don't seem natural, lettin' just any man poke me who's got the price. I been feelin' real bad about it today, wishin' I hadn't done it."

Stella pushed herself out of the chair. She walked to a window and paused there, watching the road in front of her house. "If I do let you go, George is liable to come back an' find out what I did. He'd be madder'n a nest of hornets."

Annabelle was thinking as fast as she could. "You could say I got loose on my own, that I untied these ropes while you was asleep."

"I suppose I could tell him somethin' like that." As if she had made up her mind, she came over to the rocking chair. "Just you remember it was ol' Stella Baker who helped you out, an' you best think about what I said, too. It ain't too late for you to git away from the Acre. This ain't no place for a girl like you."

Stella began untying Annabelle's wrists. When her hands were free, she jumped out of the chair.

"Thank you, Stella. An' I won't forget what you told me. I promise to think about it real hard."

Annabelle ran to the door, rushing out into a sheet of rain, slipping on the steps until her shoes were splashing through deep mud puddles. Raindrops pelted her face, soaking her yellow dress and her hair as she raced down an empty road in the dark to find Cody.

31

Inky ribbons of water twisted and turned where wagon ruts became small rivers nurtured by silvery sheets of rain falling from slate-black skies. Puddles swelled to small lakes in low spots, and even widely scattered hoofprints brimmed over here and there as the rare summer storm continued. A few window-panes glowed with lantern light along silent, empty streets, flickering when sudden squalls all but obscured them from Cody's vantage point, when to cross a side street, he and Newt and Leland Sikes left the protection of porch roofs covering vacant boardwalks. They found most of the workingman's saloons closed north and east of the Acre—all but a few had shut down when bad weather kept drinkers at home.

They halted at the intersection where Twelfth Street crossed Rusk, standing under a porch in front of the Central Apothecary Shop. Cody looked both ways, lifting the collar on a borrowed canvas duster he'd found hanging on a coat tree at the office. He wore a different badge tonight, Cordel Hull's badge. Newt and Sikes had badges Dave Watkins had given them when he organized a posse to look for Curry and Ketchum.

Cody shifted the marshal's short twelve-gauge to his right hand, looking east down Twelfth Street, soaked to the skin by so many hours walking streets in the rain. "Looks like we ain't never gonna find that woman tonight, or Curry neither. This rain has got everybody holed up. It's near like lookin' for teeth in a rooster's mouth."

"I could damn sure use a hunk of that reward," Sikes said, balancing a shotgun in his hand, squinting to see better in the dark, "but we've asked everybody we come across. Nobody's seen her, an' Curry ain't likely to show hisself."

"If we find her, we'll find Curry," Cody remarked. "He's after that map. Allene Wright's the key to everything."

"If we ain't already too late," Newt said. "Curry may have the map by now."

"I ain't gonna quit lookin' for her," Cody promised. "When I asked Rose Denadale where she might be, she claimed she didn't have no idea where to look."

"Maybe we oughta split up," Sikes said. "We'll cover more territory that way."

"Suits me," Cody replied. "I'll head due east. Newt, you keep walkin' north, while Sikes doubles back down Rusk over to Eighth Street. I'll turn up Dauphin to where the livery is, then I'll head back this way on Eleventh. Keep your eyes peeled for Curry. Take a real close look at anybody on a horse. You can be sure of one thing—Curry's still dangerous, even with a hole in him."

Sikes hunkered down inside his slicker and turned south to reach Rusk Street. Newt lingered on the corner a while longer, like he had something he wanted to say.

"I ain't real keen on bein' a deputy, Cody. Truth is, I'm not cut out to be in this line of work. I ain't all that primed to die, pardner. Wanted you to know I'm only doin' this because you an' me are friends. Pushin' steers up a cow trail ain't so dangerous as this. Not that I'm yellow, but paradin' around with a badge pinned to my shirt in a place like the Acre is askin' to get shot at, maybe killed. Eighty dollars a month don't sound like enough money for what we're doin' tonight. I got to thinkin' about it whilst I was in that posse. Got to thinkin' real hard about what I was doin'. I ain't no shootist. Come tomorrow mornin' I'm givin' you back this badge. Find yourself another deputy, 'cause I'm done with it. Hope you'll understand."

"I understand, Newt. I ain't all that sure I belong in it myself. Marshal Hull asked me to take this job till he got on his feet. Only reason I'm doin' this is because he asked."

"You've got better nerves than me. Steadier. I'm more of the type to worry."

Cody recalled the way he felt during the shoot-out at the livery. "I was plenty worried when Curry started shootin' at me. For the first time in my life I got scared. Really scared. I'll tell you somethin' I haven't told nobody else . . . I had a clear shot at Curry that night, only I didn't take it. I froze, same as if I was made of ice. I got to thinkin' about what it would be like to die right then an' there from a bullet. Maybe it never dawned on me that anybody was gonna shoot back. I just lay there on my belly till Curry an' the swindler rode off, shakin' like a newborned calf."

Newt was watching Cody's face intently. "I never knew of you bein' scared of nothin', pardner. You was always like your pa, not scared of anything."

Cody's eyes wandered up and down the street absently as he remembered the way he felt. "I was scared stiff, Newt. I told myself then it was on account of Annabelle, likin' her so much an' maybe wantin' to hang around to find out if things between us would work out, only now I ain't so sure that's what it was."

"Could be that was a part of it. You sure as hell went loco right from the first time you laid eyes on her."

He took a deep breath when a vision of Annabelle wearing a revealing dress at the Pink Lady flashed through his mind. "I saw her last night. She went to work for Rose Denadale. She decided to become a whore. When I saw her there, I got sick to my stomach over it. I figured she was a real lady, but I was damn sure wrong. She ain't nothin' but a whore after all."

"Maybe gettin' robbed had somethin' to do with it. Her ma was real sick an' they was flat broke. Maybe you hadn't oughta be so hard on her, Cody. Hard times can push folks so they make hard choices, sometimes."

"I'd have given her some money . . ."

"How come you didn't tell her?"

"There wasn't time. She was gone when I got to their

wagon that evenin'. I reckon she was already gettin' herself fitted for a whore's outfit.''

''Sounds like you're takin' it real hard.''

''I suppose I am, only it's too late to change things. She already took up with Rose. Things probably wouldn't have worked out between us anyways.''

''Appears you already gave up on the notion.''

''I reckon I have, pardner. Let's get to lookin' for Allene before Curry finds her. I've near 'bout run out of wind on the subject of Annabelle Green.''

He stepped off the boardwalk into a sea of mud as raindrops pelted his coat and hat. Slogging across the road with his head lowered to keep water from his face, he listened to the sound of his boots squishing through puddles to keep from thinking about Annabelle again, anything to take his mind elsewhere.

He thought about what Newt had told him, that he was quitting the deputy's job tomorrow morning. There was no reason to blame him for wanting out of a profession that didn't suit him. Cody pondered whether he was suited for it himself.

Keeping to the edge of the roadway, he trekked eastward as cautiously as he could without being able to see much of what lay ahead, cradling Cordel Hull's shotgun, hesitating whenever the light was so poor or rainfall was so heavy that he couldn't make out detail. Half a block away, during a lull in the rain, he saw a tiny saloon with its windows alight sitting at the corner of Dauphin Street.

With water pouring off his hat brim, he trudged down to the corner. His feet were soaking wet from holes in the soles of his boots. He came up to the building and read a sign above its door identifying the place as the Ace of Diamonds. Two hitchrails out front were empty. A pair of batwings allowed him to see that no one stood at the bar. Lanterns glowing behind the bar cast rays of golden light across what appeared to be a vacant room. A spiderweb caught reflected lamplight in a corner of the doorway as if it were spun from gold, and he wondered why he noticed such things as this, with more pressing business to attend to.

He climbed steps to the opening, pausing again to look over

the batwings, gripping the stock of his shotgun with more effort than usual when the Ace of Diamonds seemed too quiet. He told himself it was the storm, that nothing was wrong. He was being too careful.

Glancing in over the swinging doors, he found the place empty, and he relaxed his grip on the shotgun. An old man was dozing on a stool behind the bar, resting his head against the wall. As Cody walked in, he blinked and came to his feet.

"What'll it be, mister?" The bartender's eyes drifted down to Cody's shotgun. "You ain't gonna rob me, are you?"

"I'm Cody Wade, actin' city marshal while Cordel Hull is at the hospital." He stopped and gave the saloon another look. "I need to find a woman by the name of Allene Wright. She's a crib whore who used to work at the Pink Lady. Rose Denadale ran her off on account of she smokes opium. Findin' the woman's important an' I'd be obliged if you can help me."

"Never heard of no Allene Wright, Marshal, but if she's one of them pipe smokers, she could be down at Chang's place. He runs a laundry, only he makes his money sellin' opium to them who has to have it. It's plumb pitiful how folks get a cravin' for shit like that. Leave it to a goddamn Chinaman to figure out how to make a profit off shit nobody else wants."

Cody sensed he was on to something. "Where's Chang's place?"

"Right down this alley behind me. There's a big shed at the back of his laundry—ain't got any windows, so nobody can see what goes on inside. Got this door on one side. You'll have to look close or you'll miss the door."

"I'll find it. I'm grateful for the information." This was what he'd been looking for, a lead to finding Allene that could also take him to Curry. He walked out and turned for the alley, considering the possibility, that Curry had already found the woman and her map, being as how so much time had passed since Curry broke jail. But this was the only lead he had and there was no selection besides following it wherever it went.

When he came to the alleyway, he stopped for a moment to let his eyes readjust to total darkness. He had to consider the slim chance Curry might still be with Allene, and that would mean they would tangle again, a prospect Cody found disquieting as he peered down the alley through a curtain of rain. Rows of sheds and small stables lined both sides of a narrow passage behind a section of buildings, providing the only way to get to the place described by the barkeep. There would be considerably less risk if Sikes or Newt came with him, but it would take time to find them and time might be running short. Standing in the rain, weighing his chances of another meeting with Curry, he made up his mind to go it alone. He'd admitted to Newt that he was scared when shots were exchanged at the livery, and he supposed he wanted to find out if he had a yellow streak.

Walking as quietly as he could in muddy ooze, he crept along the sides of buildings, keeping his shotgun ready. Fifty yards into the alley he spotted a low-roofed shed without windows, with a door at one corner near the back. A dim light showed at the bottom of the door frame. Somewhere inside he thought he heard faint voices.

"This'll be it," he whispered, opening his duster to be able to reach his .44-.40 if he needed it in a hurry.

At the entrance he hesitated, looking behind him. Just then an unwelcome memory of Annabelle's pretty face entered his mind. He didn't want to remember her and shook his head quickly before he muttered a quiet "Damn her anyhow" and reached for the rusted doorknob.

He wasn't prepared for the harsh light or the suddenness of events when he pushed the door open. Across a smoke-filled room where a few people sat on the floor, a man in a slicker holding a gun whirled away from a far wall. He knew it was Curry before he had time to gather his senses—he recognized his flattened nose a fraction too late. The muzzle of Curry's gun came up as he let go of a woman's dark hair, sending her crashing against the wall. Someone yelled, "Look out!" Then a roar drowned out every other sound, the explosion of gunpowder at close quarters that was like no other sound on earth.

The scene before Cody tilted crazily when a force like wind drove him backward. He sat on his rump in the mud with his ears ringing. A stinging sensation across the left side of his ribs brought a rush of tears to his eyes and he felt like he'd been stung by a swarm of angry bees. Rocking to and fro on the seat of his pants, still reeling from whatever it was that had swept him off his feet, he collected himself just enough to pull back the hammers on the twelve-gauge and curl his trigger finger.

The concussion from two shotgun shells erupted in unison. A ball of smoke and tongues of fire boiled through the doorway into the roof of Chang's small building, turning wooden rafters into a spray of airborne kindling, blasting shingles toward the heavens in a widening cloud of sawdust chips shredded by buckshot. When the noise was trapped within four walls, it magnified, so screams from terrified customers went almost unnoticed. People leapt out of harm's way while bits of the roof tumbled to the dirt floor, followed by rain pouring through a gaping hole in the ceiling. The kick from both shells firing at once knocked Cody over on his back just as five more shots rang out. He heard the whack of hot lead landing in mud around his head and shoulders.

Pain spread across his chest like someone had ignited a pool of coal oil inside him. He groaned involuntarily when sharp pains grew worse, and for the first time he realized he'd been hit by a bullet.

I'm dying, he thought. Curry got me. I hope this terrible hurting don't last much longer . . .

Rain struck his face. He opened his eyes and saw a man with a gun standing over him, then he heard the soft click of a hammer as the pistol was cocked.

"You're not as smart as I thought you were, kid," Curry said as cold as ice, aiming down at Cody's forehead.

Cody winced when he heard the hammer fall, expecting things to end. But there was only the sound of metal falling on a dead cartridge, and a quiet curse before someone began shouting off in the distance, a high-pitched woman's voice coming from the alley behind him, then more voices.

Boots thudded away through the mud. He was dimly aware

his life had been spared . . . by an empty gun and whoever was doing all the yelling.

His left side was growing numb. He reached inside his coat and felt blood before he lost consciousness.

32

Shapes appeared before his eyes, then they were gone. There were times when he heard voices—indistinct, garbled words making no sense. He was alternately cold, then hot, never comfortable, while a vague sensation of pain remained constant, throbbing like a drumbeat keeping time with his heart. When he could manage to keep his eyelids open, his surroundings were a blur of light and fuzzy images, although the effort to remain awake was usually too great, and most often he succumbed to a continual drowsy feeling, drifting off into a light sleep from which he was awakened often by waves of pain somewhere in his chest.

He lost all sense of time, never knowing how long he slept or whether it was day or night. He remembered bits of events, a gun going off, falling backward, feeling pain, wondering if he might be dying from a gunshot. Things had happened so fast there was no time to think. He'd opened a door and come face-to-face with Flatnose Curry, then Curry fired and his ribs felt like they were being consumed by flames. After that, his memory was almost a blank, a scrap here and there, recollections of someone shouting and Curry bending over him, saying something he wasn't able to recall. More than anything else was a lingering sense of how badly he'd failed to do his job. Curry had gotten away, and when Marshal Hull found out about it, he'd be madder than blazes.

Someone spoke to him, and no matter how hard he tried, he was unable to understand a single word or recognize the face he found above him when he opened his eyes. He gave up and drifted off to sleep.

• • •

"You awake, pardner?"

Cody blinked when he heard Newt's voice, and forced his eyelids to remain open. "Not exactly. Where the hell am I?" His head seemed clearer than before.

"You're at the hospital. Nicest room in the whole place. A real good view from your window, soon as you're able to sit up so you can take notice. You feelin' okay?"

"Can't say for sure just yet." He glanced at his surroundings to get his bearings. He was lying in a bed near a window in a room with pale walls. Gradually, he became aware of a pulsating hurt in his left side. He looked up at Newt's beard-stubbled chin and uncombed hair, his rumpled shirt. "You look like you've been away from bathwater for a spell, pardner. I was fixin to say you was a mighty pretty sight, seein' as I figured I might be dead by now. Only you ain't all that pretty, to be honest about it."

Newt grinned. "I can tell you're feelin' better because you woke up cantankerous as hell. I warned all the nurses you'd be a double handful when you woke up."

Cody fixed Newt with a look. "I know I got shot. Tell me how serious it is."

"Bullet broke two of your ribs, but you'll mend, accordin' to that sawbones. Your wound is festered some, but you'll be up an' around pretty soon. You was real lucky. Folks who saw it claim ol' Curry fired point-blank at your chest. A few inches either way an' you'd be restin' on a plank at the undertaker's. By the time I got there, you were unconscious, layin' in half a foot of mud with blood all over the place. I seen Curry was on the run down that alley, but right then I didn't give a damn if he got plumb to Mexico. I let the sorry son of a bitch go. All I could think about was gettin' you to a doctor. That bullet glanced off your ribs, so it didn't have to come out. Like I said, you was mighty lucky."

"You saw Curry runnin' off?"

"Sure did, an' I didn't lift a finger to stop him. There ain't enough money in Fort Worth to get me in a shootin' contest with George Curry."

"How'd you get there so quick?"

Newt smiled again. "The girl found me. She'd been runnin' all over town lookin' for you, only she found me first. She told me about the Chinaman's place, so that's where we was headed when the shootin' started. We ran fast as we could, only by then you was flat on your back, bleedin' like a gourd dipper full of buckshot."

"You mean Annabelle came lookin' for me?"

"She did for a fact."

"How come she wasn't at the Pink Lady?"

"It's one hell of a story. You see, Curry snuck in the back of the Lady whilst it was rainin'. He found Annabelle in a room where he figured to find that Wright woman, so he held a gun to her head an' took her to his hidin' place until he found out just where to look for the other gal, down at the Chinaman's. But as soon as Curry left, Annabelle got herself loose an' took off so's she could warn you 'bout Curry. She found me instead an' told me the whole story, so we came runnin' to the Chinaman's, only you got there ahead of us."

Cody let it sink in, that Annabelle had wanted to save him. "I reckon she ain't all bad, even if she did decide to work for Rose Denadale."

"It's more'n likely she saved your life, pardner. If Curry had had time to reload his gun, he'd have killed you. He saw us an' lit out of there instead."

"I'll be sure to thank her, soon as I get up an' around."

Newt jerked a thumb in the direction of the door. "You can thank her whenever you feel like it. She's been waitin' out in the hall ever since they brung you here."

Cody greeted the news with a mixture of feelings. He hadn't wanted to see her again, not after finding out what she'd become. But hearing she was outside his hospital room, waiting there like she cared what happened to him, pushed him closer to asking Newt to send her in. "Don't suppose it would hurt if you let her come in for a minute or two, just so I could thank her proper. Before you do that, tell me what Marshal Hull had to say about Curry as soon as he found out what happened."

"The marshal didn't complain. Sheriff Casey tried to find
Curry's tracks, only the rain washed 'em out. Dave Watkins
got made city marshal after all, when me an' Sikes quit after
we told Marshal Hull what commenced at the Chinaman's.
The marshal said it proved what the Acre needed for a lawman
was a mean son of a bitch like Dave."

"I guess I found out the Acre was too tough for me. I had
it in my mind I could do it, only I was sure as hell wrong. It
takes somebody special to enforce the law in a place where
men like Curry walk the streets. Maybe the marshal's right,
to say it takes somebody like Dave Watkins to keep peace in
Hell's Half Acre."

"After what happened to you, I'm inclined to agree, pardner. One thing I know for certain—I'll never wear another
badge as long as I live."

"I reckon I'll take the same oath. No more badges for me.
I've got two busted ribs to remind me that I ain't suited for a
lawman's job. Soon as I get out of this hospital, we'll start
lookin' for another type of regular employment."

Newt rubbed his unshaven chin thoughtfully. "I got me an
idea whilst I was waitin' for you to wake up this mornin'. We
could start out in the freight haulin' business, if we can get
our hands on a good wagon an' a team of mules. Wouldn't
take all that much of a stake to get us started. I met this feller
who claims he makes as much as forty cents a pound, hauling
freight from Fort Worth out west where there ain't no rail-
roads."

Cody considered the freight business. "We'll look into it
as soon as I can walk. Freight haulin' don't sound all that bad
to me. I know right smart about fixin' wagons." He recalled
the day he worked on Annabelle's wagon. "I reckon I oughta
talk to the girl, Newt. No sense in havin' her sit out in the
hall all this time . . ."

"I'll tell her you're awake. Be seein' you real soon." He
waved and sauntered out of the room.

Cody turned to the window, remembering what Newt had
told him of the affair at Chang's. If Annabelle hadn't come
looking for him, he might be dead. As Newt had suggested,

the girl probably saved his life. He owed her his gratitude, but nothing more than that.

He watched puffy white clouds drift across a blue sky until he heard quiet footsteps enter his room. When he turned his head, he saw Annabelle standing at the foot of his bed.

He smiled a little. ''It stopped rainin','' he said, when he couldn't think of anything else to say. She was wearing the blue dress she'd worn to the Emporium, only it was buttoned in front to keep from showing too much of her skin. He noticed her eyes were red like she'd been crying.

''It stopped early this mornin', Cody. I'm real glad to hear you're doin' okay.''

''Newt told me the bullet broke a couple of my ribs, an' that it glanced off. It hurts, but he says the doctor thinks I'll be up an' around pretty soon. I was lucky, I suppose.''

''Very lucky.'' She looked down at the floor. ''When we found you, it looked for all the world like you were dead. You didn't appear to be breathin' any, an' I never saw so much blood in all my life.'' Her voice sounded like it was ready to break.

''Newt said it was you who brought him down to that Chinese place. He told me what Curry did to you. I owe you a big debt.''

''You don't owe me nothin', Cody.'' She sniffled and wouldn't look at him. ''I did somethin' awful to myself. You already know what it was. I wish I hadn't done it. I wish I'd have thought of a better way to make money, only I didn't. I did a real bad thing, an' there ain't no way to change it. Only reason I'm of a mind to talk about it is I wanted you to know how sorry I am that things turned out this way. I liked you a lot. I know it sounds silly but I ain't too proud to admit you turned my head. I wish I'd listened to that little voice inside me when it said you were somebody real special.''

He was a bit embarrassed to hear how she felt, since he'd felt the same way, until he found her at the Lady. ''Funny you should say that, because a little voice warned me not to become one of Marshal Hull's deputies. Only I did anyway, an' it nearly cut my life short. Maybe sometimes those voices are talkin' good sense . . .''

She smiled, but continued to avert her eyes. ''Too bad for both of us when we didn't listen. I'm glad you'll be okay after your ribs heal up.'' A tear glistened on her cheek, and as soon as she became aware of it, she turned her head.

''I'll be fine,'' he said, wishing she hadn't told him so much about her mistake and her feelings. It would be easier to forget about her if she just went away. ''I hope things turn out the way you want 'em to.''

''They won't,'' she whispered, like she knew already.

He wanted to say something kind to her, so she wouldn't feel bad. The last thing he wanted was to hurt her feelings after she brought Newt to the Chinaman's in the nick of time. ''I'm of the opinion things generally work out the way they're supposed to in the end. We hadn't really gotten the chance to get to know each other all that well.''

''I sure do wish we could have tried longer.'' She was biting her lip, looking out his window when she said it.

Now it was his turn to feel bad, when he saw her crying over something he'd said. He decided to change the subject. ''You'll be makin' enough money to take good care of your ma.''

Her head turned so quickly it startled him, and when he saw the look in her eyes, he knew he'd said the wrong thing.

''I ain't going back to Miss Rose's!'' she cried, with tears running down her face. ''There ain't enough money in the world to keep me there! I told you I made a terrible mistake . . .''

She ran from his room, choking on tears, and if he could have, he would have gotten out of bed to tell her he was sorry for what he'd said. He listened to her feet running down the hall, and regretted his careless remark.

For a while he gazed up at the ceiling with his mind on what he'd said to her, deciding after a bit that he needed to tell her he was sorry. Since he was bedridden, he would have to send Newt with his apology, and to ask that she give him another chance to talk to her.

When it came to making mistakes, Cody knew where he fit. All his life it seemed he'd been making wrong turns. But at the same time he wondered if he could ever forgive Annabelle for something far more serious than a bad choice when it came to occupations, like selling herself in a whorehouse. Thinking about it now, her mistake seemed so much worse than those he'd made.

Sometime later he closed his eyes. As he slipped closer to sleep, he saw Annabelle wearing a red dress, talking to a man with a handlebar mustache—she was smiling, listening to what the man had to say. He knew what she'd done afterward, after the two of them went upstairs . . .

33

She gathered a few wildflowers, mostly Indian paintbrushes since they grew faster after it rained. Doris liked flowers and she'd raised over a dozen varieties back in San Augustine, including pretty roses. It was going to be hard to tell her that they couldn't afford the rooming house any longer, or the medicines. There was nothing left to do but pull out of Fort Worth as soon as her ma could travel. Miss Rose had seen to their mule for a time, sending Riggs with a sack of corn. But that was over now, after she'd told Miss Rose they were leaving. Miss Rose had given her five more dollars after they talked about it, about what she aimed to do. Annabelle hadn't wanted to take it, although she did for her ma's sake. Miss Rose had said how sad she was that Annabelle was going elsewhere, but that she understood.

With a handful of flowers and her hair brushed, Annabelle started away from the campground wearing her best dress. She had put things away in the back of the wagon as best she could, the heavy iron kettles she'd lifted herself, the clotheslines and such, all neatly stacked so there was room for Doris to lie down. Their mule was tied to a wagon wheel. Everything was ready to leave.

Her mind was made up she wouldn't say good-bye to Cody. It would be too difficult to see him again. She had cried over him until she was all cried out. In place of her sorrow was an empty feeling, a hollow place in her heart.

She made the long walk across town without thinking about Cody or much of anything else, passing store windows where new dresses were on display, hardly noticing. It was a warm day for walking. After the rains everything smelled fresh and clean. At a street corner she turned for Fitsimmons Rooming House, carrying her bouquet of flowers, remembering Ruth and how kind she'd been to Doris that first day. How sad it was, that they didn't have enough money so Doris could stay there.

As she walked up the the front steps, a breeze blew her skirt above her knees, just as a gentleman in a business suit came through the screen door. He saw her and smiled, and when he did, she gasped and dropped her flowers to push down her dress with one hand and cover her mouth with the other.

"Good afternoon, Belle," he said. "Did I startle you? You dropped your flowers . . ."

His handlebar mustache only exaggerated the grin on his face, and when she saw him smiling, she felt like running away as fast as she could. "Excuse me, but you must be mistaken about my name bein' Belle," she stammered, picking up her bouquet quickly, then hurrying through the door.

"Don't you remember me? I'm Harry Longabaugh," he said as she ran upstairs.

She did not turn around until she got to a landing where the staircase turned, and even then she wouldn't look down to see if he was watching her. Her face was red and her heart was hammering when she hurried the rest of the way to her ma's room with a dry mouth.

She waited until she heard him walk down the porch steps before she continued down a hall to Doris's room. Collecting herself, she forced a smile and went in.

Doris lay on a narrow bed with her face to an open window. Her eyes were closed. Annabelle touched her shoulder gently and held out the flowers.

"These are for you, Ma."

Her eyelids parted, forming slits. "Is that you, child?"

"It's me. I picked you some flowers."

"Can't hardly see 'em. Things look mighty strange. Times, I can't git woke up all the way."

"It's the medicine makes you sleepy."

"Medicine costs a right smart of money, child. You tell 'em I don't want no more of it."

"I'll tell them. We'll be leavin' soon, Ma, soon as I get the mule hitched tomorrow mornin'. We'll head west to that place called Arizona so you'll get better. I fixed you a pallet in the wagon so you can lie down."

Doris frowned a little. "I ain't gonna git no better. May as well stay someplace closer. I'm dyin'. I can tell it ain't gonna be long now."

"Don't talk like that, Ma. If we get to Arizona, you'll be feelin' better in no time. All we gotta do is get there."

Her frown disappeared. She reached for Annabelle's hand. "I'm terrible sorry for so many things. What I done a long time ago, an' that I'm leavin' you like this. You ain't hardly old enough to make it by yourself. Life can be real hard for a girl so young."

"I'll be just fine," she said softly, squeezing her palm as Doris closed her eyes.

She placed the flowers on her pillow and left the room on her tiptoes. The medicine was making Doris so groggy she didn't wake up for long.

Downstairs, when she walked outside, she saw Harry Longabaugh waiting for her under an elm tree and she almost turned around to run back inside. He smiled and took off his bowler.

"May I have a word with you, Belle?" he asked.

"My name ain't Belle. I already told you that."

"I could never make a mistake about such a beautiful woman. I'm quite sure I'll remember you the rest of my life. May I walk with you a ways?"

"I'd rather you didn't. I'm in a hurry."

"You seem frightened of me. All I ask is for a few moments of your time."

"I ain't sellin' no more of my time, Mr. Longabaugh. I made a big mistake. Now, please leave me alone."

"I could tell you were young and inexperienced. You were so sweet. I hoped I would see you again."

"Well, you can't. Please go away!" She wondered if anyone saw her talking to him, although she was afraid to look around to see if someone might be watching. She swung away from the tree and walked as rapidly as she could.

"Wait just a moment, Belle!" he cried, saying it so loudly people would notice. She heard his footsteps following her and came to a halt, folding her arms across her chest.

"Go away!" she said, the way she talked to Tommy Joe when he wouldn't leave sometimes. "I've got nothin' to say to you an' I don't care to hear what you'll say!"

He hurried up to her and stopped a few feet away. "I've got two tickets on the evening train bound for El Paso. An associate of mine who was planning to go with me had to leave town unexpectedly. I'm going on farther west to California. There are all sorts of opportunities out west for a man, or a woman. Would you care to go with me?"

"No." She said it quickly, even though the idea of riding a train most anywhere was appealing. But she wouldn't go with him to California, or anyplace else.

"Won't you reconsider?"

"Never. I did a bad thing the other night, a terrible kind of thing, an' I'll be sorry for it the rest of my life. I won't be no hired woman again, not for nobody. So please go away, Mr. Harry Longabaugh. I ain't goin' with you to California." With that, she whirled around and ran as fast as her feet would carry her toward the center of town, with her hair flying behind her in the wind. She was glad to be leaving Fort Worth and its memories behind.

Newt held his hat in his hands, fingering the brim like he was nervous about something. She had the mule harnessed between the wagon shafts, ready to drive out to Fitsimmons right after daybreak, just as Newt came walking up.

"I've got a message for you from Cody," he said. "He asked if you'd stop by the hospital to see him. He wants to say he's sorry for some remark he made yesterday—he didn't tell me what it was. But he said it's real important that you give him the chance to make amends."

"I was headed out to pick up my ma. We'd planned to leave today."

"It wouldn't take long to stop by the hospital. It ain't much out of the way."

She thought about it. She'd hardly slept at all last night gazing up at the stars, thinking about Cody. "I reckon I could stop for a minute or two on my way to the roomin' house to pick up Ma."

"I know he'll be mighty glad to see you."

His head was propped up on two pillows. He watched her come into his room. She went to the bed and stood a few feet away, vowing that no matter what he said, she would not cry.

He regarded her a moment and the silence grew heavy. She'd begun to wonder why he'd asked her to come. She looked away when it became uncomfortable to have him stare at her; she watched leaves flutter on limbs beyond his window.

"Newt told me you wanted me to stop by."

He cleared his throat. "I wanted to say I was sorry. I was wrong, to think you'd stay at the Pink Lady. I shoulda knowed it wasn't somethin' you'd do. You're a good girl, Annabelle, only I figure it was hard times that made you work there. Needin' money for your sick ma an' all."

She decided to be completely truthful. "That wasn't it all by itself, Cody. I was tired of bein' poor. I thought how nice it would be to have money for a change, only I found out workin' there made me feel real bad about myself, about what I was doin' to make money. I felt awful, like I'd traded everything in my life that mattered for dollars. It wasn't worth it . . . losin' the chance to get to know you better, maybe to find out if we could . . . love each other. I found out too late that money didn't make no difference. I still felt bad about what I'd done, so bad I didn't hardly want to live here any longer. I decided to take Ma to Arizona today. I'm headed over to pick her up. I doubt I'd ever have come to say good-bye to you, knowin' how you felt about what I'd done. Only Newt said you wanted to see me."

Cody blinked when she looked at him then.

"You suppose we could have gotten to where we liked each other a lot?" he asked softly.

"I reckon we could have, if I hadn't gone an' done what I did at Miss Rose's. You told me straight-out how you feel about hired women."

He swallowed. "I figure just about everybody makes a few mistakes once in a while, Annabelle. Thinkin' about it now, it don't seem right to hold it against you, that you made just this one. I've made more'n my share, if the truth got told. I told you I'd shared company with a hired woman or two up in Abilene when I was there. It oughta matter that you ain't still at the Pink Lady. I've been thinkin' about it, how I'd feel, knowin' what you did . . ."

She waited, afraid to allow herself to become too hopeful.

"It's liable to be hard to think about," he continued in a quiet voice. "Maybe I'd get used to it after a spell."

"It don't seem likely you could ever love me," she said.

"I been wonderin' if I could."

"You said it would be hard to think about."

He nodded.

"That would keep you from havin' any deep feelin's for me, looks like."

"Maybe. It'd take some gettin' used to."

"Wouldn't be the same as if I hadn't done it."

A breath of wind came through the window while Cody chewed his lip thoughtfully. "I reckon, if you was willin', we could maybe give it a try. Only way we'll know for sure is to see if things'll work themselves out. If you're agreeable."

She came a little closer to his bed. "I might be agreeable if it was what you really wanted, Cody. I'd have to know it was your idea to see if we could like each other enough."

"Tell me how you feel about it, Annabelle. I already told you I'd like to give it a chance."

"I know I love you, Cody Wade. Have since nearly the first time I set eyes on you, if that matters."

A slow grin tugged at the corners of his mouth. "I reckon it does matter a whole lot." He reached for her hand, and when he held it, she had the feeling he wanted to love her in return.

34

A blustery November day turned skies gray with a cold wind blowing from the north. A casket rested at the bottom of a six-foot hole inside the cemetery fence. A preacher from a Baptist church on Fifth Street lowered his head and said, "Amen" after conducting a short funeral service over the body of Doris Green.

Cody held Annabelle's hand while she wept silently. Newt was the only other person in attendance. Fall leaves danced in colorful swirls beneath shedding oak and elm branches, shades of red and gold forming freckled patterns of orange and burnt umber and dark brown, falling like huge snowflakes where gusts ran out of breath.

He turned to her and spoke gently. "Let's go now. No sense stayin' here any longer."

She lifted her face, fingering tears away from the corners of her eyes. "She don't hurt no more. I'll try an' remember that when I think about her. She was in so much pain I think she was ready to die."

Cody took her arm, leading her slowly away from the grave. "It's best to remember what she was like before she got sick. I think about my pa that way, rememberin' him the way he was before that horse busted him up."

Newt fell in behind them as they walked toward a gate in the rusted iron fence where a covered wagon waited. In the harness a team of brown mules lowered their heads against the wind. On the canvas wagon sheet a sign read "Wade & Sims," rippling when cold air blew against it.

"Your ol' wagon don't hardly look the same, Annabelle,"

he said, feeling a bit of pride when he saw what they'd accomplished with a coat of paint and a new canvas. "How does it feel to be a partner in a freight haulin' business?"

"We haven't hauled any freight yet, Cody. You're countin' chickens before they're hatched."

Newt chimed in, "But we've got our first load contracted next week, don't forget, an' Mr. Patterson over at the gin gave me the name of a feller to contact when we get to Childress, to see 'bout haulin' cottonseed back. We'll make twice as much by workin' smart like that, haulin' plowshares one way an' cottonseed the other."

Cody nodded. "Won't be long till we'll be buyin' another wagon an' two more mules."

"You're such a dreamer, Cody," Annabelle said, and she was smiling a little now. "We hardly got the paint dry on this ol' wagon an' you're already dreamin' about buyin' another one."

"Nothin' wrong with havin' big dreams," he told her, as they halted beside the mules. "Maybe one of these days there'll be a hundred wagons with our names on 'em, rollin' plumb across Texas and no tellin' where else."

She cocked her head, giving him a mischievous look. "Can't see my name nowhere on this wagon. You said I was a full partner same as the two of you."

He grinned. "I was aimin' to talk to you about that, only I was plannin' to do it later."

"Talk to me about what? Paintin' my name up there alongside of yours?"

"Not the way you think. I wasn't gonna have Green added to what it says."

"Then how would my name be up there?"

Newt tugged his hat down, pulled up his coat collar, and shuffled off when he heard their conversation take a turn toward private matters.

Cody felt himself blush. "Can't you figure it out? We can talk about it tonight. After supper."

She took his hand. "I suppose I can wait for you to explain it." Her gaze went back to the cemetery. "We've got plenty of time," she added softly. "Good-bye, Ma," she whispered. "I just know all your hard prayin' got the attention of the Lord. He'll forgive you, no matter what you done, just like Pa did."

"What did you mean by that?" Cody asked.

She stood on her tiptoes and kissed him lightly. "I'll tell you sometime. It's got to do with forgiveness, but it ain't all that important." Annabelle stared deeply into his eyes. "What's important to me is that you love me, Cody."

He pushed his hat back on his head with a thumb. "You can be sure of it," he said. "I ain't got any doubts. If a man's real lucky, somebody special comes along before he gets old an' gray. He'd better not pass up the chance to be happy, 'cause it don't happen to everybody. I love you, Miss Annabelle Green, an' when the time's right I'm gonna ask you . . . to marry me. That way we wouldn't have to add another name to the sign, in case you hadn't already figured out what I meant."

"I sorta guessed, but I wanted to hear you say it."

He shrugged and guided her onto the seat of the wagon. "I never was much of a hand with fancy words," he said in a faraway voice, glad that he'd found the right words that day at the hospital.